MUSTARD SEED

ALSO BY LAILA IBRAHIM

Yellow Crocus

Living Right

MUSTARD SEED

LAILA IBRAHIM

LAKE UNION
PUBLISHING

Published by Lake Union Publishing, Seattle
www.apub.com

Amazon, the Amazon logo, and Lake Union Publishing are trademarks of Amazon.com, Inc., or its affiliates.

ISBN-13: 9781542045568
ISBN-10: 1542045568

Cover design by Laura Klynstra

Printed in the United States of America

In gratitude for all the known and unknown people who sowed seeds of love and justice that matured in my lifetime and for the opportunities to sow seeds of my own.
For my Maya, my Kalin, and my Rinda, I love you down to the ground and up to the sky, always.

Section 1. Neither slavery nor involuntary servitude, except as a punishment for crime whereof the party shall have been duly convicted, shall exist within the United States, or any place subject to their jurisdiction.

Section 2. Congress shall have power to enforce this article by appropriate legislation.

Thirteenth Amendment to the Constitution
of the United States

I tell you the truth, if you have faith as small as a mustard seed, you can say to this mountain, "Move from here to there," and it would move.

Matthew 17:20

CHARACTER LIST

Jordan Freedman: a nineteen-year-old teacher who lives with her parents in Oberlin, Ohio
Mattie Freedman (Mama): Jordan's mother
Emmanuel Freedman (Pops): Jordan's father
Samuel Freedman: Jordan's brother
Nora Freedman: Jordan's sister-in-law
Otis Freedman: Jordan's nephew

Lisbeth Johnson (Momma): thirty-year-old farmwife living in Oberlin, Ohio
Matthew Johnson (Poppa): Lisbeth's husband
Sadie Johnson: Lisbeth's six-year-old daughter
Sammy Johnson: Lisbeth's nine-year-old son

Ann Wainwright (Grandmother Wainwright): Lisbeth's mother
Jonathan Wainwright (Grandfather Wainwright): Lisbeth's father
Jack Wainwright: Lisbeth's brother
Julianne Wainwright: Lisbeth's sister-in-law
Johnny Wainwright: Lisbeth's nephew

Emily Smith: Lisbeth's half sister
William Smith: Emily's husband

Willie Smith: Emily's son
Ari and Winnie Smith: Emily's parents-in-law

Mary Bartley: Lisbeth's childhood friend
Daniel Bartley: Mary's husband
Emma: Mary's nurse
Mary's children: Danny, Harry, Rose, Hannah, and Freddy

Sarah: Jordan's cousin
Sophia Rebecca: Sarah's daughter
Ella Georgia: Sarah's daughter

Edward Cunningham: Lisbeth's former fiancé. Owner of White Pines

Alfie and Alice Richards: new owners of Fair Oaks, the plantation where Lisbeth and Mattie lived

Mother Johnson (Granny): Lisbeth's mother-in-law
Father Johnson (Poppy): Lisbeth's father-in-law
Mitch Johnson: Lisbeth's brother-in-law
Michael Johnson: Lisbeth's brother-in-law. Lives in California with his wife and children
Maggie Johnson: Michael's wife
Aurelia and Emma Johnson: Michael and Maggie's children

Miss Grace: owner of the boardinghouse where Jordan, Mattie, and Samuel stay

Mrs. Avery: mistress of the contraband orphanage
Tessie: lives in the orphanage

RICHMOND, VIRGINIA, 1868

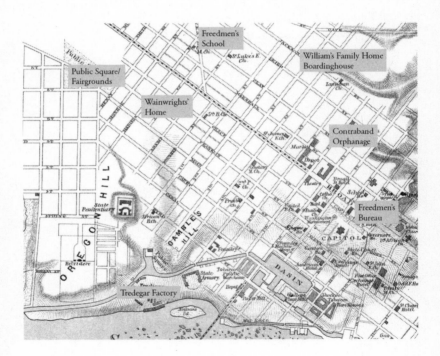

PROLOGUE

JORDAN

1868

Teachers are not supposed to have favorites, but I do. On the first day of the term last fall, little Sadie Johnson slipped her hand into mine, looked straight at me with her bright-blue eyes, and declared with a slight lisp, "It's my first day too." My affection for that sweet White girl took root and only grew throughout the school year.

Mama says I feel a special kinship with her because she's Lisbeth's daughter, but I disagree—I hardly know the woman. Once a year she arrives with a basket of holiday treats for our family. Lisbeth and Mama catch up for a bit and hug long and hard before she leaves our life until the next Christmas. Mama says Lisbeth's affection was written into my soul before I had words or thoughts, but I think Mama is speaking for herself, not for me.

Lisbeth and Mama were special to each other *before*. I know about before only from stories. The tales of the quarters, the big house, and the fields are like Greek myths to me. I was only a baby when Mama carried me off the plantation to join Pops and Samuel in Oberlin. I don't consider myself a freed slave, but Mama never lets me forget that we were *all* enslaved once, whether I like it or not. They gave me a last name that doesn't let me or the world forget it either: Freedman.

My parents are proud of their history—as they should be. I'm grateful for all that they have given to me; truly I am, but they don't understand me, and I don't believe they ever can. The gulf between our lives is simply too enormous.

CHAPTER 1

LISBETH

Oberlin, Ohio
Summer 1868

Lisbeth's hands were mixing biscuit dough for supper when Matthew walked into the kitchen with the envelope. Mother's precise handwriting jumped out at her from the white paper. She didn't break her rhythm or comment, but her body jumped to alert like a rabbit sensing a fox.

Matthew pecked her on the cheek from behind. Then he greeted Sadie, who was shelling peas at the plain wooden table, and swung her out of her chair into a huge hug, her legs dangling in the air.

Lisbeth smiled. Matthew's affection for their children never failed to touch her spirit. Her mother could not possibly understand the deep pleasure Lisbeth took in the daily routines of domestic life and the love of her family. The warmth in their cozy home in Ohio was so very different from Lisbeth's childhood home, the Fair Oaks plantation in Virginia.

Matthew held up Mother's letter. "Would you like to read it now?"

Lisbeth waved her sticky fingers and shook her head. "Would you, please?"

As he sliced open the envelope, Lisbeth steeled herself for unpleasant commentary disguised as polite news. Ever the "lady," Mother did not write anything that Miss Taylor, the comportment instructor of Lisbeth's youth, could criticize, but she never failed to point out the ways that Lisbeth's life was lacking: in financial wealth, social standing, and sophistication.

In the ten years since Lisbeth had fled Virginia, Mother had written nearly every month, but she had not once visited Ohio. Not after Sammy, her first grandson, was born in 1859, nor after Sadie's birth three years later. Lisbeth had hoped her mother would be willing to travel once the War between the States was over, but her parents had disappointed her by ignoring each of her invitations in the three years since the end of the conflict. And Mother had not extended an invitation to them.

In his calm voice Matthew read out loud:

> *Dearest Elizabeth and family,*
> *I hope this finds you well. I imagine you are readying yourselves for the harvest. That is a simple pleasure in life that has been taken from me as I continue to mourn for my lost home.*
> *You will be happy to know that Mary Bartley welcomed another son. After two daughters in a row they are delighted. Do not let it weigh on you that God has blessed them with five children. I'm sure his plan for you has a reason and a purpose.*

Jack's son had a fever last week. Johnny is still in bed but is expected to make a full recovery. He has missed many days of instruction, but since he is as bright as his father, I'm sure he will make them up in no time.

Your father is ill and is not expected to live into the New Year. It is only right for you to see him one last time to seek his forgiveness and help me with preparations. Let me know when to expect you.

Regards,

Mother

Stunned, Lisbeth collapsed into the chair across the table from Sadie. A swirl of emotion surged in her chest.

Over the years she had pushed down the hurt from her parents' rejection. She had accepted that they would have a relationship only over correspondence and had not expected to ever have an in-person visit with them again.

But in her heart she longed to see them again, to make peace and perhaps cultivate true affection. Her choice had caused them harm— she knew that now with time and maturity.

Matthew's tanned hand tenderly covered her sticky pale fingers. "You must go," he insisted kindly.

"I would be gone for weeks, perhaps months—what about the harvest?" Lisbeth asked.

"I can manage without you," Matthew replied. "He's your father. You would regret not being with him at the end."

"But he is nothing to me. He has not bothered to write me a letter." Her voice cracked, and tears pushed at the back of her eyes, her body contradicting her words. She acted as if she did not feel the sting of her father's disinterest, but in truth it hurt.

Matthew stared at her, clearly choosing his words carefully. "Any dream of moving past our wounds, past our warfare, will only come through forgiveness. The North and the South cannot be irreparably divided—whether family to family or state to state."

If she went she could apologize, and they might offer forgiveness and blessings. This would be her final chance with her father, and maybe her only chance with her mother.

"I had resigned myself to never stepping foot in Virginia again," Lisbeth said.

"Even if you do not get the reconciliation you desire, you will know you have done your duty as a faithful daughter."

Lisbeth exhaled sharply and nodded.

Sadie perked up, and her bright eyes sparkled with excitement. "You're visiting Grandmother and Grandfather Wainwright?! Can Sammy and I come too? To Virginia?"

Lisbeth hadn't realized her daughter was following their conversation. She considered the girl's question.

Matthew replied, "Sadie, your mother has just been delivered sobering news. Give Momma time, and then we will make a plan."

"Yes, sir," the girl agreed, leaning back in the chair, "but I very much want to meet Grandmother and Grandfather Wainwright. And Uncle Jack. And my cousin Johnny! Don't you think Grandfather wants to meet me? And Sammy?"

Lisbeth's chest swelled. She wished she shared her daughter's faith that they would be welcomed by her family. Sadie had a romantic notion of her Wainwright grandparents, imagining them to be like Granny and Poppy, the grandparents who had made an effort to visit them in Oberlin—Matthew's parents.

Lisbeth sidestepped Sadie's naïve question. "My father met your brother once, when I visited before the war."

"He was just a baby; babies can't do anything," Sadie explained. "Now Sammy is nine and can teach them all about baseball. And playing cards!"

Matthew laughed.

"I agree that your brother is much more interesting now than he was when we last visited," Lisbeth replied, "though babies are a blessing, even if they can't do much."

"Do they hate us because we are for the Union?" her daughter asked, worry furrowing her usually smooth brow.

Lisbeth sighed at the question. How could she possibly explain the complexity of her relationship with her parents to a six-year-old? They had run her out of their home when she had eloped with Matthew Johnson rather than wed the suitor they had chosen for her. She'd utterly betrayed them by marrying an abolitionist and moving to Ohio instead of becoming the mistress of White Pines, a large Virginia tobacco plantation. Lisbeth looked at Matthew, hoping he had a reply, but he just gave a slight shrug.

"*Hate* is a very strong word," Lisbeth stated more clearly than she felt. "Your grandparents do not hate us. Though they are unhappy with the outcome of the war."

"Will we see slaves?" the little girl asked with wide eyes.

"Slavery is over, Sadie," Lisbeth said. "It's a shameful part of the past but is no longer a stain on our country. Do you understand?"

"Yes'm," her curious child agreed, but then pushed on, intrigue in her voice. "But you saw slaves when you lived in Virginia?"

Lisbeth nodded. The children knew that both of their parents' families had owned slaves, but she and Matthew had avoided telling them her family owned one of the large tobacco plantations that had profited off the labor of nearly one hundred enslaved workers. It would cause pain for no purpose, and Lisbeth feared that they would lose respect for her if they knew the whole truth about her childhood while they were too young to put it in perspective.

"And you, Poppa?" Sadie asked.

"Yes, every home had slaves," Matthew replied.

"Many homes," Lisbeth gently corrected her husband. "Not all."

"Slaves didn't have slaves, did they?" Sadie asked.

Matthew and Lisbeth laughed.

Lisbeth said, "No, slaves did not have slaves."

"But some Negroes had slaves," Matthew explained.

Sadie looked at her father in utter disbelief; her eyebrows pulled down, and her mouth scrunched up.

"It's strange, but true," Matthew confirmed.

"Your parents had slaves"—Sadie pointed to Matthew—"but *they aren't* mad that there's no more slavery. And your parents had slaves"—Sadie pointed to Lisbeth—"but *they are* mad that there's no slaves anymore."

"Correct," Matthew replied, then looked at Lisbeth. This was a difficult conversation to have with Sadie. They'd hoped to protect her from the cruelties of the world as long as possible, but they also cherished being forthright with their children.

"There's people who used to be slaves still living in Virginia, right? If I get to go, I'll see some," she declared, excitement filling her voice.

Lisbeth was taken aback by her daughter's attitude. "Sadie, there is nothing to celebrate about the cruel treatment of other people."

Sadie nodded earnestly.

Lisbeth's child would have been surprised to learn that the very chair she was sitting on and the table she was working at were made by former slaves. Sadie knew Emmanuel and Samuel Freedman, the woodworkers who crafted this table. But she didn't know that Lisbeth and Samuel had known one another as children. Until he'd escaped when he was ten years old, Samuel had been forced to work on the plantation owned by Lisbeth's father.

Each winter Sadie accompanied Lisbeth to deliver a Christmas package to the Freedmans, believing it to be a thank-you to Samuel's mother, Mattie, the midwife who had delivered Sammy and Sadie. But Lisbeth brought the basket in gratitude for so much more.

Mattie had been Lisbeth's nurse from the moment of her birth until Lisbeth was twelve years old. As a child Lisbeth was utterly devoted to Mattie, feeling more connected to her than to her own mother. Jordan, Mattie's daughter, was the first baby Lisbeth had ever loved. Lisbeth had doted on her in the afternoons whenever she could get away from her lessons. When Mattie took Jordan and escaped from bondage, Lisbeth lost the two people she loved the most. Her life had been irrevocably turned upside down in an instant. That they both ended up in Oberlin, Ohio, was not entirely a coincidence, as many forward-thinking people chose to make this progressive community their home before and after the war. Their lives did not intersect often here, but Lisbeth was forever grateful for Mattie's love and guidance, which had shaped her into the woman she had become.

Sadie had no idea that their church and her school were unusual in their mingling of the races and in the roles of women. For her it was normal to have a colored teacher and classmates of every hue. Jordan Freedman had started teaching there last fall—the same year that Sadie had begun her schooling. Lisbeth was amused and delighted at the strange turn of events that caused her daughter to admire Mattie's daughter so very much.

"Will we get to stay with Granny and Poppy too when we go to Virginia?" Sadie asked.

"I will be sure to see them when I go, but we have not agreed that you or your brother will be coming with me," Lisbeth told her daughter.

But in her heart she knew that it was time for both of her children to meet her parents.

An hour into her first train ride ever, Lisbeth's pulse was returning to normal. The blur of scenery outside the window was so dizzying that she had pulled down the wooden shutter, much to her children's disappointment. She desperately needed a pause from the stimulation. The car was overly warm, but she kept the window closed tight because of the deafening noise and the bits of soot that flew in. One passenger, sitting just a few seats in front of them, had a hole burned into her traveling gown when a spark from the engine landed on her before it had fully extinguished.

The interior of the train car was cheery, with shiny crimson paint that perfectly matched the velvet-covered benches and made a lovely contrast with the yellow upholstered ceiling and bright-yellow shutters. Currently the car was nearly filled to capacity, but the number of riders changed at every stop. They were surrounded mostly by men, but Lisbeth was not the only unaccompanied woman.

Matthew had assured her this was a safe form of transportation, but it seemed unbelievable that traveling forty miles per hour wasn't harmful to their health. By the miracle of this modern invention, the five-hundred-mile trek from Columbus, Ohio, to Washington, DC, on the B&O Railroad would take less than twenty hours. She had never traveled this far without Matthew and hoped that they would not run into any unforeseen difficulties that she could not handle on her own. She wanted to appear confident to her children and took comfort in their company, but she continued to question the wisdom of bringing Sammy and Sadie on this journey.

They were scheduled to arrive at the capital before dark. In Washington, DC, they would stay in a hotel for the night and then travel the following day on the Richmond and Potomac line to Richmond, Virginia, to her parents' new home.

In reality it wasn't a very new home for them. They'd been living there since being forced to sell Fair Oaks eight years earlier. When Lisbeth had made the decision to escape from the plantation, she hadn't considered that the family she left behind might be shunned by their neighbors, causing them enormous financial hardship.

She had entirely overestimated her parents' place in society and underestimated the cruelty of the Cunninghams, the family she'd nearly married into. Lisbeth never regretted her choice to leave, but she felt shame for the harm she'd brought upon her parents and her brother, Jack.

Sammy was bent over, his brown hair practically touching the pages, reading a printed brochure he'd picked up at the train station. "Did you know that the Baltimore and Ohio Railroad provided transportation for Union soldiers during the war?" he asked. Without waiting for an answer, he continued. "It was raided by the Confederacy a bunch of times! Bridges were blown up, and then they had to be rebuilt." He looked up at the closed shutters. "I wonder if we will be riding over some of the new bridges."

Despite herself, Lisbeth smiled at her son's enthusiasm. For him the battles were like a grand story, but she was painfully aware of the human cost of the war. It had been taxing to have Matthew away for months, fighting for the Union while she tended to their small farm. She'd lived in constant fear while he was soldiering, but she had done her best to shelter her children from her anxiety, carrying on as if it were but an adventure. Matthew had returned home with all of his limbs and only a small cloud over his spirit. So many families were not as fortunate. Too many were devastated by the conflict, their men coming home beaten down in body or soul, or never returning at all. When a man simply disappeared, and the family members never learned the circumstances, it was especially haunting.

"Sammy and Sadie, I have a request," Lisbeth began, and Sammy's hazel eyes and Sadie's blue ones jumped to her. She'd been wrestling with how to bring up a difficult subject, but she knew she had to address it before they arrived. "Do not mention the war when we are in Richmond. It is a disturbing topic that will be painful to our family. Please do not speak of it."

They nodded. Sammy asked, "Uncle Jack was a Union prisoner, wasn't he?"

"Yes. It cannot have been pleasant. And Aunt Julianne lost her father and two brothers. As you can imagine they are not very sympathetic to our cause."

Sadie's eyes got big. "Did Poppa kill them?"

Lisbeth took a deep breath. "No. The One Hundred and Fiftieth Infantry defended Washington, DC. Poppa was not stationed near her home. My understanding is her father and brothers were killed in North Carolina."

"She must be very sad," Sadie said.

Lisbeth nodded in agreement. "One never gets over a loss such as that. You simply learn to live with the ache."

"We'll meet our auntie, won't we?" Sadie asked.

"Uncle Jack, Aunt Julianne, and Cousin Johnny live with Grandmother and Grandfather Wainwright," Lisbeth explained. "We will be staying with all of them."

"Is their house grand?" Sammy asked.

"I haven't ever been there," Lisbeth replied, "so I can't say, but they have servants' quarters, as well as room for us, so it must be quite large, though Mother describes it as cramped."

"Why did they leave the home you grew up in?" Sammy asked.

Once again Lisbeth wrestled to find an honest, but discreet, answer.

She spoke carefully. "You know that I did not marry the man my parents chose for me. When I went to Ohio with your father, it was like I chose to be on another team."

"The Union team?" Sammy wondered.

"I didn't realize there would be a war when I left," Lisbeth explained to her children, "and that we'd be on different sides, but, yes, that's essentially what happened. They are angry for all that they lost, and blame me. They became bitter and scared."

"Why is it your fault?" Sammy asked.

Lisbeth took a deep breath. It was hard to put into words. Her son stared at her, waiting for an answer.

"I said yes to an engagement to a man named Edward Cunningham, which is a promise to get married. When I broke that promise everyone shunned the family I left behind in Virginia."

"What's *shunned*?" Sadie asked.

"Their neighbors ignored them, wouldn't buy or sell from them or invite them to parties. Your uncle Jack lost all of his friends."

Sadie's mouth turned down in empathy. "Poor Uncle Jack. He must have been very sad."

Lisbeth nodded in agreement. It was hard to admit to her children that her choice had hurt her brother.

"*You* broke a promise?" Sammy looked like he'd learned a precious secret about his mother. Her lessons about keeping one's word had sunk in.

Edward's traumatic betrayal was something she avoided speaking of or even thinking about, and she had certainly never told her children. Lisbeth considered her words carefully. "I broke a promise because I found out that Edward did something horrible to someone he should have protected," she explained.

"What did—" Sammy started to ask.

Lisbeth interrupted. "You are too young for the specifics, but know that it was so awful that I knew that I could not have a husband like him."

"What did he do?" Sadie looked so curious.

The horrible image of Edward raping a field hand forced its way into her mind. Picturing the desperation in the young girl's brown eyes caused a knot in her stomach and made her physically ill.

Lisbeth steadied herself with a slow breath. "When you are fifteen I will tell you," she said firmly. "You are too young to learn about such things. Breaking my word was a very hard decision, but it was the right one given the circumstances. Keeping your word *is* important, very important, but sometimes you learn new information that makes breaking your promise the right thing to do."

"I was almost born in Virginia?" Sadie asked, seemingly excited and fascinated by this possibility.

Lisbeth smiled, glad to be moving to a new topic. Realizing she was about to challenge her daughter's understanding of herself, she gently replied, "You would not have been born at all if I hadn't married your father."

Sadie drew her eyebrows together, evidently wrestling with the possibility of her own nonexistence. She stared at Lisbeth, her face changing expressions as she thought through the implications of this information.

"That hurts my head to think about," Sadie finally replied.

"It hurts my heart to think about no you!" Lisbeth replied, smiling at her daughter. She looked at Sammy. "And you too!"

"Did you tell them about the bad thing that man did?" Sammy asked.

"Who?" Lisbeth asked.

"Your parents," Sammy replied.

Lisbeth flashed back to Mother's utter disregard when Lisbeth had told her about the scene under the willow tree. She had insisted that part of becoming a mature woman was accepting that this behavior was a common part of life for men, which had added to Lisbeth's horror. Edward's actions and Mother's casual acceptance of his brutality utterly shook Lisbeth's understanding of the world and ultimately led her to abandon that community along the James River.

"I told my mother, but she did not share my concern," Lisbeth explained.

"Oh," Sammy said, worry in his eyes. "Like they didn't understand that slavery is bad."

Lisbeth nodded. "Yes."

"Do they understand now?" he asked, still looking concerned.

"Let's hope enough time has passed for them to come to peace with my decision," Lisbeth said, sounding more confident than she felt.

"Cousin Johnny won't be mad at you, will he?" Sadie asked, putting her own priorities first, as children so often did. Sadie planned on being dear friends with her cousin.

"No." Lisbeth chuckled.

"You don't think Cousin Johnny has a baseball glove already, do you?" Sammy asked.

"Unlike Ohio, baseball is new to Virginia," Lisbeth reassured Sammy. "It is unlikely he will have one, and I think he will be very excited to have something as modern as a baseball glove."

"I promise I won't talk about the war. Now can we watch outside, please!" Sadie begged.

Sadie's enthusiasm was infectious. Lisbeth nodded and opened the shutters. Blurry cornfields rushed by. Her children watched ahead to where they were going with excitement, while Lisbeth gazed out at where they had been with trepidation, preparing herself for what was to come.

CHAPTER 2

JORDAN

Oberlin, Ohio

Jordan slipped the opened letter into her pocket and opened *Harper's Weekly* on the wooden table in front of her. She read news from the world beyond Ohio while her mother cooked bean soup and biscuits for supper. When Jordan came across a story about the treatment of freedmen anywhere in the South, she read out loud, Mama hanging on to every word.

Jordan didn't share her mother's interest in the former Confederacy. Many years had passed since Mama had carried her daughter to freedom, but despite the abolition of slavery, her mother was still obsessed about the safety of their last remaining relative in Virginia.

Jordan was educated enough to understand that the conflict was over and they had won. The war ended three years ago, and the federal government was righting the wrongs of the past. Despite the last few gasps of protests by backward-thinking Whites, equality was now the law of the land. The Thirteenth Amendment had abolished slavery throughout the United States, not just in the ten states in rebellion covered by the Emancipation Proclamation, and the Fourteenth Amendment would soon grant equal protection to all Americans. America was moving forward.

She read out loud an article about the Freedmen's Bureau that proved her thinking. It concluded:

> Congress is providing that the Bureau, which was in its nature temporary, shall cease its work. It has taught the freedmen that they are citizens of a government which recognizes their equal manhood. It has taught the late master class that all men have rights which must be respected. Clad in the armed authority of the United States, it has been a true minister of peace, and as the occasion for its service disappears, the Freedmen's Bureau passes into history with that highest crown of praise, the pious gratitude of the poor and unfortunate.

"They closing up the bureau?" Mama questioned, panic in her caramel-brown eyes. She rushed over from the stove to look at the paper, as if she could make any sense of the letters. She pointed to the paper with her dark-brown finger and asked, "When they gonna do that?"

"It doesn't say, but, Mama, there is no need for concern. So long as Grant is elected president, the liberty of the Southern Negro is assured." Then, to assert her deepest interest, she added, "At least for the men."

While she was speaking Samuel entered the room. Like Jordan, Samuel had been one of the few Negroes to attend Oberlin College, though he had studied law, not education. Born ten years before her, at thirty he was settled into life as a husband and a father. He married Nora soon after he returned from fighting in the war. Their baby, Otis, was the most cherished member of their household. There wasn't much demand for lawyers in Oberlin, so Samuel used his hands as well as his mind, working part-time as a lawyer and part-time with their father, making high-quality furniture.

"Are you fussing about women's suffrage again?" Samuel asked, his deep voice somewhere between taunting and teasing.

"Men—their rights and nothing more! Women—their rights and nothing less!" Jordan retorted, citing her favorite slogan from *The Revolution*, the women's rights weekly newspaper.

"You don't need the vote." Samuel shrugged. "I'll vote on your behalf, Sister."

"And your father gonna vote for me," Mama said, giving her two cents. "It just fine so long as Negro men get to vote . . . everywhere."

"I wish to express my views for myself," Jordan responded, her cheeks heating up.

It was infuriating that her family cared less for her own rights than the rights of faraway freedmen. For her, women's freedoms mattered as much as those of the formerly enslaved. She had even memorized Sojourner Truth's magnificent speech, "Ain't I a Woman"—the original one delivered spontaneously at the Women's Rights Convention in Akron in 1851, not the version revised and popularized by Gage more as an argument for abolition than women's rights. Jordan's favorite lines were from the opening:

Well, children, where there is so much racket there must be something out of kilter. I think that' twixt the Negroes of the South and the women at the North, all talking about

*rights, the White men will be in a fix pretty soon. But
what's all this here talking about?*

Her family appreciated the eloquence and passion behind the
words, but they did not share her devotion to women's suffrage.
Mama wished Jordan were more enamored with Harriet Tubman
and less devoted to Sojourner Truth.

Mama ignored Jordan's comment. "Your sister say they closing
the Freedmen's Bureau," she said to Samuel. "It gonna get ugly—well,
uglier. We gotta go back to Virginia to get Sarah out safe."

Jordan shook her head. For years Mama had been begging her
"niece"—Jordan's "cousin" Sarah—to move from the plantation to
Ohio. Sarah's mother, Rebecca, had been taken into Mama's family
when Rebecca was bought by the Wainwrights, and Mama called
Rebecca her sister even though they didn't share any blood. Rebecca
had died suddenly a few years back, but Mama was determined to
bring her last remaining Virginia relative to freedom, even though
Sarah had been freed by the Emancipation Proclamation for five
years.

Mama gave Jordan a sharp look and scolded, "You owe everthin'
to Sarah. Your cousin wrote the pass that got us free. Never forget
that!"

"Mama, she is not going to come live with us. How many times
have you had me write to her, asking if she wants to move to Ohio?"
Jordan said, keeping her voice calm and respectful, though she
wanted to shout. "She can *still* read. When she writes back she never
even responds to your suggestion to relocate."

"If'n we go with a wagon, she gonna say yes," Mama said. "I feel
it in my bones."

Jordan looked at Samuel. He shrugged. Typical Samuel. He
pretended to go along with Mama, but then he just did what he
wanted, leaving Jordan to take care of their mother. Mama's "feeling

in her bones" was nearly impossible to reason with, but Jordan was going to try.

"It will take weeks, maybe a month, to get there. Virginia is more than five hundred miles away," she reminded her mother.

Mama stiffened and tipped her head forward. Jordan saw a quiet storm was about to rain down on her.

"I may not knows how many *miles* we is from the James River, but I know just how far away it is," Mama chastised, putting on her thickest dialect. "I done walked most of the ways . . . with *you* on my back. I don' need you to tell me it will be a hard and long journey."

"Yes, Mama," Jordan said, annoyed at being reminded, once again, about the hardship her mother had endured to bring the two of them out of slavery. The way Mama talked about it you'd think it happened last year, not nineteen years earlier.

Seeing her mama's mind was set on this fool's errand, Jordan switched strategies so she would not have to go along on the journey. She did not want to take up the rest of her summer break traveling to Virginia to rescue a reluctant stranger. "We can take care of everything here no matter how long you and Pops are gone."

Mama shook her head slowly. "We *all* gonna go. You gonna get a chance to see what you come from."

Dread trickled into Jordan's stomach. The set look on her mother's face told her that she had to come up with a compelling reason to remain behind. Quickly she thought through counterarguments.

"I fear I'll miss the start of the term if I travel with you," she said. Nothing mattered more to Mama than education.

Mama retorted, "Well, then, we better get goin', so we gets you back in time."

"All of us?" Samuel asked. "You want to bring Otis to the South?"

Mama shook her head. "No, we ain't taking my precious granbaby on that long trip. Your son and wife can stay back. They gonna be fine without you for a bit."

"Pops just got a big chair order," Samuel said. "He asked me to work extra time until it's done. He won't want either of us to be gone for weeks."

It sounded like Samuel had finally realized Mama's plan might affect him too. Jordan was glad to have an ally in her brother.

But a fierce look covered Mama's face; her mind was made up. "With or without any of you all, our wagon headin' to Virginia."

Samuel shook his head. "Mama, we can't let you go alone."

"You jus' told me that your pops too busy to come. Besides, he already spent plenty of time in Virginia. He know where he come from." Mama's eyes bore into Samuel. "You forgettin'."

Then Mama looked at Jordan with those intense eyes. "Maybe you don' wanna know what you come from, but not knowin' don' make it so. You ashamed of your past, of me and your pa."

Mama's words hit Jordan hard in the belly because they were true. She did her best to hide it, but she *was* embarrassed by her parents. They didn't understand that the world had changed; they were stuck in backward thinking, still concerned about the rights of Negro men when that had already been earned. Jordan was going to be a part of moving the nation forward, on behalf of all women.

Mama took a deep breath and declared, "Church on Sunday. Then I gonna leave on Monday . . . alone or with company."

"In three days!" Samuel exclaimed.

"It the right time," Mama replied. "I feel it in my bones."

Samuel sighed. "All right, Mama. I'll be in that wagon too," he acquiesced. "Pops can get the order out by himself."

"Ain't that nice." Mama nodded slowly, a small victory smile on her face. She turned to Jordan, her dark eyebrows arched in expectation, clearly expecting a specific answer.

Jordan knew when she'd lost a fight with Mama. "Me too," she submitted.

"Don' you worry. We gonna be back in time for the first day of school!" Mama patted Jordan's hand in reassurance.

Jordan's heart skipped a beat; her argument was a ruse. She wasn't going to be teaching the children of Oberlin next fall. She fingered the letter in her pocket from Lucy Stone, responding to her request to work for the American Equal Rights Association. Like her hero, Sojourner Truth, Jordan was going to be "keeping the thing going while things are stirring"—she was moving to New York City to ensure women's suffrage wouldn't be left behind in this changing time. She just hadn't yet figured out when or how to break the news to her family.

Now that they were going to Virginia, she'd put off telling them. She didn't need the weight of her mother's disappointment added to this stressful journey.

Her family didn't understand Jordan's absolute fury that women's rights were ignored. It was an utter betrayal to the cause of liberty. "Too much, too soon" was a refrain she'd heard, but she couldn't disagree more. She was not going to stand idly by and watch the world advance only for Negro men. She was going to dedicate her life to moving the world forward for women too.

Sunday night the whole family gathered outside to eat supper in the hot evening, the air heavy with moisture. Collard greens with bacon and johnnycakes sat on Jordan's plate. Samuel's son, Otis, pulled himself up using his mother's thigh. On shaky limbs he reached for Pops's outstretched hand. Grabbing tightly with his pudgy fingers, he moved first one leg, then the other, making his way across the divide between the two adults.

Pops cheered. Otis opened his mouth wide in a huge grin, and his dark-brown eyes sparkled with pride.

"He's walking!" Nora exclaimed.

Mama snorted. Nora looked at her, puzzled and hurt by Mama's judgment.

"Don't mind Mama. It's one of her *beliefs*," Jordan explained to her sister-in-law. "She says that's shuffling, not walking."

"Walkin' is when you do it all on your own," Mama said, defending her stance. "Our Otie need a little help. Ain't nothing wrong with that. We all need a hand when we first do somethin'. It jus' need a diff'rent name, that all."

Mama reached her fingers toward the little boy. He grinned up at her, stretching out one brown arm while still holding on to Pops with the other.

"Come on." Mama wiggled her fingers to coax him, a huge smile on her face. The little boy grabbed Mama's finger with his left hand and let go with his right. His body wobbled, first too far to the left and then to the right, but he steadied himself with the support of Mama's hand. Mama nodded encouragement at him, her eyes sparkling with love. Otis toddled across the space into his grandmother's waiting arms. She scooped him onto her lap and gave him a series of quick kisses on each cheek. Mama rubbed her face in his fuzzy black curls until he squirmed and giggled with joy.

Despite being annoyed with her mother, Jordan smiled at the scene. *She sure loves that boy.* Her stomach sank with the sudden realization that she had only a few more days with this little one. Moving to New York meant she was going to miss most of his growing up. The summer in Virginia was cutting short the time she'd thought she would have with him.

Jordan reached out a hand and said, "Come to Auntie Jordan," in the singsongy voice reserved for babies. Otie smiled at her from Mama's arms. He scooched himself to the ground and crawled to his aunt. Jordan lifted him onto her lap and gave him a squeeze, kissing his warm temple. She took in his smell, her heart tender, savoring this moment with her nephew.

Mama turned her attention to her children. "You gonna laugh at me, but I got to prepare you for our journey."

"Mama, Jordan and I arranged the food and the route. Pastor Duhart gave me a list of congregations we can turn to if we need anything. You can just relax in the wagon," Samuel told her. "Mr. Brown says the roads are so good now that it may only take two weeks to get to Fair Oaks." Samuel sounded confident, but Jordan knew he was anxious about returning to the South, the place he'd escaped as a boy and fought in as a man. He didn't share the details about either difficult experience, but Jordan suspected he harbored pain about both.

"I ain't gonna relax until we all back in Ohio," Mama said.

"Then why are we going on this fool's errand?" Jordan questioned gently, hoping she could say something to change Mama's mind. She looked at Samuel; perhaps he would join her protest.

"I gonna die much easier knowin' I tried. I gotta know I tried," Mama said, her voice tightening up. "When we get there, you gonna understand. We got everythin', and they got nothin'. It ain't right."

Pops interjected, heat in his voice. "Listen to your mama. She knows what she talkin' about. Even though the paper says it's fine there right now, you got to be careful."

Jordan nodded passively. Pops hadn't accepted that the world had changed either.

"Nowhere like Oberlin. Nowhere. Not even other parts of Ohio," Mama lectured. "You do like I do. If I step out of the way for a White person, you do the same. If I say, 'Yes, suh, no, suh; yes, ma'am, no, ma'am,' you do the same. Don' look a White person in the eye, and never *touch* 'em, unless they go to touch you firs.'"

Samuel looked at Jordan, exchanging a private eye roll. Jordan thought they were being subtle, but she was wrong.

Pops sat up straight and glared at them both. His whole body moved as he shouted, "Yo' mama tryin' to save yo' life! No White person in Virginia respect you. Yo' clothes, the way yo' talks, that yo' come from Ohio. All that just gonna make 'em hate you more. No education from Oberlin College gonna save you from that hatred."

Jordan's pulse sped up at the intensity of her father's outburst. She hadn't meant to hurt him or show disrespect.

"Sorry, Pops," she muttered.

"Yes, sir," Samuel said.

Nora grabbed Samuel's arm, her brown eyes wide with fear. "You be careful!" she begged him. "Get there. Get them. And come home. No heroics. No fighting for justice."

Samuel agreed. "I promise. We'll keep our heads down."

Pops sat back with a sigh and nodded. The energy visibly left his body now that they were taking his fears seriously.

"Pastor Duhart gave me something special for our journey," Mama said, excited.

She pulled a small velvet pouch from her bodice. Placing it on her palm, she carefully opened it to show them a handful of perfectly round tiny yellow balls.

"Seeds?" Jordan nearly snorted, but she worked to keep her voice even and respectful.

Pops paraphrased from the Bible. "If you have faith as big as a mustard seed, you can move mountains."

"Come close. Hold out yo' hands," Mama told them. The family formed a small circle, with Pops holding Otis. Each put out a hand, the little boy mimicking the others though he didn't know what they were doing. Mama carefully placed a small pile of the little orbs into each palm. "We all gonna have some of these to remind us to keep the faith, and maybe spread some around too. We each get to be like the Sower."

Despite herself, Jordan was touched by the image of all the little mustard seeds in their outstretched hands. Rolling the ones in her palm around, she felt all that they contained: Pastor Duhart's blessing and the support of their whole church, the connection they would give her to Pops, Nora, and Otis while they were gone, and her mama's outspoken faith that they were all sowers, each in their own way doing something to make this world a bit more righteous and loving.

"Thanks, Mama." Jordan smiled. "I'll keep these close on our journey." She looked around at the faces of her family. In their eyes she saw mirrored her own emotions: gratitude, fear, and hope.

Then Otis turned his hand over, scattering his seeds onto the ground and causing them all to laugh. He broke the spell of the moment. Their sacred circle broke apart, and they went on with their night, cleaning up and finalizing their packing.

Despite the sweet feeling from receiving the seeds, Jordan was annoyed. She bristled at the thought of traveling for weeks with her brother and her mother, taking their orders, and she resented that she was being forced to go on this trip at all. Jordan had no interest in acting subservient to White people when they got to Virginia, all to rescue a woman who didn't care about escaping her situation.

Jordan loved her family, and she respected what her parents had done to give her a "better" life, but they just didn't understand her and what she wanted. Mama didn't hide her hopes that Jordan would soon choose among her suitors, get married, and have children—just like Samuel. But she was different from her brother. She wanted more from life than Oberlin could offer. Jordan was going to make a meaningful contribution to the world, a contribution that mattered. She was going to sow her seeds in New York.

CHAPTER 3

LISBETH

Richmond, Virginia

"Now it's the South?" Sammy whispered the question to Lisbeth.

"Yes," Lisbeth replied. "We are in Virginia."

It was hard to take in that the capital of the Union and the capital of the Confederacy had been only one hundred miles apart. The sky, the plants, and the railway were identical in the North and in the South. The enormous boundary between Washington, DC, and her former home state was emotional and political, not physical.

As the train sped through the forest, Lisbeth was touched to see the landscape of her childhood. The trees, the moisture in the air, and the undulation of the horizon were so familiar. She was startled to realize that her body felt at home here.

Sadie poked Lisbeth, interrupting her thoughts, and pointed at a wet spot on the floor with a sour face. Lisbeth snorted with a smile.

"Chewing tobacco," Lisbeth explained. "We'll be seeing it everywhere down here."

"Like baseball players!" Sammy said.

"It is a nasty habit, even if your heroes are enamored with it," Lisbeth lectured.

She watched as a few men spit into the aisle, not even bothering to aim for the spittoons. The pungent smell took her right back to her childhood, when the smell of tobacco was always in the breeze.

Dread rose in Lisbeth as they traveled through the countryside. She remembered the shame and frustration that had shadowed her last visit with her family. Lisbeth had been so utterly delighted with every aspect of her baby that she'd been naïve enough to think that the blessing of a grandchild would be her ticket to forgiveness, but her parents' disinterest in her precious son quickly dashed any hopes that the visit would be a source of happy reconciliation. The monthlong stay had been a thinly veiled display of disappointment and hostility. At every meal Jack and Mother railed against Northern interference in states' rights and attacks on their way of life. Father was distant and preoccupied, hardly speaking anything beyond niceties.

Lisbeth had no illusions that the trauma and losses in the intervening years would have improved their attitudes.

A few hours later they were pulling into the bustling station in Richmond. The city had grown enormously since she had last been here, nearly doubling in size. Fearing she might lose her children, she held their hands tightly on the busy platform and waited for the crowd to clear. Fortunately she didn't have to take any action, but simply accepted the offer of an eager porter, a young light-skinned Negro man, to get their baggage and find them a suitable carriage.

They followed him outside into the bright sunshine. Sammy poked her and pointed to a large white building sparkling in the sun on a nearby hill. She sucked in her breath, taken aback by the sight.

"Is that the . . . ?" Sammy asked.

Lisbeth nodded at her son and replied, "Yes, that's the White House of the Confederacy. Jefferson Davis lived and worked right there."

"Whoa!" Sammy exclaimed.

"What?" Sadie asked.

"The war happened *right here!*" Sammy said, sounding excited rather than anxious about that fact. They climbed into the waiting carriage and set out to find her parents' home.

Sadie and Sammy gawked out the window at the passing scene. Lisbeth's dread grew as they drove west through the commercial and warehouse districts. The children pointed to the charred remains of buildings burned during the Confederate evacuation of Richmond. Much of the debris had been cleared away since April 1865, but the rebuilding was far from complete. More than one pristine Confederate flag hung in the air, the last gasps of a lost cause.

Lisbeth projected calm, but her heart pounded in her chest. She suddenly feared again she'd been naïve to bring her children on this trip. She felt too young and unprepared to shield Sadie and Sammy from the pain of the nation's and her own history.

The business district gave way to a residential neighborhood of well-manicured, stately homes. Brick buildings, set close to one another, rose two and three stories high, very different from the prairie-style wooden farm homes in Oberlin. The carriage stopped in front of a brick house with a shiny black door.

The children ran up the walkway, but they stood back once they arrived at the door, waiting for Lisbeth to take the lead. She closed her eyes and breathed in to steady her nerves. Then she took Sadie's hand on her left, knocked three times, and braced herself for what was to come.

───────── ❧ ─────────

"Emily?" Lisbeth exclaimed at the unexpected ghost from her past standing in the doorway. A rush of conflicting emotions flooded her already-alert nervous system; embarrassment, delight, and surprise swirled in an unusual combination. Mother had written that they had taken Emily with them when they were forced to sell Fair Oaks, but she had not mentioned her name in a number of years. Lisbeth hadn't imagined Emily when she thought about this reunion with her family, nor the complex reaction their unusual relationship would invoke.

Emily was as beautiful as ever, still tall and lithe, though the years showed in the spread of her face. Her light-brown skin was smooth, and no gray showed in the dark hair pulled back into a neat bun.

Lisbeth was startled at the intensity of her own emotion at the sight of this person. Her initial impulse was to hug the woman who had cared for her dutifully after Mattie left, but they had never hugged before. It would seem strange to start now. Her relationship with Emily was unlike any other, and she had a hard time reconciling this part of her past with her current life.

Mother and Father had planned to give Emily to Lisbeth after she married Edward Cunningham. Emily would have moved to White Pines with her, and instead of being a part of her history, she would have been Lisbeth's closest daily companion. Though the war might have ended that arrangement too.

In addition, Lisbeth harbored a suspicion that she and Emily might be related by blood, though she had never confirmed that belief, nor spoken of it. Lisbeth was mindful of the strange situation she was walking into. Emily's wry smile showed Lisbeth she might feel the same way.

"Hello, ma'am. Welcome. It's nice to see you again, and meet your children."

Emily ushered them into the foyer. Lisbeth noted the shiny parquet floor and the cherrywood staircase to the right leading upstairs. To the left was a closed door, presumably to the sitting room.

"Emily, it is so very nice to see you too. You look very well." Lisbeth smiled. "You are married? With a son?" When Emily nodded, Lisbeth said, "Congratulations. How old is he?"

"Willie turned seven last month," Emily replied. "Close to your age, I think," she said to Sammy.

"Emily, this is Sammy. Sammy, this is Miss Emily," Lisbeth introduced. She started to say more, wanting to explain her relationship with Emily to her son, but found no familiar terms were adequate.

"Nice to meet you, Miss Emily," her son said, reaching out to shake hands.

Emily looked taken aback and stared at Sammy, then glanced at Lisbeth with her brows slightly furrowed. She looked back at Sammy and slowly reached her hand out to him, a sad smile on her face. Lisbeth felt the unspoken poignancy of the moment, and she let the complex silence stand until Sadie tugged on her hand.

"And this is Sadie," Lisbeth said. "My six-year-old."

Coming out of her thoughts, Emily said, "Sorry, ma'am."

"How do you do?" Sadie said cheerfully with a tiny curtsy, something she'd learned about recently and decided was the most elegant way to greet people.

Emily smiled and nodded to Sadie. She looked back up at Lisbeth. "Your family is right through here. They are expecting you."

Lisbeth's pulse quickened. She and Emily exchanged a glance as she opened the door; then Lisbeth grabbed Sadie's hand and walked over the threshold.

Mother sat on the familiar blue upholstered couch. Jack and a young woman with dark-blond hair sat nearby.

Mother had aged enormously in the last eight years. The stress of the war showed in her gray hair and gaunt face. She stared at Lisbeth and the children, unmoving, her face unreadable. Lisbeth felt Sadie's little hand tighten in hers. She gave it a small squeeze and put an arm around Sammy's shoulder.

Jack's face was stony. Gray shot through his brown hair, and his blue eyes had sunk into his leathery skin. Her apprehension that he neither had forgiven her nor now welcomed their visit grew.

Julianne—wearing an unreadable expression—appeared just as Lisbeth had imagined, with a lovely sweetheart-shaped face and smooth skin. Julianne's dress was shiny green taffeta with lace trim. Her waist was tiny, due to a tightly cinched corset. Lisbeth flushed with embarrassment as she realized how dowdy she must look in her blue cotton gingham and single petticoat. Only rare formal occasions caused her to bear the pain of a tight corset. She hadn't even considered it for this day.

Lisbeth gazed around the room, taking in the rug, furniture, and pictures. It was disconcerting to see her childhood belongings in this unfamiliar room. A flood of memories cascaded through her brain: counting the flowers on that rug, playing clapping games on that davenport, Father arguing with the paper in that chair.

"Elizabeth, you made it," Mother said without rising. "I hope your journey wasn't too tiresome."

Being called Elizabeth caused her to feel like an insecure child again. Only her parents, her brother, and Emily had ever called her by that name, and no one had used it in the years since she left Fair Oaks. In her mind, she'd been Lisbeth for as long as she could remember. Sadie's head whipped around; her daughter was probably amused and confused to hear her called by a new name.

"It was fine. Thank you, Mother," Lisbeth said.

Even with the difficulties between them, she'd expected to be welcomed with some sort of embrace. Mother was breaking protocol, leaving Lisbeth feeling awkward and uncertain about what to do or say.

"You are staying, are you not?" Mother asked, her voice short.

"Of course . . . I just," Lisbeth stuttered. She sank down on the davenport across from her mother, Sammy and Sadie close on each side.

"Mother, this is Sadie. And you remember Sammy," she said.

Mother looked at them, her eyebrows arched in anticipation. When they didn't understand her unspoken hint, she sharply asked, "You are not going to greet your grandmother with a kiss?"

Lisbeth's heart dropped. She'd had no idea what her mother wanted from her or her children. She patted Sadie and Sammy on the back, silently encouraging them to do as their grandmother asked.

"That's better," Mother said after they had each taken a turn kissing the cheek she offered. "Now kiss your aunt and greet your uncle."

Lisbeth watched her children slowly walk over to Julianne, looking somewhat wary. The petite blond woman accepted their kisses with a smile. In a strong North Carolina accent she said, "Johnny will be here soon. He is looking forward to meeting his only cousins."

Lisbeth felt the sting in her sister-in-law's words, and her eyes traveled to the black mourning locket around Julianne's neck. The fashion rose during the war as a means to proclaim one's loss to the world. There were no cousins on Julianne's side because her brothers were killed before they had children.

Jack reached out a hand toward Sammy and said, "I am glad to meet you, young man."

Sadie put her hand out to shake Jack's as well. Her uncle took it, but then turned her hand sideways, leaned over, and kissed it.

"In Virginia," Jack explained in a deep voice, "a gentleman does not shake the hand of a lady."

Sadie smiled at her uncle, looking very proud, and then looked over at her mother to make sure she was watching. It was surprisingly sweet for Lisbeth to watch Sadie with her long-estranged brother.

Apparently Jack's anger toward Lisbeth might not be directed at her children. Lisbeth nodded in encouragement to Sadie.

"How is Father?" Lisbeth asked.

Mother cleared her throat and blinked a few times. "He is fading, as I mentioned in my letter. The doctor has given him drops to keep him comfortable, so we are deeply grateful that he is no longer in pain. He sleeps most of the day."

Lisbeth nodded, but before she could ask more, the door opened. In walked a child with bright-blue eyes and golden-brown hair who was the spitting image of Jack when he'd been a boy. A new layer of sediment settled onto Lisbeth's already-complex emotional landscape as she thought of her brother from so long ago.

She'd felt a disconcerting mixture of fear and pity toward Jack for most of her childhood. When he was a very young child, he'd seemed confused and sad, and was too often a target of their grandmother's anger for simply having the energy of a child. Lisbeth had felt compassion for him but had been helpless to shield him from their grandmother's wrath. In time Jack toughened up, becoming a shrewd and cruel bully himself. Lisbeth had steered clear of him as a rule, making a point to never be alone with her brother. They had been virtual strangers living in the same home until she left.

Neither Lisbeth nor Jack had made an effort in the intervening years. Lisbeth learned of his life from Mother's regular correspondence and Julianne's periodic notes. She'd written him the expected congratulations on his marriage and the birth of his son. She felt none of the sisterly affection for Jack that others seemed to have for their siblings. When she was honest with herself she realized she was as much to blame as Jack for the ongoing distance between them. She hadn't considered that her decision to leave the plantation would affect him so dramatically, but it had—yet she'd never spoken of it with him.

The boy walked straight up to Sammy and said, "I'm Johnny. You're my cousin!"

"I'm your cousin too," Sadie declared.

The adults chuckled. Amused at how forthright children could be, Lisbeth was grateful to stop thinking about her estranged relationship with Jack. Johnny sucked in a cheek and rolled his eyes at Sadie's introduction. Suddenly Jack's hand shot out, and he grabbed the skin on the boy's small arm between his thick fingers and pinched hard.

"Ow!" Johnny's body jerked, and he cried out.

"Be a gentleman, and greet your cousin Sadie like the young lady that she is," he scolded his son.

Lisbeth's mouth went dry, and her heart wrenched for Johnny. She and Matthew did not pinch or hit their children to teach them lessons. Jack's behavior was an overreaction and unnecessarily cruel. It would do nothing to increase Johnny's affection for Sadie; in fact it might produce the opposite effect.

The moment of affection she'd felt for Jack vanished. She felt as helpless and confused watching him lash out at his son as she had when their grandmother had slapped Jack. Sadie and Sammy looked at her, pleading in their eyes. Lisbeth's stomach sank. Her children were getting a vivid lesson about the household she'd grown up in.

Johnny blinked back tears and said, "How do you do? It's nice to meet you, Cousin Sadie." Then he took a step away from his father and turned back to Sammy. "Wanna play with my top?" he asked.

Sammy looked at Lisbeth for permission. The tense moment had passed, though Lisbeth's stomach still churned. She nodded, and the two boys started to leave. Sadie returned to her side and cuddled close to Lisbeth.

"Do you want to go with them?" Lisbeth asked the girl quietly.

Sadie shook her head. Lisbeth patted her daughter's leg.

"While the boys play, I can show you to your room and acquaint you with the routines of the house," Julianne said with a smile. "Perhaps there will be time for me to braid your hair before dinner,

Sadie. I do so enjoy arranging hair and seldom get the chance, since I have no daughter."

Sadie nodded vigorously. "Of course you may braid my hair, Aunt Julianne."

Lisbeth smiled at her sister-in-law. It seemed there would be moments of sweetness interspersed in this tense visit. Perhaps Sadie would help her family thaw the chill that was between them.

Julianne brought them first to Father's room. Lisbeth paused in the doorway, breathing deeply to calm herself in preparation for what she might see, before slowly rounding the doorjamb.

Father looked peaceful in his sleep, though he was utterly changed. His thin face was hardly more than a layer of skin over his skull bones, his bright-white hair like a halo of dandelion seeds around his head.

In the many years since she had visited, he had written short greetings at the bottom of Mother's letters, but that was the extent of their contact. They had never been close, so it was not surprising that he did not make an effort once she had moved to Ohio.

He had always been more interested in the newspaper and the Bible than his children, but tenderness toward him welled up in her. This was her very own father.

Lisbeth walked over to the bedside and took his hand. It was bony and warm, with veins popping out from under the thin skin. The quilt that covered his diminished body was the one he had slept under when she was a child. She rarely went into his room back then, but still she recognized it. She ran her fingers across a dark-blue triangle and felt the history contained in the cotton fabric, and she was struck by the poignancy of this situation. She'd returned to tend to her parents, who were virtual strangers, but she felt a deep obligation toward them, as well as a desire to finally earn their affection.

Lisbeth gestured for Sadie to join her at the bedside. Her daughter approached slowly, looking serious, but not too frightened.

"This is your grandfather, Sadie," Lisbeth said.

"Is he really dying?" the girl whispered.

Lisbeth's throat swelled, and she nodded. "Yes. We're here to give him comfort in his final days."

"Yes'm, I will." Sadie leaned into her for support, and Lisbeth wrapped an arm around her daughter.

"I will be spending most of my days in here with him. You can help Cook in the kitchen."

"We do not have a cook," Julianne corrected. "Emily prepares our meals, as well as doing the cleaning."

"This whole house? By herself?" Lisbeth asked, instantly regretting that she sounded judgmental.

"Yes. This whole house. By herself," Julianne snipped back. "Times are difficult for all of us."

"Of course," Lisbeth said. "I'm sorry."

Father stirred in the bed and opened his eyes, looking at Sadie. They widened, seemingly in wonder. Still lying down he said in a raspy voice, "Elizabeth? Is that you?"

Lisbeth's throat was too tight to speak. She cleared it and swallowed hard.

"Father, this is my daughter, Sadie," Lisbeth said.

He looked at Sadie, then at Lisbeth. His eyes filled with water. "You've come to see your father in his last days?"

He reached out a shaky hand and patted Lisbeth on the arm. "I am so relieved you are here. Thank you for coming." A small smile passed over his face. He closed his eyes, and in moments she could hear his heavy breathing again. Tears welled up in Lisbeth's eyes—her father *was* glad for her presence.

Julianne was staring intently at Lisbeth. "He hasn't spoken that many words in weeks," she said, rancor in her voice.

Lisbeth was confused by her hostility until Julianne spoke again.

"It must give you peace of mind that *you* will be there to comfort *your* father at the end. Many of us are not so fortunate."

Lisbeth reached a hand out to pat Julianne's arm, intending to provide a modicum of support to her sister-in-law. Of course Julianne felt pain knowing that her brothers and father had died without the solace of home and family in their last moments.

Lisbeth said, "We are blessed to be able to be here. And I'm grateful to you for allowing us into your home."

Julianne pulled in her lips and exhaled a sharp snort. "It's kind of you to imagine this is my home, but your mother does not ever let me forget that I am a guest here."

Lisbeth was surprised at her sister-in-law's plain language and at the sentiment. Mother described them as a unified and happy family living under one roof. Apparently she'd been misrepresenting the situation in this home.

Julianne led them to the small bedroom they would be sharing for their stay. The marble-topped washbasin was the familiar one from Lisbeth's childhood room. She ran her fingers over the cool, smooth stone.

"After you wash up and change your clothes, I can fashion your hair," Julianne explained to Sadie. "The children will join the adults for supper, since your arrival is a special occasion."

"Where do we usually eat?" Sadie wondered, looking confused.

Julianne replied, "With Emily in the kitchen—except for Sunday supper."

Sadie looked at Lisbeth and shrugged.

Lisbeth replied, "That's different than how we take our meals at home, but you can adjust, can't you, Sadie?"

The little girl nodded, looking earnest and eager to please.

Julianne directed her gaze at Lisbeth. "You would be wise to prepare your children for your mother's standards."

Then she turned and left them alone. Lisbeth exhaled in relief for the moment, but she knew that the next few days of getting her children accustomed to fitting into this household would be exhausting. She and Matthew practiced a modern form of child rearing, eating their meals together and allowing their children to speak up with questions or thoughts. Sadie's and Sammy's habits would need to change if they were going to fit in here.

With Father too weak to sit up at the table for meals, Jack presided at the head of the well-worn cherrywood table. Mother sat at the foot. Lisbeth, flanked by her children, sat across from Julianne and Johnny. Lisbeth rubbed the wood, remembering the many meals she'd eaten at this very table—bored as a young child, nervous that she or Jack would provoke an angry outburst as she grew older, and finally scared of divulging secrets that would harm Mattie or herself.

Fearing Sadie and Sammy would be confused by the rituals of the meal, before they sat down she had instructed them to take their cues from Johnny to know when to speak or from her to know what utensil to use. Sadie proudly showed off a new look, her hair held back by a lovely mother-of-pearl headband with two sausage curls hanging down the sides of her head. At the start of the meal Sammy put his hands out for grace, but he quickly returned them to his lap when he saw that no one else was reaching out. There were so many little differences in this home that reminded them they didn't really belong here.

Emily came out of a swinging door with a plate of fish. She moved around the table to serve each seated person. Sammy had no problems getting the food to his plate. Lisbeth offered to serve Sadie, but her daughter waved her off, whispering that she could do it herself. A few drops of sauce landed on the tablecloth, but otherwise she was successful.

Lisbeth felt a combination of familiarity and discomfiture being served. Her childhood had prepared her well for it, but in Ohio they did not have any help in the house. She wanted to signal to Emily that she found this whole system barbaric, but didn't know how to without drawing unwanted attention to herself, or to Emily.

She could not recall her children ever having the experience of being served, but they handled it without embarrassment. The adults made polite conversation of no consequence, while the children sat quietly. Lisbeth was proud that Sadie and Sammy ate the bass with oyster sauce and young greens without complaint, though they were unfamiliar tastes. Lisbeth searched for a topic of conversation when they fell into an awkward silence while eating their dessert of burnt custard.

"Mother tells me you are now a justice of the peace?" Lisbeth directed the question to her brother.

Jack nodded, but didn't elaborate.

Julianne filled in the details. "He was appointed to honor his service to the great cause. We make a special effort to reward the sacrifice of *our* prisoners of war. We take care of our Southern heroes."

Lisbeth didn't miss the not-so-subtle slight in Julianne's words.

Sammy perked up and asked, "You were a prisoner of war, right?"

Jack nodded.

Respect and fascination in his voice, Sammy asked, "Did you have to eat any rats?"

Jack's face contorted in disgust. "No! How could you think that?"

"Timmy's pa said they ate them at Andersonville, 'cause there was no food," Sammy explained.

"We had food," Jack replied quietly.

Mother spoke up, heat on her cheeks and in her voice. "*Our* soldiers did not invade *your* lands, burn crops, and slaughter animals without mercy, leaving everyone, including women and children, to starve. That cannot be said for Union soldiers, who have no thought of human decency. Your soldiers went without food because your Mr. Lincoln was a cruel and heartless man."

Lisbeth felt heat rising in her and tension building in her neck. She was dismayed that their exchange had taken this turn. Her goal had been to steer clear of controversial topics. She had asked her children to avoid talking about it, and on their first day here she herself was responsible for leading them directly into it.

Lisbeth deflected the conversation. "Tell me what your job entails as justice of the peace."

Jack turned his head slowly and stared hard at Lisbeth. Her stomach dropped at the intensity of his gaze. "I keep the peace, just like it says in the name," he drawled without emotion.

"Jack makes certain the social order is maintained, even in these trying times," Julianne said. "Large number of niggers have deserted the plantations and congregate in cities."

Lisbeth flinched at the word. Subtly she looked in turn at each of her children. Each was staring at her with eyes wide in horror. They had been firmly taught that word was absolutely forbidden to ever be spoken.

Julianne seemed not to notice their reactions though, blithely continuing. "They are overburdening the towns and depleting the agricultural regions of labor. They do not believe that they need to work and expect we will simply provide for all their needs. Jack ensures they have lawful employment."

Sadie leaned over to whisper in Lisbeth's ear. "Aunt Julianne used a bad word."

"Sadie Ann!" Mother shouted.

Sadie jumped. Lisbeth's heart sped up. Lisbeth's and Sadie's heads turned to the foot of the table.

Mother chastised, "We do not whisper in this home. Anything you have to say, you must say out loud."

All eyes turned to Lisbeth's child. Sadie's small head bobbed up and down, her eyes wide with fear and her chin quivering.

Mother Wainwright continued to glare at Sadie, waiting for her to speak up. Lisbeth's chest hammered hard; her daughter was trapped in an impossible dilemma. Sadie would be rude to share her observation out loud or keep it private. Either choice would further infuriate Mother.

Lisbeth spoke up to protect her daughter. "Sadie noticed that we use different language in our home than you use in yours."

Lisbeth stared down her mother. Mother stared back, but finally looked away without further comment.

"May I be excused?" Sadie asked in a quavering voice.

"Yes, dear." Lisbeth nodded, feeling bad for Sadie, but wanting to put this interaction behind them as soon as possible.

Sadie stood up to leave.

Mother asked sharply, "Sadie Ann, what are you doing?"

Looking distressed, Sadie turned to Lisbeth. Lisbeth shared her daughter's hurt. She smiled in empathy and nodded an encouragement to the girl to speak up.

"Leaving the table after being excused?" Sadie said, more question than statement.

"What is in your hand?" Mother rebuked, contempt in her voice.

"My plate, ma'am," Sadie replied, on the edge of tears.

"Put it down. *Now*," Mother ordered. "In this home you will not touch a dish. Do you understand?"

"Yes, ma'am," Sadie squeaked out. "I won't make that mistake again."

"You *will not* make that mistake again," Mother corrected.

Sadie gave a slight, shaky nod. Lisbeth's heart welled up into her throat. She was embarrassed at her mother's reaction to her child's manners and angry at herself for not better preparing Sadie for this world. She wanted to apologize to her daughter and give her a reassuring hug, but that would simply draw further attention to them both. Instead she patted Sadie's arm and whispered, "Go on now. It's over. You can play in our room. I'll be up soon."

"It is no wonder they sound like servants," Mother hissed to Lisbeth. "You speak like one as well."

Lisbeth was relieved for the peace that came when she and the children were alone in their bedroom. It felt like forever since they had left Oberlin, but it had not even been two days. This was going to be an exhausting visit, full of traps to be avoided.

Sadie and Sammy were tucked into bed. Lisbeth shared the details of their day in her letter to Matthew, grateful to have an opportunity to unburden her heart in this nightly ritual. Thanks to the new innovation in the postal system, the Railway Mail Service, Matthew would get her letter just a few days after she posted it. It was worth the expense to experience a connection despite their physical distance and to hear one another's news.

"Momma?" Sadie asked from bed. Sammy lay next to her, reading *Alice's Adventures in Wonderland*.

"Sadie?" Lisbeth replied in the same emphatic tone.

"Was your mama nice when you were little?"

Lisbeth inhaled and considered how to answer the question. Sadie stared at her mother intently, waiting for a reply.

"My mother did not spend very much time with me when I was a child. As I have told you before, Mrs. Freedman took care of me."

"All of the time?" Sadie asked.

Sammy put down his book and turned his attention to their conversation. Lisbeth nodded to both of them.

"Who put you to bed?" Sadie wondered.

"Mrs. Freedman," Lisbeth replied.

Sammy asked, "Who prepared your meals?"

"Cook."

"Did your mother do anything for you?" Sammy asked.

"As I grew older I joined them for meals, and in the parlor after supper. We went to church without Mattie." Lisbeth dug in her mind for memories. "Mother taught me to cross-stitch," she explained. "I'm sure she taught me other things as well, but I do not have many recollections of being with her."

"Did she hug you when you were sad?" Sadie wanted to know.

Lisbeth shook her head slowly. "No. My mother was never affectionate like that."

"I'm sorry, Momma," Sadie said. Concern filled her eyes.

"Thank you, Sadie. I am very fortunate that I had Mrs. Freedman to care for me," Lisbeth replied. She was ready for this conversation to end. She could not explain something to her children that she did not understand herself.

In nearly all of Lisbeth's memories, her mother was cold and distant. The only time Lisbeth felt that she pleased Mother was when Edward Cunningham had taken an interest in her. "It has been a long day. Time to sleep; no more questions."

Sadie closed her eyes, and Sammy returned to his reading. Lisbeth kissed her daughter's forehead and hummed "Go to Sleepy Little Baby" until the soft sounds of slumber emanated from Sadie.

In the morning, Lisbeth walked the children to the kitchen. Emily stirred a pot on a small black cast-iron cookstove. The nasty smell that filled the air told Lisbeth it was heated by coal. A platter with fried eggs and grits sat on the table where Johnny and another boy were seated kitty-corner to each other.

Emily introduced the light-skinned child. "This is my son, Willie."
Willie was so fair that Lisbeth had first believed him to be White. His
father, William, must be mixed like Emily.

Lisbeth stared at the boy, struck by the fact that he could be her
nephew or her cousin, but she would never know the answer to that
lingering question. Looking for a family resemblance, she decided
that Sammy and Willie had the same eyebrows. Though it could
simply be a coincidence, a trick of her own mind.

Sammy put out his hand. "Nice to meet you. I'm Sammy."

Johnny snorted. "You don't shake hands with a niggra. Don't you
know anything?"

Sammy looked at Johnny and then at his mother, confusion in
his eyes, his hand still reaching out like a bare branch, vulnerable and
brittle. Lisbeth hurt for her son. She took a deep breath.

"Johnny, in our family we shake hands with all people, and
Sammy knows it," Lisbeth said firmly.

Willie looked to his mother for guidance. Emily nodded at him.
He shook Sammy's hand once without saying a word.

Johnny glared, and he muttered under his breath, "I thought you
were in *our* family."

Lisbeth heard the comment but ignored it, deciding against
arguing with a child.

"I will leave you to breakfast in here," she told her children. "After
I eat I'll be upstairs with my father. Emily will help you if you need
anything."

Emily replied, "If you come looking for us and we aren't here, we
will have walked to the public square. It's only a few blocks away and
a nice place for the children to run. Anyone can direct you there."

"That sounds lovely," Lisbeth said. "Thank you, Emily."

"You're welcome, ma'am."

Lisbeth sat by her father's bed. He spent most of the day sleeping, but she stayed by his side in case he needed assistance. She offered him sips of water when he stirred and wiped his brow. When he appeared to be in pain, she put drops under his tongue, which soothed him immediately. This was why she had come to Virginia, and she found herself incredibly grateful and touched to have this opportunity. She'd sat vigil with more than one person in Oberlin, but she'd never cared for a family member before.

Even though she and her father had had an unreconcilable moral conflict and she felt hurt by his lack of effort over the years, she nevertheless believed there might be some true healing by her providing solace to her father in his last days. Sitting alone with him in this room, she felt at peace.

A Tale of Two Cities by Charles Dickens was open on her lap, and she was reading it out loud even though Father seemed to be unaware of the words coming from her mouth. Her mother had left the book by the bed for them, and Lisbeth was grateful that her mother's literary choice was a story she enjoyed as well. She doubted that Mother would approve of Dickens's message, though it was most likely that her mother had never read this novel.

Lisbeth was intrigued by the sentences her father had chosen to underline. She felt they gave her some clues about this man she knew so little about. She had grown up with him, but she had no memories of being alone with him as a child and could not even say how he occupied himself during the days when she lived with him. Unlike some fathers, he was not frightening or harsh; rather he seemed almost invisible.

She was interrupted by the click of the door latch. She turned to see Emily carrying a fresh tray. Lisbeth lifted the old tray littered with damp cloths and half-empty glasses from the bedside table. She moved out of the way to make room for Emily to set down the dented and worn silver-plated tray.

"Thank you, ma'am," Emily said.

Lisbeth set the used tray on the bureau and walked back to her father's bedside.

"Emily, I'd prefer that you didn't call me *ma'am*. I realize you must when Mother is around, but please know that I find it unnecessary."

Before Emily could reply, Father stirred in the mahogany bed. His lids slowly blinked open. His cloudy blue eyes focused on Emily and suddenly opened wide, a huge smile springing to his face. Lisbeth did not know what to make of his peculiar attitude.

"Lydia! You came. I prayed that you would change your mind." He grabbed Emily's hand and kissed it. Emily pulled her hand away, looking disgusted.

He struggled to sit up. Excitement lighting up his face, he exclaimed, "We can depart right now. Do you have everything you need?" He looked around like he was searching for an escape route.

Emily looked like Lisbeth felt—confused and uncomfortable.

Lisbeth interrupted, "Father, this is Emily. Who is Lydia?"

Father looked first at Lisbeth, then at Emily, bewilderment rolling over his face.

He looked back at Lisbeth and asked in a hoarse voice, "Am I dreaming?" Without waiting for an answer, the dying man shook his head and mumbled as if he were explaining to himself, "But I see her, right here, before me."

Father blinked slowly in thought. He grabbed Emily's fingers again. "I feel her hand in mine; she must be alive," he declared, longing filling his voice.

"This is Emily, Father. She *is* alive," Lisbeth explained slowly and patiently, as if she were talking to a child. "I do not know Lydia, so I cannot tell you if she is alive or dead."

Lisbeth took her father's hand and pried Emily's fingers from his desperate grip. The sick man sighed and lay down. He rolled to his side and curled into a C shape. Lisbeth watched, her heart twisting as a tear seeped from his eye, slowly traveled across the bridge of his nose, and then fell onto the bed.

He mumbled to himself, "She can still come. There is more time."

Father closed his eyes, and in a matter of moments, Lisbeth was relieved to hear quiet snores coming from his mouth.

"I apologize for his outburst," Lisbeth said to Emily. "It is close to the end; he is agitated and confused."

"Lydia was my mother," Emily stated plainly, her face expressionless.

Lisbeth didn't understand what Emily was telling her; then a hot wave of emotion passed through her as she grasped the implications of Emily's statement. "Lydia?" Lisbeth asked.

Emily nodded. Lisbeth's mind was clouded. She searched for the right words.

"So my father is also your . . ." Lisbeth stopped speaking, not comfortable saying the word out loud.

"I believe so," Emily confirmed.

Lisbeth let out her breath, a chill traveling down her spine. She'd suspected Emily was her sister or cousin when she'd discovered an ambiguously marked family tree: Emily's name was followed by a question mark—with lines to both Lisbeth's father and deceased uncle. Having it confirmed was a mixed blessing. To speak of it outright made her extremely uncomfortable. She had never spoken of her shameful discovery, not even with Matthew. But it was a measure of relief to know the ugly truth.

"Is my mother aware of the situation?" Lisbeth asked.

"She has never been kind to me, so I imagine yes."

"Was he . . . affectionate to you?"

"Extra food, and clothes," Emily stated without emotion. "A pat on the hand now and then. I worked in the house instead of the fields. He insisted I not be sold with Fair Oaks. Your mother was extremely angered. It is the only time I heard them quarrel."

Mother's seething fury took on a whole new meaning. When Lisbeth had revealed that she'd seen her fiancé with a field hand, Mother had dismissed it outright, expecting Lisbeth to accept such behavior, just as she had.

Lisbeth looked at her father. How did he live with such a heavy contradiction in his life? She didn't know what to make of the information. She supposed this made Emily a sister of sorts, but she did not believe that what she felt for Emily were sisterly feelings. She imagined sisters felt trust and affection, but she felt only reserved and uncertain around Emily.

"I don't know what to say." Lisbeth was flustered. "This is a peculiar situation."

Emily's lips tugged into a small, tight smile. "There is nothing to say. It's no stranger than many folks deal with."

"Do you think they loved each other?" Lisbeth wondered aloud.

Emily's eyebrows furrowed, considering her reply carefully. Lisbeth's mind flashed to the scene under the willow that had caused her to flee her childhood home. She'd learned all too graphically how common it was for masters of houses to force themselves upon unwilling field hands. She recalled the horrible sight of Edward's violent thrusting, and the young girl's caramel-brown eyes filled with pain and shame. Her mother could not even consider the hurt to the child, insisting it was welcome attention.

Lisbeth took back her question. "Never mind, Emily. We cannot possibly uncover the truth, can we?"

Emily nodded. "Please do not speak of this with your mother. She will only become more cruel if you do. As it is, I fear we'll be turned out when your father dies."

"Wouldn't that be preferable?" Lisbeth asked. "To work somewhere else?"

"We don't have other options," Emily explained. "We have looked. There are so many freedmen that housing and work are scarce.

William's family home is overcrowded. They cannot fit us in as well. William's employment at the Tredegar Iron Works pays for clothes, school for Willie, and church. My work gives us a room to sleep in and food to eat. Our life has its complications, but we are doing better than many."

"My parents don't pay you?" Lisbeth asked, shocked that such a thing was even possible.

Emily snorted and stared at Lisbeth, looking incredulous. After a moment, she asked, "You imagine they would pay me for housework? In money?" She shook her head. "Is it really so different in Ohio?"

"We pay for labor . . . with money. On occasion with livestock or other goods," Lisbeth explained, "but mostly with money."

"Ohio sounds nice," Emily replied, longing in her voice.

"We are happy there," Lisbeth agreed. She considered telling Emily that White and colored children attended a publicly funded school together in Oberlin, but realized that would only be cruel. There was no point in adding to Emily's pain.

A few days later Sammy came into their room and told Lisbeth, "I wish I had brought two gloves as gifts."

"Does Johnny need one for each hand?" Lisbeth teased.

"No." Sammy's hazel eyes rolled up at her. He explained, "Willie wants to use the glove and Johnny refuses."

"I hope you gave him a turn with yours," Lisbeth told her son.

"Yep, but it ain't the same as having your own."

"No, it's not the same." Lisbeth nodded in agreement, subtly correcting her child's grammar.

"Willie does whatever Johnny says. You say slavery is over, but I don't think Grandmother Wainwright or Uncle Jack or Johnny knows that." Frustration filled her son's voice. "Yesterday, Grandmother

Wainwright told Willie he couldn't go to the park with us because he had to clean the kitchen stove. Like he's her servant. So he stayed and cleaned while Emily took me and Sadie and Johnny to the fairgrounds without him."

Lisbeth sighed.

"Today he went with us, but Johnny wouldn't talk to him or give him a turn with his glove." Samuel was on a roll. He went on, venting his outrage. "When we were at the park a White lady told Miss Emily she wasn't allowed to be there. But when Miss Emily told the lady she was watching us, the White lady said it was okay. You hoped they figured out by now that slavery is bad, right?"

Lisbeth nodded. "Yes."

"They haven't," he said, looking dejected.

Lisbeth hurt for her son. He was losing his faith in humanity and her family. As she feared, this trip was costing him much of his innocence.

Sammy continued. "And I don't think your family has forgiven you for marrying Poppa. They all hate us."

"*Hate* is a strong word," Lisbeth reminded her child.

"Then they don't like us very much," Sammy said.

Her throat swollen, Lisbeth nodded in agreement. "Sammy, I fear you are right."

"Except Sadie," Sammy clarified.

Lisbeth furrowed her brow and tilted her head in an unspoken question.

He shrugged. "Uncle Jack and Aunt Julianne like Sadie."

"She does seem to have captured their approval," Lisbeth agreed. "I'm sorry, Sammy. We just have to make the best of it while we are here. Be kind to Willie and to Cousin Johnny," she said. "Maybe our kindness will help Johnny to see a new way."

Samuel shrugged. "Mr. William says he can take me and Willie to Tredegar if you say it is okay."

"The factory where Mr. William works?" Lisbeth asked. "Is it safe?"

Samuel scrunched up his shoulders and said, "Miss Emily thinks it's fine." He stared up at her, hope in his eyes.

"All right. You may go," Lisbeth agreed.

"Thanks, Momma!" Sammy said.

Sadie came running into the room, excitement in her eyes.

"Look, Momma! Auntie Julianne gave me a *real* locket!"

Sadie held the treasure out to Lisbeth. The silver locket had spiraling swirls engraved around a tiny diamond. Lisbeth pried it open with her fingernail. She choked in fury when she saw a small Confederate flag squirreled away on one side. A picture of a baby looked up at her from the other.

Sadie went on, oblivious to Lisbeth's outrage. "Auntie Julianne says we are her only living relatives, so she wanted me to in—inhere?" Sadie changed tactics. "She wanted me to have it. To keep!" She twirled around and pulled up her hair, freshly braided in the French style that was becoming so popular. "Put it on me," she demanded.

Lisbeth was torn. She didn't want her daughter wearing that symbol around her neck. Sadie turned around and looked at her mother, telegraphing a silent message to hurry up. Lisbeth sighed. Her daughter was too young for a political conversation. Lisbeth would simply trade out that image for another.

Sammy grunted and repeated, "They do like Sadie! And I think she likes them right back."

"Of course I do!" Sadie said. "They are *my* family, and I love them!"

Before coming here, Lisbeth would have been pleased to hear that sentiment from her daughter, but now she was uncomfortable with their influence on Sadie and her attachment to them. She'd prefer that both of her children were more neutral when it came to the Wainwrights. Sadie's adoration was as unsettling as Sammy's disdain.

CHAPTER 4

JORDAN

Ohio

Contrary to Mama's worries, the trip from Ohio to Virginia was more tedious than scary. The roads were so muddy that they had to free themselves from puddles more than once, but they didn't meet any hostilities on the route. The hardtack, dried meat, and dried fruit grew tiresome, but they were adequate to keep hunger at bay. Mama taught them to keep an eye out for edible plants to add to their meals. Wild mustard greens were the most common addition.

At the end of each day, getting the wagon a safe distance into the forest wasn't easy. One night they stopped traveling so late that it was full dark by the time they were tucked into the trees. They made certain to leave more time after that. Sleeping crowded together in the back of the wagon took some getting used to, but after the first few nights Jordan learned to sleep outdoors, and she even came to appreciate it a bit.

This journey was certainly the farthest she had ever traveled from home. She'd been as far as Columbus, the state capital of Ohio, to the south and Cleveland to the north, but she had no memories of being so far east. She enjoyed seeing the changes in the scenery and found herself recognizing the differences between the various plants. For years Mama had been trying to teach her to recognize them and learn their uses, but she'd never taken an interest. Without much else to do on this journey, she found herself thinking about plants and grew excited each time she successfully named one.

Mama and Samuel both grew visibly agitated as they crossed the Ohio River into West Virginia. This part of the country wasn't its own state until 1863, when it stayed in the Union rather than seceding with the land to the east. Seeing the tense look on Samuel's face, Jordan realized he probably had more feelings about Virginia than he usually let on. Nothing changed dramatically on the other side, but the geographic marker meant something to Mama and Samuel that it didn't mean to her.

Once they crossed into Virginia, though, the road changed dramatically. Some parts of it were even paved, and occasionally they were forced to pay a toll to proceed through turnstiles that were protected by pikes. Vestiges of the war showed along the turnpike. Samuel pointed out the clear-cut fields that were a telltale sign of troop camps. Guns, planks from broken-down wagons, and decomposing cloth dotted the road, and cannonballs were half buried in the dirt and shrubbery. A skeleton of a horse still attached to a rotting wagon by leather straps was particularly disturbing to Jordan. She looked at her brother to see if he was alarmed by this situation too.

"Is this close to where you fought?" Jordan asked Samuel.

"We were farther south, and east," he said. "But it looked like this. And the air felt like this, the heat and the moisture."

Samuel was confronting two painful parts of his past by coming back to Virginia. Like most of the returning soldiers, he kept the details of that experience buried deep, but Jordan knew it still affected him. He continued to have nightmares on occasion, though they had lessened over time, and none of them ever spoke about the sounds coming through the planks.

Instead of continuing east to the capital, they traveled the southern route, coming to the James River from the west. Soon they would be at Cousin Sarah's on the Fair Oaks plantation. The dirt road that ran to Mama's old home cut through thick forest. Behind the elm trees Jordan made out workers in the tobacco fields. The landscape was broken up by charred fields and trees that proved that Union soldiers had not simply passed through here, but had fought with fire, as well as guns and cannons.

"This here one a the first, an' one a the last places there was fightin'," Mama said, clicking her tongue in disapproval.

"It shows," Samuel said.

"Here!" Mama directed Samuel. "This the way. Turn before we get to the big house."

They started to turn off the main road onto a rutted trail. In the distance Jordan saw a huge columned house. Suddenly her heart hammered as she felt the enormity of where they were and what they were doing. Ahead was an actual plantation house, these workers had been enslaved, and blood had been spilled right here.

Mama's eyes were round in fear, and she was biting her lip.

"Stop," Mama whispered. "Don' turn here; it too open, and we gonna get noticed. Go past the big house, and hide the wagon in the woods. We gonna walk back."

Jordan noted Samuel's hands shaking as he guided the horses along the muddy road.

"Do you remember this place?" Jordan asked her brother quietly.

His small nod told Jordan that he did. And his tight face showed her that he didn't want to talk about it.

Samuel let out an audible sigh after he stopped the team in a stand of elm trees. Jordan looked at him with sympathy.

"I didn't realize it would be so hard to be back," he whispered.

His hands were still shaking. Jordan patted his arm, but she couldn't think of any words of comfort. Being here elicited such strong emotions in her mother and her brother. She didn't want to do or say anything that would cause them more concern.

Mama leaped out of the wagon. "Me and Jordan gonna walk over to get Sarah. You stay with the wagon, Samuel."

A look of relief passed over Samuel's face, but he asked, "You sure that's safe, Mama?"

"We safer without a man. Less of a threat. You stayin' put," she declared.

Mama looked Jordan up and down, then surprised her by picking up a handful of dirt and rubbing it into Jordan's dress, front and back.

"Muss up your head cover, and your shoes too," Mama directed Jordan. "Then get on yo' knees and crawl around a bit."

"Mama, I'm filthy from traveling. Do I really need to get dirtier? What I actually need is a bath."

Mama snorted. "You don' know nothin' about really needing a bath. And travelin' dirty ain't the same as hard-work dirty."

Jordan sighed. She looked back and forth between her mother and brother. They stared at her, waiting for her to comply.

"You want me to entirely ruin my dress?" Jordan asked.

"I tol' you to wear yo' oldest one," Mama replied.

"It's old, but I still like it," Jordan replied.

"Well, you gotta like fittin' in more than yo' dress."

Jordan took a breath. She reminded herself that she would not have to take orders from her mother for very much longer. She felt ridiculous getting down on her knees and disgusted crawling around in the dirt. She thought to herself that her mother was being overly cautious, and that this trip would soon be over.

After she stood up, Mama examined her, smeared a bit more dirt on her face, and nodded in satisfaction. Then Mama dirtied herself up. Watching her mother crawl on the ground, Jordan was flooded with humiliation. Moisture pushed at the back of her eyes. How could this woman, Sarah, possibly be worth this indignity?

"Take your shoes off. Leave 'em in the wagon," Mama said, bending over to unlace her boots.

"No! Mama, no." Tears burned in Jordan's eyes. That was going too far. "I'm not walking barefoot. Please!" she begged.

Mama sighed. "All righ'. We gonna keep our shoes on."

Jordan exhaled in relief. "Thank you, Mama."

The older woman turned her attention to Samuel. "I hoping we jus' find Sarah and walk out a there with her, but I don' think it gonna be quite that easy. Don' you fret if we gone awhile."

Jordan's brother looked up to heaven and back down. He seemed like he was about to say something when Mama spoke up again.

"Of course you gonna fret," Mama corrected herself. "But jus' sit tight. I know how to get back here. We gonna be gone over the night, maybe two. If we ain't back by the day after 'morrow, then you head to Richmond for help."

Samuel stared at her, looking overwhelmed with worry and confusion. He asked, "Who's going to help me in Richmond?"

"The church," Mama said. She pulled the piece of paper from her bag and handed it to Samuel. "Pastor say they help folks like us."

"You are certain you want me to stay here?" Samuel asked.

"You gonna raise more questions than we are," Mama said. "So, yes. We *all* gonna be better off if you stay here."

Samuel pulled Mama into a long embrace, then opened his arms to Jordan.

After he released them, Samuel looked at Jordan intently and reminded her, "If you see a White person, pretend you're stupid. *Never* let them know you can read. The rules are different here."

Samuel's breathing was shallow, and he wiped his brow. His fear penetrated into Jordan more than Mama's caution. She nodded and gave him a tight smile; then she followed her mother away from her brother.

CHAPTER 5

LISBETH

Richmond, Virginia

Lisbeth heard a thud come from the drawing room. She rushed in to find her mother standing over a glass. Mother stared in horror at the liquid seeping into the carpet.

"I will get a rag," Lisbeth reassured her.

"I dropped my medicine!" Mother screeched. She barked to Lisbeth, "Get me more from your father's bedside."

Mother's whole body shook. Ignoring her command, Lisbeth walked to the older woman's side and wrapped an arm around her shoulder, hoping to be a calming influence. The twitching and panting did not lessen.

"I will send Emily for the doctor," Lisbeth soothed, hiding her alarm at her mother's demeanor.

"I do not want to see a doctor," Mother growled. "I need my medicine! Get it *now!*"

Lisbeth stared at the frantic woman, uncertainty wrestling inside her.

"I know what I need, Elizabeth!" Mother grabbed Lisbeth's wrist and dug in so hard it hurt. "Get me my medicine at once, or I will force you to leave this home, never to return again." Hatred burned in her mother's eyes. Lisbeth started to panic in the face of her mother's intensity, but she took a deep breath. She would get the drops and then call for the doctor if need be.

Wrenching her arm free, she acquiesced with a small nod. "Please sit while I get it, so you do not fall."

Mother clenched her jaw tight, ready to fight, but she let Lisbeth guide her to the davenport.

As Lisbeth walked to the stairs, rubbing her wrist, Mother called, "The dropper with the brown liquid!"

Lisbeth knew what her mother was asking for: the laudanum the doctor had brought to soothe her father's pain. She returned with the glass bottle and started to pass it to her mother, but the older woman's arms shook too intensely to take it.

"Give it to me!" Mother begged.

"Should I get a glass of water?" Lisbeth wondered.

Her mother answered the question by leaning forward with an open mouth, like a desperate baby bird. Lisbeth sat down on the sofa, unscrewed the top of the bottle, pulled the brown liquid into the dropper, and squeezed the serum under her mother's quivering tongue. Mother closed her eyes and finally took in a deep breath. She nodded in satisfaction. Tension slowly left both women's bodies.

"One more," Mother urged.

Lisbeth complied.

"Usually one is enough," Mother explained. "But your visit is impinging upon my calm."

Lisbeth's heart sank. For a week she'd worked hard to be helpful to her mother, encouraging her children to be lovely guests and keeping her differences of opinion to herself. But no matter her effort, Mother was disappointed by her, just as she had been during Lisbeth's childhood.

"What is this medicine?" Lisbeth asked.

"It is for my nerves." Mother's voice took on a challenging tone. Lisbeth noticed she did not answer the question.

"The doctor prescribed it for you as well as Father?"

Mother nodded slowly. "Like him, I am often in need of calming these days."

Mother's eyes took on a dreamy quality. Her shoulders dropped, and she leaned back into the sofa. The quivering stopped, and her breathing slowed. Lisbeth shared her mother's relief.

Mother studied Lisbeth's face for far too long.

"I did not think you would come," Mother said, breaking the uncomfortable silence. "I thought that you would feel no obligation toward us, despite all we have given you."

"I am glad that you asked," Lisbeth replied, realizing it was true. "I wish there only to be mutual fondness between us."

"Why did you not come before?" Mother challenged.

Lisbeth felt heat rise in her. "I visited when Sammy was young, but you did not invite me again."

"A mother should not have to beg for her daughter's company."

The words felt like a horse kick to the chest. Lisbeth bit her lip. She did not wish to engage in an argument.

"You are right. I should have visited sooner," she agreed, hoping to appease her mother, "but the . . . conflict made it unsafe."

"The conflict!" Mother snickered. "It sounds so harmless when you say that word. You have no idea the horrors, the absolute horrors I have lived through."

"I am sorry, Mother. Truly I am," Lisbeth said, and she meant it. She'd never wished any ill will to the family she left behind.

"When the inmates broke out from Libby Prison, I was so terrified that I did not sleep for days. Do you know what I lived through?"

Lisbeth shook her head. She hadn't heard about her mother's experience, but she knew that conditions at Libby had been horrific. It was second in notoriety only to Andersonville in Georgia. Union soldiers were kept in a former warehouse. The windows on some floors had bars but no glass to keep out the elements. The prisoners of war regularly suffered from outbreaks of diseases and malnutrition. Their newspaper celebrated when 109 Union soldiers escaped in 1864.

"I did not want us to be murdered in our beds," Mother explained, venom in her voice. She pointed her bony finger at Lisbeth. "In that very seat . . . I sat up all night . . . with a *gun* on my lap, ready to kill any Union soldier intent on harming us."

Lisbeth took her mother's hand, a spontaneous act of comfort. She'd never considered that the Libby prisoners would seem a threat to her family, though it was understandable now that she thought about it.

Mother continued without taking a break, grabbing her hand away from Lisbeth. "My son, my beloved son who stood by us, was put in prison, and we simply had to bear it. His crime? Protecting our way of life from invaders. I imagine you celebrated when you heard the news that your brother was in prison," Mother hissed. "You certainly did not express outrage or do anything, *anything*, to help secure his release."

The force of Mother's anger was nearly a physical blow. Lisbeth repressed the urge to defend herself. Contrary to her mother's charge, she had not celebrated Jack's imprisonment. She'd been concerned for him throughout the war. However, she was also aware that the prison that held Confederate officers, where Jack had been confined, was warm, with adequate food and medical supplies. In fact Lisbeth had worried less about Jack's safety once he was a prisoner. And there was nothing she or Matthew could have done to secure his release.

Not wanting to argue or provoke her mother, Lisbeth sat quietly in the face of her mother's fury. Mother stared at Lisbeth, her mouth pinched tight. After a long, uncomfortable silence, she relaxed against the davenport, her head leaning back, her face softening and her lids shut. Perhaps she was finished speaking of the war.

Her eyes still closed, Mother mumbled, her tone changing entirely, "I can see the flames in my mind's eye. The doctor says I should put them out of my head, but it is nearly impossible—the drops are the only way to do that."

Confused, Lisbeth waited for more, but when it didn't come she quietly probed. "Flames?"

Mother brought her head forward. She blinked her eyes open, and she seemed surprised to see Lisbeth in the room. She furrowed her brows, then drawled out, "April 3, 1865, was the end—Richmond was no longer the capital, but an occupied city."

Lisbeth understood. Mother was speaking of the evacuation fire. She knew of it from the newspaper account, but her mother had never mentioned it in a letter. Or perhaps she had, but the correspondence hadn't arrived. The post had been increasingly unreliable toward the end of the war.

"I'm sorry, Mother," Lisbeth said. "It must have been very alarming."

Her mother continued, ignoring Lisbeth's condolences. "President Davis must not be blamed for the destruction. The fire was necessary to prevent the Union troops from following." She blinked at Lisbeth. "You must have celebrated the news, but I feared for my life."

Indignation smothered Lisbeth's compassion. How could her mother believe her to be so indifferent to her suffering? She started to defend herself, but her mother interrupted.

"Then"—contempt filled her mother's voice—"your Mr. Lincoln dared come here with his son. Flaunting his cruelty! Celebrating."

Lisbeth believed Lincoln's tour of Richmond was a peace offering, to show respect.

"He got his due ten days later," Mother snarled. "We kept our celebrations private, but no one loyal to the South mourned the day Mr. Booth brought us justice."

Lisbeth felt like a boat being tossed around in a harsh storm of her mother's emotions and accusations. President Lincoln's assassination was as painful as losing a dearest family member. She'd heard there were many people who sympathized with Mr. Booth, but she hadn't let herself believe her own mother was one of them.

Mother stared in challenge, waiting for a reaction. Lisbeth would not give her the satisfaction of showing outrage nor defending the outcome of the war. Lisbeth waited patiently for the next outburst, but Mother dropped her shoulders and looked away.

Changing the subject and her tone, Mother said, "Elizabeth, please help me upstairs. I must rest before supper."

Lisbeth exhaled in relief. This had been a confusing, though informative, conversation. She appreciated the frank words about Mother's experience of the war, but it was exhausting to be chased by her mother's intense emotional states. Mother vacillated between being pathetic, polite, and cruel at such a quick rate that Lisbeth felt like a jackrabbit jumping in all directions.

After Lisbeth guided her mother into bed, Mother cooed, "I have longed for just *this*, Elizabeth. A daughter to comfort me in my time of need."

"I hope Julianne has been a good surrogate," Lisbeth ventured.

"She is too nervous. It is simply not the same." Mother actually smiled tenderly at Lisbeth.

Lisbeth felt wary at the change in Mother's attitude, but perhaps her unburdening was serving to bring peace between them. Cautiously Lisbeth said, "I have always wished to be close with you too."

"Elizabeth, I always felt motherly affection for you. I just did not know how to express it."

Lisbeth's heart swelled at the news.

"You hoped for kisses and pats, but I am not demonstrative like you. Your desire was confusing and overwhelming." Mother sighed. "But I only ever wanted the best for you. Which is why we went to such extremes to ensure your marriage to Edward."

Lisbeth steeled herself for criticism.

"We were shunned, entirely ignored by our dearest neighbors. Your father never recovered. When he passes, the creditors will take everything. Once again, I am going to lose my home. Soon I will be a homeless pauper."

Without thought, Lisbeth offered as reassurance, "Mother, you are always welcome to live with us in Ohio."

She regretted the words as soon as they left her mouth, but tears already pooled at the corners of Mother's eyes and seeped out the edges. Lisbeth had no memory of seeing her cry before.

"You are a dear child. Thank you for bringing comfort to this mother's heart."

Giving in to a yearning to hug her mother, Lisbeth leaned forward, her arms held out wide in an unspoken invitation. She waited in anticipation for her mother to accept or reject her offer. Mother looked back and forth between her two arms, seemingly puzzled, and then finally bent forward, resting her head against Lisbeth's shoulder. Lisbeth sighed in relief. She wrapped her arms around the thin shoulders. Mother reached up and patted Lisbeth's arm. A rush of warmth and tenderness filled Lisbeth. Her eyes moistened. She took in a deep, grateful breath. After so much time perhaps she finally made some real peace with her mother.

After a time, Lisbeth felt her mother's body go slack. She laid her down and tucked her under the covers. She even ventured a tender kiss and brushed the gray hair off Mother's cheek. As she walked out of the bedroom, Lisbeth felt the bottle in her pocket. She opened the door to her father's room to return the laudanum to his bedside table. He was alone, asleep under the quilt.

Father rolled onto his back, his lids open. "Elizabeth? Is it really you?" His voice was still raspy, but his eyes were clear and looked right at her.

"Yes, Father," Lisbeth replied. Apparently he'd forgotten that she was in Richmond.

Still lying down, he said, "You are brave . . . to visit, to face your mother's venom. But then you have always been . . . brave."

He sounded like the man she knew as a child, his voice stronger and more coherent than it had been since her arrival. Lisbeth had sat with the dying before and had experienced the changes in mood and energy, so she wasn't surprised.

She replied, "I came to be of support, for you and Mother."

Father asked, "You do not regret your choice, do you?"

Lisbeth sat on the edge of the bed. She'd never been so familiar with him, and it was strange to be so physically close, but she wanted this conversation—to know a little more of her father while there was still an opportunity.

She replied, "I'm glad to be here with you in this time, after all these years."

Father shook his head and corrected, "I mean your choice to abandon this life. You do not regret that?"

Her neck tingled. She knew the dying spoke honestly, but that question was a startlingly frank and complicated one to answer.

Lisbeth considered her words, striving to be kind, but honest. "I do not regret leaving Virginia, though I am sorry for the harm my choice caused you, Father."

Father replied, "I was not brave in this life, and now I will burn in hell for all of eternity."

"What? No!" Lisbeth challenged, saddened to hear his fear. "Why do you say that?"

"I only hoped to be a simple minister preaching truth. Seminary was the happiest time of my life," Father said.

"You were enrolled to become a minister?" Lisbeth asked, shocked at this new information.

"I was never concerned or jealous that I would inherit nothing. I was grateful for the role God had put me in as a second son, but then he tested me with Alistair's death." Her father sounded defeated. He went on. "I was not brave enough to refuse the evil of my inheritance, and I will pay the price for my cowardice forever. Please pray for me when I am gone, though it will be too late to do me any good."

Lisbeth longed to find words of comfort for her father before he died.

"Father, surely God knows your heart," Lisbeth said.

"Actions matter, not words," Father said, resigned. He stared off into space, lost in thought, his brows furrowed.

She patted his arm, wishing there was something more she could do. Lisbeth felt compassion and sorrow for him, but she couldn't argue for his salvation when she didn't believe in it herself. She thought of the more than ninety slaves that her father had owned. He spoke of himself as a benevolent master, but privately he understood it was a sin. He had lied to her, and to himself, when he'd explained that the enslaved were an inferior race who needed his care. For years Lisbeth had believed that myth—until she discovered that men like him forced themselves upon girls for their own pleasure and power.

She thought of Emily, and the layers of deceptions that were hidden in her childhood home.

A smile split her father's face. His affect totally changed, he said, "I know! I will free all my slaves upon my death. Surely that will give God cause to bring me to heaven!" He smiled a dreamy smile.

Lisbeth considered telling him that he no longer had that power, but he looked so delighted with his solution. What purpose would it serve to tell a dying man that he did not have a route to heaven? He would learn soon enough.

Father whispered urgently, "Lisbeth, do not tell your mother, for she would be furious. Bring paper, quickly! I must do this today!"

Disdain joined the sorrow in Lisbeth's heart. Even this close to his death her father was a coward, unwilling to do what he knew was right in God's eyes.

"But first I must rest, for I am so tired." He rolled to his side. Lisbeth wondered if he would say more, but when the soft sounds of heavy sleep came from his throat, she gave up on him.

CHAPTER 6

JORDAN

Fair Oaks plantation, Virginia

Jordan and her mama cut through the brush back to the main road toward Fair Oaks. Trickles of sweat ran down Jordan's back as they walked. With each step she regretted that the wagon was so far away from their destination. On the hot, deserted dirt road Mama's caution felt undue.

"Keep your mouth closed, and your eyes down!" Mama lectured Jordan. "I gonna do all the talkin' if we see anyone beside Sarah. And keep your shoes hid. They a dead giveaway no matter how much we mussed 'em."

Jordan nodded absentmindedly and took in the scenery. She'd imagined only harsh ugliness, but this was lovely. Elm and hickory trees lined the road. Beautiful shrubs with yellow flowers dotted the ground, contrasting with purple aster. Breaks in the trees revealed fields of tobacco plants nearly six feet tall. The huge leaves were striking in the sun.

"It's gorgeous here, Mama. I had no idea tobacco grew so high."

"It sure is." Mama got a wistful look in her eyes as she took it all in. "So much beauty and so much ugliness all mixed together. My heart don' know what to make of it."

Jordan hooked her arm through her mother's. Her spirit was confused too. It felt peaceful, walking on this road past these plants. Mama had lived right here for nearly thirty years. This was Samuel's childhood home. In all the stories that she had heard, Jordan had never pictured the plantation as appealing in any way, only horrific, but this was idyllic.

They turned onto the wide dirt path that led to the cabins. Mud filled the ruts left by wagon wheels. Rows of tall plants blocked the view of the big house. Heads poked up and then disappeared behind the tobacco leaves. In the distance Jordan saw a dozen or so small shacks lined up in two rows. Past them there was a dark smear, probably the James River she had heard so much about.

As they walked past a break in a row of plants, Jordan saw a White man on a dark-brown horse. She quickly turned her head away and whispered to her mama, "There's an overseer! Right there." Her mouth went dry as fear replaced her enjoyment of the scenery.

"I seen him too," Mama replied. "Maybe he ain't noticed us."

"You! Turn around!" a deep voice shouted behind them.

Mama patted Jordan's hand and hissed, "You stay quiet!" Then, "Yes, suh," Mama said with her head bent and her eyes turned down. Jordan mirrored her mother's stance.

The man growled from his horse. "Where do you think you're going?"

"We here to see Sarah, suh," Mama said. Jordan bristled, but she understood her mother's obsequious tone. "She my husban's cousin."

"Where you visiting her from?" he challenged, looking them up and down slowly.

"Shirley, suh."

Jordan's heart pounded fiercely in her chest, and her breathing got shallow. Suddenly, mussing up her clothes didn't seem like an adequate disguise. The quality of the cloth and the style of her shoes were a glaring betrayal. Her father's warning echoed in her ears; her nice clothes would make her a target. Not wanting to draw attention to herself, she ever so slowly pulled the hem of her gray skirt over her feet, wanting to hide the most conspicuous evidence that she didn't belong in this land.

The man snorted. "They may let their niggras come and go at Shirley, but at Fair Oaks ours work to earn their keep."

"Yes, suh."

"Go back to the road and wait until sunset." He smirked. "You can have your *visit* then."

"Yes, suh."

They walked in silence until they got to the T at the main road.

"Should we go back to the wagon?" Jordan asked. "Wait with Samuel?" She wanted to get away from that man. If he came back to question them, Jordan was certain he would figure out she was not a worker.

"No. He gonna be watchin' us," Mama explained. "We gonna do jus' as he says and sit right here until the sunset."

"Mama, you were right," Jordan replied. "This is awful."

Her mother gave her a bittersweet look. "Honey, you ain't seen nothing awful yet."

Jordan had never been so hot or so thirsty, but she didn't complain out loud because there wasn't any point in mentioning it. The minutes crept by. Just sitting here she was miserable; it was hard to imagine what it was like for the workers in the fields, including Cousin Sarah. She looked over at her mother.

"Is that what you used to do? Work in the field like that?"

Mama nodded. "Until I was brought in. I missed being in the quarters, but I didn't miss workin' the field. It was so hot and awful." Mama looked directly at Jordan, like she knew her soul, and said, "That why I so grateful just to be *free*. I ain't never, ever taken it for granted."

In the distance they watched the workers moving through the fields. Two men on horseback patrolled the area. Jordan was disgusted by the long leather whips tied to each saddle, and grateful neither was being put to use. She'd read enough slave narratives to be jarred by seeing overseers and whips. The scene was perversely calm given the history of these fields and these people.

"Why do they stay? These workers?" Jordan asked.

"Uprootin' ain't easy. Mos' of them been here they whole lives. They don' know anything else. They think they don' got a choice."

Eventually the sun hit the horizon, and the overseer yelled out a signal that work was done for the day. The field hands walked through the rows of tobacco toward the quarters. Jordan started to stand, but Mama grabbed her arm, shook her head, and stayed sitting. Jordan settled back onto the log. Mama didn't make a move until it was fully dark, long after the field hands had trudged away. Alone they walked on the road through the empty fields and cut down the path into the quarters. Rows of small, rickety huts lined the path. They saw no one on their way to Cousin Sarah's. Jordan would have thought the huts were abandoned, except there were a few open fires with pots held up by tripods. It was depressing and unsettling, sad and haunting at the same time.

"It too quiet," Mama practically whispered. "It used to be filled with folks getting their supper ready after working all day."

Jordan felt Mama's nerves as they reached the fifth cabin on the right. The crooked little shack could hardly be called a house. No more than ten by fifteen feet, it was made of gray weathered planks with open cracks and knotholes. A hole in the door had a piece of frayed rope through it instead of a metal latch. Slavery was over, but these people were still living in shacks. Jordan understood it was hard to start anew, but she still could not fathom why anyone chose to stay here.

Mama tapped quietly. They didn't have to wait long for the portal to swing open.

"Hello?" an old woman asked, worry and uncertainty covering her wrinkled brown face.

Mama stared hard and then gasped loudly. "Sarah?"

The woman nodded, looking skeptical. Jordan kept a neutral expression on her face, but she was stunned and slightly disgusted by this grungy woman, with her yellowish weathered skin and sunken, rheumy eyes. Dirt, scars, and sores covered her body. *This* was her mother's cousin?

Mama put her hand to her chest. "It me, Mattie." Mama's breathy voice shook.

The woman's dirty hand flew to her mouth. "What! No . . ." She stumbled backward.

Mama took Jordan's hand and led her into the dark space. Sarah looked back and forth between them, shock and confusion covering her face. "What you doin' here?" Sarah asked. Gaps in her teeth showed swollen gums.

"We came for you, like I said I would," Mama said.

The woman studied Jordan, who stood there, feeling uncomfortable. "Jordan?" she asked, incredulous.

Jordan nodded.

"Oh my!" Sarah's eyes filled with tears. "I ain't seen you since you were a baby. Look at you. So grown. So lovely." She patted Jordan's smooth brown skin with her calloused and swollen fingers. Jordan resisted the instinct to pull away from the rough scratching on her cheek.

"Oh, Mattie." Sarah's hoarse voice filled with awe. "You did it! You got yo'self a good life."

The wonder on the woman's face was touching.

"And we got that waitin' for you too!" Mama exclaimed. "I brought a wagon. We gonna take you to Ohio. Samuel waitin' in the trees with it."

Panic overran Sarah's face. She challenged, "Anybody sees you?"

Mama sighed and nodded. "The overseer."

"He talk to you?"

Mama shrank into herself, nodding her head.

"What you say?" Sarah challenged.

"You my husban's cousin, and we visiting from Shirley."

Sarah scrunched up her lips, disgusted. "You know he know you lying!" she rebuked. "Look at those clothes. Ain't no way you a field hand!"

Jordan watched in silence. The woman chastising her mother had been born only a few months before Samuel, but Sarah looked older than Mama.

"You cain't come here and jus' take me away," Sarah scolded. "It don' work like that!"

"You're free!" Jordan burst out. "Haven't you heard of the Thirteenth Amendment?"

"Course I *heard* that I free," Sarah replied, heat and indignation in her voice, "but I don' know what good it do me."

"You can do what you like, and you can go where you like," Jordan replied more gently.

"Freedom don' come with a house. Freedom don' come with a horse. Freedom don' come with land. Freedom don' come with food," Sarah hissed.

Jordan's stomach lurched at the truth of the rebuke: freedom didn't mean very much without the means to exercise it.

"Have you managed to save any of your pay?" Jordan asked carefully, not wanting to sound judgmental.

Mama threw Jordan a harsh look and said quickly, "You don' need any money to come with us. We gonna take care of you till you get on yo' feet."

Sarah shook her head, snorted, and then clicked her tongue.

"You 'magine things so diff'rent now? The only thin' that change is they ain't so many of us to do all the work. Massa don' give us money. We gets food, cloth, and"—Sarah waved her hand around—"this place to live. We don' get no *pay*."

Massa. That word pierced Jordan. Sarah still had a massa, and she didn't get paid?

"Massa don't take well to anybody that say they want anythin' diff'rent than he say we get." Sarah shook her head, then looked resigned. "Well, you here now. We gonna have a nice visit tonight, and in the mornin' I gonna fix up the mess you made by comin' back where you don' belong anymore. Maybe Massa gonna say you can stay for a visit, but I ain't gonna leave with you when you goes. I 'preciate your carin', but I tol' you in that letter I ain't movin' to Ohio!" Sarah declared. "I go get us our supper now. I got a nice stew cookin' that'll stretch jus' fine." She patted Mama's hand.

Jordan's heart sank. They'd come all this way for nothing? She looked at her mama, concerned that Mama was hurt by this news, but the woman watching Sarah leave through the worn door looked more determined than hurt.

After Sarah left, Mama hissed at Jordan, "You ac' like her food the bes' thin' you ever ate. You understand me?"

"Of course, Mama! I'm not going to be rude." Jordan was indignant that her mother thought she would be disrespectful. "I'm sorry that Sarah won't take you up on your offer to move to Ohio. As you said, it's too scary for some people to give up the familiar."

"This ain't over yet," Mama insisted.

Sarah returned carrying a heavy metal pot. She ladled a greasy brown liquid into three dull wooden bowls sitting on the table lit by a small oil lantern. Jordan's stomach lurched at the thought of spooning the slimy mess into her mouth.

"Thank you, Cousin Sarah." Jordan smiled, doing her best not to show the trepidation that she felt.

Sarah reached out her hands to each side and spoke grace. "Thanks to God fo' bringin' Mattie and Jordan to me safe. Watch over Samuel in the woods. We glad for this food and for yo' mercy. Amen."

Jordan and Mattie followed with *amens* of their own. Jordan steeled herself for the meal. She held her breath as she spooned the brown liquid into her mouth, swallowing quickly, hoping to bypass her taste buds. She worked to keep a neutral look on her face as the flavor hit her despite her precautions. The stew was as distasteful as she feared.

She forced a smile. "Thank you for supper, Cousin Sarah."

"It ain't much, but I happy to share what I got with you," Sarah replied.

"After so long on the road, this hit the spot," Mama said.

Jordan wanted water to wash down the food, but there wasn't any on the table. She considered asking for it but realized that might be rude. She'd have to get through this meal without it.

"I can tell you ain't from here by the way you talk," Sarah said to Jordan. "Do all the color folk talk diff'rent there?"

Jordan considered the question. Did Sarah even know about college . . . or high school? She didn't want to be insulting—either underexplaining or saying too much. Before she could formulate a response, Mama spoke up.

"Jordan and Samuel both went to college. That the most schooling you can get. Emmanuel and I so proud of 'em." Mama smiled at Jordan.

Wonder on her face, Sarah shook her head. "You really got yo'selves a good life." Her chapped lips pulled up at the edges. She took a slow breath, and Jordan saw her eyes well up with tears. Jordan watched various emotions cross over Sarah's face. It was hard to know exactly what she was thinking or feeling, but it seemed that pain and awe, uncommon companions, were wrestling in her heart and mind.

Jordan felt bad that their presence was so unsettling to this woman. She looked at Mama, hoping she would have soothing words, but Mama didn't disrupt the quiet. The three women sat in the discomfort of this strange situation.

Eventually Sarah gestured with her head and said, "You born right over there."

Jordan's stomach flipped. Too many times over the years she'd heard that she was born in a slave shack, but here? In her mind's eye she'd never imagined something as dreary and primitive as this. She looked at Mama, who nodded. Jordan took in the dirt floor and the rough wood walls. It was hard to see in the dim light, but she doubted the morning sun would make this space less of a dirty cave.

"Right there on that bed stand." Mama grew wistful. "I held you in my arms after a long night's work and swore to God we was gonna join yo' brother and yo' father. I done it too!"

A chill ran down Jordan's back as she felt the enormity of what Mama had done. She'd been alarmingly close to having an entirely different life—one where her fingers would have picked worms off tobacco plants rather than turned pages of books. Her head was dizzy with the thought. She gazed at her own smooth hands and then studied Cousin Sarah's swollen and gnarled fingers. If Mama had stayed here Jordan's life would have been preoccupied with survival, not emancipation and the women's franchise.

"You live here all 'lone?" Mama asked Sarah.

Sarah nodded slowly. "Ever since the girls lef' . . ." Her voice cracked. She cleared her throat and went on, "And Ma died."

Mama leaned in and put her hand over Sarah's. She said, her voice tight as well, "You ain't never tol' me how my sister passed."

Sarah took a deep breath and then sighed. "Four summers ago Massa say Sophia and Ella—they my daughters." She looked at Jordan as she gave that explanation, then went on. "Massa say they gotta go south. He say he sold them . . . to pay for a wedding!" Sarah hissed, indignation filling her voice. "Can you believe he think a fancy wedding more important than my family!"

Sarah continued. "Mama say, 'No!' She say right to his face that *they free*. We knowed the Emancipation Proclamation say so, that he can' just make 'em leave. Quick as a flash Massa swung his walkin' stick at her. He hit Mama hard with that big metal bird."

Jordan flinched.

"Like I say, he don' take no stock in our *freedom*. The next day he grab my girls, put 'em in a wagon, and they driven away. They tears didn' change anythin'. Mama's yelling didn' change a thing. Her head swolled up big, and there weren't nowhere for the swellin' to go."

Sarah fell silent, lost in thought. Jordan waited, anxious for the ending, though she knew the excruciating outcome.

"My mama died three days later." Sarah swallowed hard. Her face was stony, but Jordan sensed she was overcome with intense emotion.

"Oh, Sarah," Mama exclaimed. "That's jus' awful—the saddest thin' I think I ever heard."

"How old were they?" Jordan had to know. "Sophia and Ella?"

Sarah bit her lip. "Sophia had just made eight. Ella still five years old. Just a baby really."

Jordan imagined the two little girls, crying as they were being driven away, while Cousin Sarah watched helplessly. Her eyes burned at the thought of those children forced from their home and family—without anyone to care for them.

Sarah looked straight at her and said, "I don' even know if they was kept together."

The agony in Sarah's voice cut straight into Jordan's heart. Tears spilled onto her cheeks. Jordan's throat swelled up so tight that she felt like she couldn't breathe. She took a shaky, deep breath through her nose. Reading about the conditions of the Southern slaves never felt like this. Even the intense and painful details of slave narratives did not compare with hearing this story firsthand from her cousin.

Sarah whispered through a tight throat, "I can' never leave Fair Oaks till they come back. That hope the only thing keepin' me going all these years. Maybe they got real freedom where they gone to. Maybe they gonna come lookin' for me."

Jordan searched for the right words to say to her cousin, but nothing could be remotely adequate in the face of such horror. Mama was right. Sarah had to get out of this horrible place. She laid her hand over Sarah's, wiped her cheek, and declared through taut vocal cords, "We will find your children and take you *all* to Oberlin."

She looked at her mama for affirmation. Mama gazed back with her intense and kind caramel-brown eyes and nodded. Jordan smiled a tender, moist-eyed smile back at her mother.

CHAPTER 7

LISBETH

Charles City County, Virginia

Lisbeth and her children traveled on a tree-lined dirt road close to the James River. They were taking a few days away from Richmond to visit Lisbeth's childhood friend.

Lisbeth had left Virginia before Mary Bartley's wedding to Daniel. In the intervening ten years, Mary gave birth to seven children, five of whom were still alive, and she was the mistress of a large plantation along the James River. Somehow Daniel seemed to have acquired more land during the conflict between the states.

Strong emotion arose in Lisbeth as they journeyed: excitement or fear, perhaps a mixture of the two. She and Mary had corresponded regularly, but they avoided unpleasant topics like the war. Lisbeth worried that Mary would feel Lisbeth was a traitor to their cause, like her family did. Mary had been nothing but enthusiastic when she invited Lisbeth and the children for a visit—in fact she'd absolutely insisted that they take the time away—but nevertheless, Lisbeth was wary.

"As I've mentioned, Mary and I were dearest friends growing up," Lisbeth told her children.

"Were you desk mates at school?" Sadie asked.

"We did not attend school," Lisbeth explained. "We each had tutors in our homes. Though we did have comportment lessons together, with all the other girls in the area."

"Comportment?" Sammy queried.

Lisbeth shrugged. "Lessons on manners and dancing to prepare to be young women."

"Will I have compamortment lessons?" Sadie wanted to know.

Lisbeth laughed. "Comportment. No, thankfully we don't have the same kind of system in Ohio. And here we are." Lisbeth pointed to the grand house.

Sammy's mouth literally dropped open. The brick façade and large white columns were very impressive. This was the largest house he'd ever seen, and it showed on his face.

"Whoa!" he blurted out. "I thought Grandmother Wainwright's house was big."

The glossy white front door opened, and Mary flew out to greet them.

"My dear Lisbeth!" she exclaimed.

She looked just the same and yet so different from the girl Lisbeth had left ten years earlier. Seven pregnancies had left some gray in her hair, and a hint of sadness hid in her sparkling eyes. It looked like a slight breeze could bowl her over because she was so thin, but she greeted Lisbeth with such joy that any fears Lisbeth had about their reunion evaporated instantly.

The two women shared a long embrace. Lisbeth's heart opened up even wider when Mary hugged Sadie and Sammy as well.

"Come in!" Mary said to the three travelers. "I have arranged for tea in the garden. The children are so excited to meet you, my dearest childhood friend and her children! We can watch the river, and the children can play with one another."

"Should I get my carpetbag?" Sammy asked Lisbeth in quiet tones.

"Oh, no!" Mary replied. "Leave everything. It will all be taken care of."

As they stepped into Mary's grand entry, Lisbeth looked back to see a brown-skinned servant lead her wagon away. Mary hooked her arm through Lisbeth's and led the way through the back of the house to the grounds. Sadie held Lisbeth's left hand, and Sammy followed from behind.

"My brother Robert has been living with us since the end of the war," Mary whispered in her ear as they walked on the wide gravel path. "He will join us until he tires. Please do not comment on his appearance—or mention the conflict. We are striving to bolster his spirits."

Lisbeth nodded, grateful for the direction to avoid the topic of the war. She breathed in the familiar damp air as they walked in silence toward the river. She took in the trees and the grass. A shiver passed through her when the slow-moving James River came into view. This was home. She hadn't realized how much she missed it until this moment.

Robert was sitting at a small table by the bank. Lisbeth had seen many young men returned from the war, but never one she'd known as a boy. Robert was utterly transformed from the mischievous young man who had always made others laugh. His shoulders hunched up to his ears, and his chin was curled over to his chest. His eyes darted sideways to watch them approach but returned to stare at the ground as they drew close.

"These are my children," Mary announced cheerfully. "Danny, Harry, Rose, Hannah, and baby Freddy."

The children lined up to shake their hands; even Hannah, who couldn't have been two yet, followed her siblings.

"Oh, Mary. They are precious!" Lisbeth exclaimed. "May I?" Lisbeth gestured toward the baby in the servant's arms.

"Certainly." Mary grabbed the baby and passed him to Lisbeth.

Lisbeth cuddled Freddy. She loved the feel of the baby's warm, soft head against her chest.

"Can I touch him?" Sadie asked.

"Just his toes," Lisbeth instructed.

"Nonsense," Mary corrected. "He cannot afford to be fragile. Not as the youngest of five. You can hold him if you like."

"Really?!" Sadie looked eager.

"He is not a toy," Lisbeth admonished her daughter. "You must take care."

"I will. I promise!"

Mary pointed to a blanket a few feet away. "Louisa will help you hold him on the blankets. Truth be told, my children are as comfortable with her as with me. She's been their nurse since they were born."

"Like me . . . with Mattie," Lisbeth told Mary. Her childhood friend nodded with a small smile.

Lisbeth passed the baby to the tall woman with light-brown skin and watched her herd Mary's children to the blankets. Like being served by Emily, it was familiar, but surprising that the end of slavery hadn't impacted their household more dramatically. Lisbeth wondered if Louisa was paid, or if she too worked for room and board like Emily.

"You too," Mary instructed Sadie and Sammy. "Your mother will be right here if you need anything. Go on!"

Lisbeth nodded in agreement, and her children scampered off to join the others who were playing a chasing game.

"Louisa is such a dear. My life would be intolerable without her. You traveled without your nurse?"

"We do not have one."

Mary's blue eyes went wide, and then she blinked away her surprise. "Life *is* different in Ohio! Tell me everything!"

"It's not *so* different. We have a nice home and farm. Since the war ended we've grown flax, which is highly in demand, as well as oats, in rotation." As soon as the word *war* was out of her mouth, Lisbeth regretted mentioning the conflict. She continued quickly, hoping her error would go unnoticed. "As I wrote, Sadie started first grade in the autumn, so the house is quiet in the middle of the day. We have a public school system in Oberlin divided by grades. We attend church as a family on Sunday."

Robert looked up suddenly. He'd been stony silent since they arrived, and she had nearly forgotten about him. He stared hard at her, giving her a good look at his craggy face. He had the scared, angry, and confused look of so many returned soldiers. Once again she felt the terrible cost of the conflict.

"You! Had the war? In Ohio?" he challenged.

"There was no fighting near our home," Lisbeth said gently, "but so many men were gone that we felt the effects."

"Felt the effects," Robert whispered. "Felt . . . the . . . effects," he continued slowly. He nodded. "Me too. Your husband? He was in the war?"

Robert's eyes bored into Lisbeth as if his life depended upon her answer. She nodded silently.

"Blue or gray?" he asked, his voice charged with emotion.

Lisbeth's heart skipped a beat. She was trapped between the evil of a lie and the harm of the facts. In Ohio the Union felt entirely noble. She never imagined she'd feel shame about Matthew fighting in the war, but here, along the bank of the James River, telling the truth to Robert was problematic.

Lisbeth looked at her childhood friend. "Sorry," she mouthed. Mary gave a small shrug.

"Blue or gray?" Robert insisted, fury in his question.

Fortunately Mary spoke up so Lisbeth did not have to select the correct path. "Robert, I think you know the answer to that question." Mary patted her brother's hand. "It's over now, dear."

"Is it?" he asked, staring off into the distance, his eyes watching something visible only to him. Robert shook his head and slowly turned his gaze to his sister. "It may be over to you, but not to me. It will never be over for me."

Robert stood up and joined the children on the blankets.

"Oh, Mary. I am so sorry."

"This is actually a good day for Robert. Some days he is so agitated he frightens the children, and others he doesn't speak a word."

"How long has he been like this?" Lisbeth inquired softly.

Mary looked at Lisbeth, her fingers twisting the white cloth napkin on her lap. She seemed to be wrestling with herself.

"You can confide in me, if you wish," Lisbeth said. "Or we can speak of other topics. As you like."

Mary took a breath. Quietly she told Lisbeth, "Robert witnessed our brother Albert's death. He does not speak of the details, but I believe it was neither fast nor pain-free."

A knot developed in Lisbeth's stomach, and she took Mary's hand between her own. Mary had written of her brother's death, but not the circumstances. Albert and Robert had been nearly twins; no two brothers had ever been closer.

Mary gazed off to the river as she spoke. "Robert was sent home to recover, but his state worsened after the Union troops stationed on our land burned all of our stores and crops." She looked into Lisbeth's eyes. "The war may have ended, but I fear it will live in him forever."

Sammy ran up to them, interrupting the conversation. "May I have the playing cards?"

Lisbeth dug them out of her bag. "Who are you playing with?"

"Uncle Robert and I are going to teach Danny and Harry how to play Go Fishing."

Lisbeth smiled at her son as she passed him the deck of cards. She watched him run back to the blanket. In this setting he reminded her of Jack as a boy. With more kindness in his life, perhaps Jack would have been as thoughtful of others as her Sammy.

"Sitting here is so familiar and comfortable it is hard to believe that I have not seen the James River, or you, in ten years," Lisbeth said to Mary.

"I was utterly distraught when you left," Mary remembered. "I feared your life had been ruined. Now I believe you and Matthew were wise to leave."

Surprised, but curious and willing to speak plainly, Lisbeth replied, "But your home and children are lovely."

"It looks pleasant, but Daniel hardly sleeps at night with the worry. We do not have enough seed to plant all of our acres, and we cannot get any more credit to purchase more. Even if we had more seed, we do not have enough workers. A few have been loyal, but most have abandoned us. Without workers we will be ruined. He fears we are going to lose everything to a carpetbagger."

Lisbeth was astounded. Mother had given her the impression that Daniel Bartley had profited off the war. Lisbeth considered that her mother might have been intentionally misleading her.

"Enough feeling sorry for myself," Mary said. "I have arranged a surprise for you. Tomorrow we are visiting Fair Oaks! Alice and Alfie Richards, the current owners, are delighted to have us for dinner."

Lisbeth's heart leaped. It would be bittersweet to return to her childhood home, and complicated to show it to Sammy and Sadie. They'd been raised to understand that slavery was abhorrent, and she'd been too ashamed of her family's relationship to that travesty to be entirely honest with them. Her children were always begging her to tell them about her experience growing up. They'd heard stories about the willow tree, hunting for yellow crocuses, and picnics by the river, but they didn't have the full understanding of her childhood home.

CHAPTER 8

JORDAN

Fair Oaks plantation, Virginia

Mama, Sarah, and Jordan squeezed into the only bed in the shack. It was more cramped than the wagon, and the straw under the ticking poked through in spots, making for a long, uncomfortable night. Jordan was grateful to her mama for taking the middle. Sleep came in fits and starts, her mind jumping between worrying about Samuel alone in the woods and searching for a way to find Ella and Sophia. The only information Sarah had was that her children had been taken to Hope Plantation in North Carolina, not much to go on.

When Jordan woke up, she was alone with Mama. Sarah was already at work in the fields, having instructed her guests to stay inside unless they needed the facilities. Sarah planned to assure the overseer they would be gone soon, and that they were no threat. After supper with Cousin Sarah, they'd leave her, head back to join Samuel, and work to find those girls. Though Jordan hadn't thought of a way to go about doing that.

By daylight this space was more depressing. It hardly seemed fit for livestock, let alone humans. Slits of light came through the cracks in the walls, highlighting the dust dancing in the air.

"There's no floor," Jordan remarked. "You and Pops really lived here?"

"You know your father lived on another plantation," Mama corrected her. "Jus' me and Poppy and Samuel were here, until I was brought in to feed and care for Lisbeth."

Jordan had heard these stories her whole life, but they took on a whole new meaning after seeing this place.

"And you," Mama reminded her sharply. "You lived here too, though not for long. We lef' before you made one. You know that!"

"Oh, Mama," Jordan exclaimed. "You told me, but, I just . . . I just had no idea. I don't know what to say, except thank you. Thank you so much for getting me out of here."

Mama smiled at Jordan. "That the hardest, and best, thin' I done in my whole life. Traipsin' through the forest, you on my back." Mama shook her head, remembering. "You nearly died. That's *the worst* moment of my life . . . when I thought you was gone."

Mama had tears in her eyes at the memory. Filled with tenderness and awe, Jordan looked at her mother with new respect.

"Did you plan for a long time?" Jordan asked, suddenly interested in the details.

"Mm-hmm," Mama confirmed. "Took me months to save up jus' for the paper. We got *Sarah* to thank for writin' the pass that got us to freedom."

Jordan recalled, "Lisbeth taught Samuel to read and write. Then Samuel taught Sarah. Did Lisbeth understand what she was doing?"

"No." Mama shook her head. "She only a little thing that jus' wanted to please me," Mama explained. "We was always under that willow for naps and for reading. I don' think she thought twice about Samuel joining us." Mama paused and got a far-off look in her eyes. Then she said, "I wasn' much older than you are now when I was brought in to be her nurse."

"Twenty used to seem so old to me," Jordan said, "but you were hardly more than a child yourself."

"You grows up fast round here," Mama agreed.

Jordan dug behind the bed for her head scarf, which had come off in the night. She pulled up the ticking and was stopped short by what she saw on the wall.

"Look!" Jordan said, pointing to the rough wood plank.

"Hmmm," Mama said in wonder. "Somethin' even I can read: *Samuel*. Guess he jus' wanted to leave his mark—remind God he was here. I had no idea he done that."

Jordan ran her fingers across her brother's name, carved into the wood hidden behind the bed she was born in.

"Where's the willow tree and the window that Samuel waved to?" Jordan asked. "Putting his fingers up?"

Mama drew her eyebrows together into a scowl. "I don' think we need to be showin' ourselves in the direction of the big house . . . rubbin' it in that we here."

Jordan pleaded, "Just a quick peek."

"All right." Mama opened the door and looked into the distance. A wistful expression covered her face, and she pointed.

"The graveyard way up there. You can' see it from here, but you can when you up high. That where Poppy and my mama have markers. I sorry you can' see it, but I don' wanna show ourselves so much." She pointed again. "And there's the willow, on that rise."

Jordan sucked in her breath. It was beautiful. The bright-green canopy reached up to a beautiful blue sky and all the way down to the ground. The James River sparkled in the background, and birds flew in and out of the branches.

"Was this your whole world, Mama?" Jordan asked.

"What you mean?"

"This cabin, that tree, the fields. Did you know anything else?"

Mama pulled in her lips, biting the lower one in thought. "I had stories from the Bible, once or twice a year a dance, and eventually the big house, but nothing like you seen growing up." Mama got a far-off look in her eye again.

"What?" Jordan asked.

"I jus' remembered that I didn' even knowed what a mirror was when I was brung in," Mama said with a snort.

"A mirror?" Jordan thought about Sarah's shack. Of course, Mama hadn't ever seen a mirror.

"My own reflection scared me." Mama laughed. "I actually jumped."

Jordan smiled at the story, but it broke her heart too. "Where's the window? To your room with Lisbeth?"

"That one, right on the corner. Ten years I spent caged in that pretty room, takin' care of her and washin' laundry for the big house."

Jordan looked at the building, sun glistening off the window her mama pointed to. She looked back at Mama, her face pinched with sorrow.

Mama said, "Ain't no pain as awful as the one that come from bein' away from your own chil'. Seein' through that window helped a bit. Samuel knowed I checked on him two times ever' day, but it ain't the same as holdin' him and being his all-the-time mama, you know?"

After talking with Sarah last night, Jordan understood her mother's anguish in a whole new way. The stories from her childhood had happy endings with the four of them reunited. Mama and Pops always reminded them to count their blessings, not their sorrows. But Mama had borne years of loneliness, separated from Pops and Samuel. Her mama was strong in a way Jordan had never had to be and had lived with loss Jordan had only read about. Jordan put an arm around her mama. A small, though so inadequate, comfort was all she could do for the woman who had been brave enough to give Jordan so much.

CHAPTER 9

LISBETH

Fair Oaks plantation, Virginia

"You lived here? With Grandmother Wainwright and Uncle Jack?" Sadie exclaimed when the driver stopped in front of the white façade with tall white columns.

"No wonder they're so mad," Sammy said. "They lost *this*."

"Money is not nearly as important as human kindness," Lisbeth reminded her children, uncomfortable with their attitudes. She did not want them to romanticize her childhood, but she also did not want them to think less of her because of it.

They gave quick nods but didn't take their eyes off the building. Lisbeth studied the façade, looking for changes. The trees were the same, only taller. The paint on the front door was a new shade of deep blue. And the path had been filled in with bits of rock gravel, making it less muddy.

Nervous and excited for the memories and questions this home would stir up, Lisbeth followed Mary to the familiar front door. Her friend knocked and waited. It felt strange to be locked out of her first home. Her instinct was to simply walk in as she had always done before.

An unfamiliar Negress with dark hair pulled into a tight bun greeted them and led them to the Richards family, who was waiting in the sitting room. It felt at once familiar and wrong. The drapes and walls were exactly the same as the day she'd left home, but the furniture was entirely different, and too modern for this space. The daguerreotypes on the mantel displayed the faces of strangers.

"Elizabeth," Mary said, interrupting her thoughts. "Mr. and Mrs. Alfie Richards, this is Elizabeth Johnson and her children, Sadie and Sammy."

"Thank you for opening your home to us," Lisbeth said. "You are very generous to allow me to return to Fair Oaks."

"Nonsense," Mr. Richards said. "We are so glad to meet you. Cook speaks of you very fondly."

"Cook is still here?" Lisbeth asked. She remembered the large dark woman with a mixture of fear and admiration. Cook had been a powerful fixture in Lisbeth's childhood household, seeming to answer to no one but herself. Though on reflection, Lisbeth understood it must have been more complicated than that for Cook.

"Absolutely," Mr. Richards replied. "She is a treasure. We would never part with her. Please, sit. Make yourselves comfortable."

Once they were settled, Sadie tugged on Lisbeth's hand and pointed to one of the images on the mantel.

Mr. Richards responded to Sadie's gesture. "That is our daughter, Cora, in her wedding gown."

"She looks like a princess!" Sadie said, awe in her voice.

"That day was a much-needed respite during the difficulties," Mr. Richards replied. "It was well worth the sacrifice we incurred to cover the costs. I hope your journey here was pleasant."

"It was. Mary's carriage is very comfortable. And the roads are much improved from when I lived here," Lisbeth replied.

"I hate the Yankee invaders, but I appreciate the roads they paved to get here," Mr. Richards said with a chuckle. He continued speaking without pause. "I see you have good taste, young man."

Sammy had been studying Mr. Richards's cane.

"You may take a closer look." The jovial man passed the cane to Lisbeth's son. "My grandfather had that made eighty years ago—in 1788. Do you understand the significance of that date?"

Sammy shook his head.

"That was the year the Constitution was ratified," the man proclaimed proudly. "My grandfather's great-great-grandfather was a part of the original Jamestown settlement. Have you learned about Jamestown?"

Sammy nodded. "We studied United States history last year."

"I am glad to hear that even in Ohio they are teaching you about the founding of our great nation," Mr. Richards said. "My grandfather was an officer in the Revolutionary War. He had this cane crafted to remember the sacrifices that must be made for freedom. I trust you know the eagle is the symbol of our great country. My grandfather passed it to my father, who in turn passed it to me." Mr. Richards looked intently at Sammy, clearly serious about conveying his words of wisdom. "Son, you must remember that *liberty* is a most precious gift from God. No one has the right to wrest it from you, though many will try. As the greatest of us all wrote in the most magnificent document of all, 'we hold these truths to be self-evident, that all men are created equal, that they are endowed by their creator with certain unalienable rights, that among these are life, liberty, and the pursuit of happiness.'"

"Do you know where those words are from?" Mr. Richards asked.

"The Declaration of Independence, sir," Sammy answered.

"Do you agree?" Mr. Richards asked in a way that left no room for opposition.

Sammy nodded his head.

"What is the most precious gift from God?" the man quizzed Sammy.

"Liberty, sir," Sammy parroted.

"That's right, Son," Mr. Richards praised him.

Lisbeth had to bite her tongue to keep from asking Mr. Richards whose liberty he would fight to defend. She hated to let his ideas go unchallenged in front of her children, but even more she did not wish to be rude by having a political argument with her host. She would be sure to bring up this conversation when she was alone with her children to tell them where she and Matthew stood on this issue.

Mr. Richards continued. "You can go back to Ohio and tell your friends you held a piece of United States history in your hand: the cane from a Revolutionary War hero!"

Mr. Richards put his hand out to get the cane back. Sammy passed it to him.

"May I hold it?" Sadie asked.

Mr. Richards looked at her, his eyebrows pulled together in surprise. "I suppose there is no harm."

Sadie ran her fingers over the intricate eagle feathers.

"Is this for my liberty too?" Sadie asked the old man.

Mr. Richards laughed and looked at Lisbeth. "You have a little spitfire there! Honey, you have no need for liberty," Mr. Richards said condescendingly to Sadie. "Your husband will take care of you. You'll understand when you are older." He reached for the walking stick.

Lisbeth patted her daughter's arm and telegraphed a silent request to stay quiet. She was grateful when Sadie returned the eagle without saying more.

Mr. Richards sat back, looking satisfied, and changed the subject. "Dinner will be ready soon; however, we thought you might enjoy a tour before we eat."

A shiver, likely from excitement, shot through Lisbeth's spine. She smiled at Mr. Richards. "That would be wonderful, if it is not an imposition."

"No imposition at all. I am quite sentimental myself, so it is what I would want if I were in your position. Lucie can show you around while we visit with Mary. We will catch up on the news."

Sadie squeezed Lisbeth's hand. "May I come too?"

"Of course," Mr. Richards said. "You must learn about your history, but first . . . have a sweet." He opened a small dish with a flourish and revealed hard candy in bright colors. "Lemon, mint, or sassafras," he announced.

The children looked to Lisbeth for permission, who nodded her consent.

"Thank you!" they exclaimed, and chose pieces for themselves.

"You too," Mr. Richards insisted to Lisbeth.

Feeling like she could not refuse, Lisbeth took a lemon piece and expressed her gratitude as well.

The petite Negress who had let them into the house gestured to them from the doorway. Lisbeth, Sammy, and Sadie followed Lucie's gray skirt up the wide staircase. Lisbeth's chest hammered in anticipation.

"Mr. Richards is very kind," Sadie declared.

"He seems nice," Lisbeth replied, though she knew very well the appearance of courtesy was a separate issue from true kindness.

"Mrs. Richards is shy," Sadie decided. "She doesn't like talking to us."

Lisbeth had also noticed that the older woman hadn't said a word to them. She doubted it was Mrs. Richards's own temperament that kept her quiet, but instead assumed Mr. Richards's attitude silenced her. Lisbeth had been raised around men like him. They were jovial and kind until they were crossed. So many wives found it best to simply stay silent rather than risk the storm that came from saying the wrong thing.

At the top of the stairs the maid asked, "Which room did you stay in?"

Lisbeth pointed to the right. "The last one."

Lucie nodded and led the way down the rug-covered hall, which was narrower than in Lisbeth's memory. She opened the door, and Lisbeth stepped into her childhood. She looked around, taking in all that was the same and all that had changed. The mirror, the windows, and the wallpaper were familiar. She walked around the space, opening the door to Mattie's small antechamber, which was hardly more than a closet. Crossing to the door on the other side, she opened it and looked down. Her children squeezed their heads past her arms to peer into the dark.

"What's down there?" Sadie asked.

"These are the back stairs. They lead outside, to the kitchen," she explained. "At least they did. Is the kitchen still a separate building?" she asked.

Lucie nodded.

"Peculiar!" Sammy said.

"Different, not peculiar," Lisbeth corrected.

They went back to the main room.

She pointed and said, "My bed was there, my dressing table was there, and I used to look out this window every morning and every night. With my nurse."

"What were you looking for?" Sammy asked.

Lisbeth remembered the twice-daily ritual soon after sunrise and just before sunset when the workers were going out to or coming in from the field. She had stood by Mattie, and together they would search for Samuel in the dots of people. As he got closer they both grew excited. Each evening he would hold up a different number of fingers. Lisbeth liked to predict what number he was going to do ahead of time. She wrote it down each day, so Mattie could report on the various numbers on her Sunday visits.

As a child it was an entertaining game. As she thought about it from her adult vantage point, it was unspeakably cruel. Mattie must have gone about her day accompanied by worry for Samuel.

Lisbeth had never explained that kind of detail from her own childhood to her children. It filled her with shame, and sorrow, to know that Mattie had been forced away from her own son because of her. Now that she was a parent, she could barely imagine the torment that Mattie had lived with for ten years. While Matthew and Lisbeth were vocal about their opposition to slavery, Lisbeth did not want Sadie and Sammy to know such contemptible details from her past.

Out loud she answered Sammy's question. "We saw many things. The sunset, the sunrise, the workers in the fields, people in the quarters."

"That's where the slaves lived?" Sammy asked, suddenly very interested.

Lisbeth nodded. Sadie and Sammy walked over to the glass and stared out.

"It doesn't look very nice," Sammy said.

"The workers had to live somewhere," Lisbeth justified without thought, but then she thought better and agreed. "No, it wasn't very nice."

"You had lots of slaves, didn't you, Momma?" Sammy looked so disappointed.

Lisbeth took in a deep breath, then nodded.

"How could you? Didn't you know it was wrong?" he asked, pain in his voice.

"It wasn't my choice. Grandmother and Grandfather owned them, not me," Lisbeth replied, sounding more defensive than she liked.

"Momma! It's Miss Jordan!" Sadie cried out.

"Pardon me?" Lisbeth asked.

"I see Miss Jordan. Out there," the girl explained.

"Sadie, that is impossible. I imagine you are seeing someone who looks similar to your teacher," Lisbeth explained. "Miss Jordan is in Ohio, not Virginia."

"Come see. Really, it *is* Miss Jordan. I promise!" Sadie pointed at the glass.

The children parted to make room for her. Lisbeth followed the direction of Sadie's finger. Sure enough, standing outside Mattie's old cabin, Miss Jordan was looking up at them. And Mattie was by her side. Lisbeth's heart did the familiar lurch it made every time she saw her old nurse.

"Can I go see her?!" Sadie asked, excitement filling her voice.

Lisbeth's head was spinning. It was surreal to be standing in her childhood room, looking down upon Mattie in the quarters. Time took on a peculiar quality, causing her to feel like a young girl and a mature woman at the same time. What strange circumstances would bring them both back to Fair Oaks after all these years? Lisbeth was torn. She wanted to let Sadie run down the back stairs to greet them, but her head told her that would be unwise—for all of them.

"Momma?" Sadie interrupted Lisbeth's musings. "May I go?"

Lisbeth glanced at Lucie. The young woman's face looked horrified at the suggestion. Lisbeth shook her head and composed herself.

"No, Sadie," Lisbeth told her child. "It would be rude to intrude on the quarters without an invitation."

Sadie tugged on Lisbeth's hand. "Pleeease?"

Lisbeth gave her a sharp stare, and Sadie stopped speaking at once.

"Let's return for dinner. We have seen enough," Lisbeth said.

Just as they were sitting down at the table, Lisbeth realized she should have taken Sammy and Sadie aside and told them to avoid mentioning that they had seen Mattie and Jordan. It was too late now, so she silently telegraphed the message to her children.

"Is this the mash-potato table, Momma?" Sadie asked.

"You think our table is made from mashed potatoes?" Mr. Richards teased, feigning outrage.

Sadie laughed. "No! My momma spilled water into the mash potatoes when she was a girl, but her brother was blamed. She says it's best to tell the truth because otherwise you may regret it for the rest of your life."

Mary said, "I had forgotten about that event, but I was eating dinner here that night. You taught me that hand-clapping game after. Little Sally Walker!"

"This is the room where that happened, but not the table," Lisbeth said. "That table is in Richmond with Grandmother and Grandfather Wainwright."

"They took many of their belongings, leaving just the ones that would not fit in their new home. We were satisfied with that arrangement," Mr. Richards said. "Right, Mother?"

Lisbeth was unsettled to hear a grown man using that term for his wife. Mrs. Richards silently nodded her agreement.

Out of the blue Mary asked, "Do you understand the rules of baseball?"

"Sammy knows all about it!" Sadie proclaimed.

"Then please explain it to us," Mary requested. "All the soldiers returned enthusiastic about it. My children have asked, but I cannot explain it to them. I wish to keep up."

Sammy launched into a detailed description, and for once Mr. Richards listened more than he spoke. He interrupted only to ask questions. Thankfully they managed to get through the rest of dinner on that one topic, and the children did not make any uncomfortable proclamations.

While Sammy was speaking, Lisbeth thought about Mattie and Jordan just a few feet away. She feared that being here at the same time might put them at risk somehow. There was nothing *wrong* about the fact that they knew one another in Oberlin, but she didn't believe Mr. Richards would find it an amusing coincidence that they were visiting at the same time.

When supper ended Mr. Richards led them outside to the kitchen. The old man boomed from the wooden doorway, "Cook! We have a visitor for you!"

"Miss Elizabeth!" Cook exclaimed. "Look at you all grown-up!"

Cook marched over and wrapped Lisbeth in a giant hug. She pulled back and asked, "These your chil'ren?"

Lisbeth nodded. She was too choked up to speak. She hadn't realized that Cook meant something to her, but it was so good to see her. As a child Lisbeth had been intimidated by this woman who had firm control over her own domain. Her knees had always shaken a bit on the rare occasion when she had to speak to Cook directly.

"She looks just like you! I could call you little Elizabeth," Cook said to Sadie. "And you have your grandfather's eyes," she said to Sammy. "Your ma was a precious child, always thinkin' of others as much as herself," Cook told them. "She probabl' too modest to tell you herself, but she was."

Lisbeth cleared her throat, smiled, and said, "Thank you for a lovely dinner. I was especially appreciative of the oyster soup and young greens like you used to make when I was young. We don't have oysters in Ohio."

"My pleasure. Absolutely my pleasure! I 'membered you love those mustard greens!" Cook declared with a smile. "Have you looked around outside?"

Lisbeth shook her head.

"Well, you should," Cook said. "Don' you agree, Massa?"

That word was like a slap across the face. Cook seemed so happy; Lisbeth liked to think she would have been this friendly even if Mr. Richards weren't watching, but there was no way to know how she would have behaved if he weren't with them.

"Please, walk to the river, enjoy the view. I have correspondence I must attend to, so take your time," Mr. Richards said.

Mary joined them as they explored outside. Lisbeth led them toward the James River and away from the quarters. She didn't want to chance bumping into Mattie in case it would cause unwelcome tension or strife. She hoped the children had forgotten about seeing Miss Jordan.

They walked to the bank overlooking the river. She watched the muddy-brown water flow quickly to the east. Once again Lisbeth was thrown into a sentimental state. So many sweet memories flooded into her mind, most of them involving Mattie—hunting for yellow crocuses in the early spring, and picnics overlooking the river in the fall.

"Do you remember where this river starts?" Lisbeth asked Sammy.

"The Appalachians?" He answered her question with a question. Lisbeth nodded. "And it flows to?"

"Jamestown and the Atlantic?" Sammy guessed.

"Mostly correct." Lisbeth smiled at her son. "It flows into the Chesapeake Bay, which is attached to the Atlantic Ocean."

"Can we go see the ocean?" Sadie asked.

"I'm sorry, Sadie, it's too far." Lisbeth shook her head. "I've never seen it myself."

Sammy said, "This is the same river that is in Richmond, right?"

"Yes. The barges we see there pass by here on their way to the Atlantic, to the rest of our nation, and to the world," Lisbeth said.

"If we wait here long enough will we see a barge?" Sadie asked.

Mary laughed. "My goodness, you have curious children. Mine don't ask nearly so many questions. And I'm sure I would not have answers to them."

"Momma, look." Sadie pointed to the ground.

Lisbeth stared where her daughter pointed but did not see anything remarkable. She looked at Sadie with a question in her eyes. Sadie waved her closer and pointed down.

Sammy laughed. "Crocus leaves!"

Lisbeth didn't see what Sammy was talking about, and then suddenly they popped out at her. Thin blades with a strip of white lay limp against the dirt among the grass. She smiled at her children and nodded.

"I wonder what color it was?" Sammy said.

"Yellow. I'm sure!" Sadie said. "I feel it in my bones."

Lisbeth smiled at her daughter's faith in the magic of the world, and her own certainty.

"Is that *the* tree, Momma?" Sammy asked, pointing to a large willow tree situated on a rise. Lisbeth looked at the impressive tree in the distance. Another wave of nostalgia crashed hard onto her.

"Yes," Lisbeth said quietly.

"Where you took your naps when you were little and studied when you were older?" Sadie asked.

"That very tree," Lisbeth said.

And where I taught Mattie's Samuel to read, she thought to herself. At the time she had no idea that she was being rebellious by doing so. She'd often wondered if she would have done it had she realized she was betraying her parents—and the law. She liked to think she'd be brave enough to make that choice. By the time she understood the full ramifications of what she had done, she only wanted to keep it secret.

"Can we go under it?" Sadie pleaded.

Lisbeth looked at Mary, who nodded her agreement.

"Lead the way," Lisbeth told her daughter.

Parting the long green branches was another step back into childhood. The smell, the shade, and the feeling of the air brought her to the many afternoons under this tree. She felt safe and at peace here. Deliberately she walked toward the center, feeling the spring of the moist earth under her feet. She rubbed her palm across the sturdy trunk, leaned her cheek against the rough bark, and gave the tree a hug.

"You were always so sentimental," Mary said.

"I have missed being here," Lisbeth said. "I cannot let it go so long next time."

"I shall be glad to have your companionship once again." Mary sounded pleased. "Letters are not the same."

"I agree," Lisbeth said. She took Mary's hand, squeezed it, and smiled at her dear friend. It was reassuring to confirm that the politics of the day were not going to interfere with the fondness that they held for one another.

Lisbeth turned at the sound of laughter. Sammy and Sadie were chasing each other around the tree, darting in and out under the branches as they ran in a circle around the wide canopy. It was bittersweet to see them enjoying this sanctuary that had meant so much to her. If she had made a different choice, her children would have also grown up playing under this very tree. However they wouldn't be Sadie and Sammy, these people that she loved so much.

Sadie ducked through the branches as she ran away from her brother. Lisbeth's eyes traveled around the circumference to catch her reappearance. Sadie didn't dart back into sight. Sammy stopped running; he looked at Lisbeth and shrugged.

Lisbeth walked to the edge where Sadie had disappeared. She parted the branches and stepped through. Sadie wasn't there. Lisbeth's pulse sped up. She twirled around to look for her daughter. No Sadie. She peered back under the branches but didn't see her. Lisbeth frantically scanned the horizon and saw Sadie running down the slope, toward the quarters—straight to Jordan and Mattie.

CHAPTER 10

JORDAN

Fair Oaks plantation, Virginia

"Miss Jordan!" a high voice exclaimed.

Jordan spun around. Her head and her heart had a hard time reconciling what her eyes saw. Sadie Johnson was skipping straight toward her with a huge grin on her face. Before Jordan fully understood the situation, Sadie's small arms were wrapped around her waist in a sweet hug, just like she greeted her at school.

Sadie beamed up at Jordan. "I can't believe *you* are *here*! Where my momma used to live."

Jordan looked up. Sure enough, Lisbeth Johnson was walking toward them with another White person. The very baby that Mama had been brought in to breastfeed and care for was also visiting Fair

Oaks right now. Jordan was flustered by this improbable turn of events.

"Momma! Like I told you, it's Miss Jordan and Mrs. Freedman," Sadie said, pointing out the obvious.

Mama got that bittersweet look on her face that she always got when she saw Lisbeth Johnson. Kind of happy. Kind of sad. Today there was fear too.

"Hello." Lisbeth nodded a simple greeting. Apparently she was nervous to be seeing them too.

"You are acquainted with these people?" a small White woman asked, contempt dripping from her voice.

"Mrs. Bartley, this is my teacher! Miss Jordan," Sadie innocently and enthusiastically explained, unaware of the tension between the adults.

Lisbeth's discomfort grew more visible.

"Oh," the woman drew out. "Just one more *difference* between Virginia and Ohio."

"She is my *faaavorite* teacher," the little girl replied.

Jordan smiled at the six-year-old. "Thank you, Sadie. And you are one of my favorite students."

The little woman got a puzzled look on her face and said, "Jordan?" Then she looked over at Mama with dawning realization. Slowly she said, "Mattie! My goodness. This *is* a strange turn of events." She shook her head as if to clear it.

"Yes, ma'am," Mama said, head bowed. "Nice to meet you, ma'am."

Her voice completely changed, the woman said, "Mattie, I am Mary. I knew you when I was a child."

The submission in Mama's eyes was replaced by wide-eyed wonder.

"Oh my," Mama said. "I 'member you. Never was there such a well-behaved little girl. Look at you all growed up!"

"Thank you, Mattie. Yes. I am 'all growed up.' With children of my own now," Mary said, as if she were talking to a child. "You look very well. What brings you back to Fair Oaks?"

Jordan felt indignant on her mother's behalf. This woman had gone from rude to patronizing in an instant.

"We here to see family. Jus' a real quick visit. My son—you 'member Samuel—had some works in Richmond," Mama lied, "so I say I gonna come along to take a little time to visit with my kin that still livin' here."

"Well, we do not want to intrude any longer upon your short time together," Lisbeth said. "Sadie, say goodbye to Miss Jordan. You'll see her soon enough," Lisbeth directed her daughter.

Jordan knew she should just stay quiet, but she couldn't help herself from challenging that White woman's attitude by saying, "Bye, Sadie. See you at school. Remember to work on your letters."

"I will. I promise."

"You too, Sammy!" Jordan called out.

"Yes, ma'am," he replied.

Jordan got more than a hint of satisfaction having the White woman hear Sammy call her *ma'am*. It reminded her that whatever that Mary woman thought, it did not affect her accomplishments.

Mama watched the White people walk away. Once they were out of sight she let out a deep sigh.

"Well, that ain't good. It only gonna cause trouble for Sarah. Why you rubbin' it in that you they teacher?"

"You worried about Lisbeth?" Jordan asked.

Mama shook her head. "Not her. She smart about a thin' like this. But little White girls don' know not to talk. And that Mary always was one to keep to the rules." Mama sighed.

The knot already in Jordan's stomach got bigger. She didn't fully understand why, but her mother believed they had put Sarah at risk. She prayed that Mama was wrong, but feared that she was right.

Mama and Jordan boiled up greens with some beans in a pot over an open fire. They had supper waiting on the table when Sarah got home from the fields. It was fresher than last night's meal, but bland since there wasn't any salt or meat to flavor it. Jordan was on edge, waiting for Mama to tell Sarah about the encounter with Lisbeth Johnson.

"It look like there ain't so many folks livin' in the quarters anymore," Mama said. "That why you get this place to yourself?"

Sarah nodded and replied, "They bring men in for planting, then back again to harvest. Jus' a few mens live here all the time."

"When that change?" Mama asked.

Sarah shrugged. "Few years back."

"It feel wrong," Mama said.

"The war change ever'thin'. The men leave, and they don' come back, not even for visiting, it seem like. Not like before."

Mama asked, "Where they go?"

Suddenly the door to the shack banged open; the three women flinched. A large White man stood in the door frame holding a silver-topped walking stick.

"I heard there were intruders at my home," the man bellowed. "I came to see for myself."

Jordan, heart pounding, started to rise up and introduce herself. "Hell—"

Mama kicked her hard under the table. Jordan stopped speaking. Mama and Sarah rose without raising their eyes. Jordan followed their lead, adrenaline surging through her body.

"Good evenin', Massa Richards," Sarah said.

"Who are you? And what are you doing on *my* land?" he shouted. "And do not tell me any lie about being from Shirley!"

"We only here for a visit with Sarah, suh," Mama said. "My son, suh, he had to go to Washington. And we came with him."

The man walked up to Jordan and stood so close that his hot breath covered her face. Her mouth went dry, and her palms moistened. Terrified, Jordan needed all her self-control not to step back in retreat. She felt his gaze traveling up and down her body. Her eyes averted, she looked toward the eagle-topped walking stick he gripped in his hand, but in the periphery of her vision, she was fixated on his every movement.

"Where do you live?" he hissed. She flinched when spit from his mouth landed on her cheek.

Jordan, eyes still down turned, looked sideways at her mother, hoping for rescue. She feared she would make this situation worse by speaking.

"Do not look at her for your answer!" he shouted.

"Ohio," Jordan said in a shaky voice. Then she remembered to add, "Sir."

"Sir, huh? That does not come easily to you."

Fury built in him, his whole body tightening, scaring her more. He forcefully tapped his cane up and down against the floor as his hand troubled the metal eagle that topped it. Jordan stared at the sharp beak, fully aware that a stick just like this, perhaps this very cane, had struck and killed Mama's sister, Rebecca.

"*You* are not welcome here, disturbing our way of life," he said, continuing to hover threateningly close to Jordan. "Sarah, I thought you knew better than to invite these people to *my* home."

"Yes, suh," she agreed. "I ain't asked for them to come. They jus' showed up."

"Are you happy here, Sarah?" he demanded, all the time staring at Jordan.

"Oh, yes, suh! Very happy."

"Would you like to stay here?"

Sarah confirmed, "Oh, yes, suh. I never wants to live anywhere else, suh."

"Do we treat you well, Sarah? Fairly?"

"Oh, yes, Massa!" she said, sounding enthusiastic, though Jordan heard the fear underneath the words.

He leaned in even closer to Jordan and hissed, "You go back to Ohio, and you tell them that *everyone* is happy here and that they can stop intruding upon our freedoms."

Jordan nodded rapidly, her mouth dry and her heart nearly exploding in her chest.

"Yes, suh," Mama said.

The man's eyes bored into Jordan. Her heart thumped so loud she heard it in her head, and her legs quivered so hard she feared she might collapse. Jordan stood frozen, staring at the cane, watching for a cue from her mama.

"Now!" he barked. Jordan flinched.

"'Scuse me, suh?" Mama asked.

"Leave now!" he ordered.

Jordan felt Mama's body jerk. "Yes, suh."

Mama grabbed their carpetbag and walked to the door. A mustard seed fell from her hand. Watching it bounce on the ground broke Jordan's terror, giving her a bit of courage.

The man stood firmly in Jordan's path. She slowly inched to the left, mindful of the cane. He didn't move. Jordan rushed past him into the dark night, abandoning Sarah to the evil man who had killed Aunt Rebecca.

CHAPTER 11

Lisbeth

Charles City County, Virginia

"Momma, what's a scalawag?" Sammy asked. The three of them were alone, traveling back toward Richmond. They were going to stop for two nights to visit with Matthew's parents, Granny and Poppy.

The insult hit Lisbeth like a blow to the stomach. "Where did you hear that word!"

"Johnny said, 'Granny and Poppy are scalawags,'" he replied.

"That is not language we use in our family," she chastised. "It's a disrespectful name for Southerners who support the cause of the Union."

"Are they? Scal—" He stopped himself. "On our side?"

Lisbeth nodded. "Yes. And it has not been easy for them or your uncles. Some of their neighbors are unkind."

"What do they do to them?"

"After your uncle Mitch joined the Union army, Uncle Michael was put in jail."

"That's not fair!" Sammy exclaimed.

"People aren't fair, or kind, during war. One Union tactic was to burn fields. Poppy's crops were spared by the Union troops, but someone set fire to them after the Northern soldiers retreated."

Sammy slumped his head over and thought for a while. Eventually he said, "I never thought about what it was like here. For our family."

"It's difficult to think too long or too hard about the other side when there is a conflict. It's easier not to be too sympathetic to their sorrows."

"Is that why Uncle Michael and his family moved to California?" Sammy asked.

"Yes. He didn't believe he would have opportunities if he stayed here."

"Why do Granny and Poppy stay?" Sammy questioned.

Lisbeth chose her words carefully, explaining to him what they had told her. "This is their home, the only place they have ever lived. Their brothers and sisters live here. They are proud Virginians and proud to be a part of the United States. Like us, they hope we leave this conflict in the past and move forward together, as one country."

"You keep saying that we won, but it doesn't seem like it," Sammy observed.

"Why do you say that?" Lisbeth asked.

"Mrs. Bartley spoke so rudely to Mrs. Freedman until she realized she was your Mattie. Then she acted like she was glad to see her, but I could tell she wasn't. And Mr. Richards was *furious* when Sadie said she saw Miss Jordan. You pretend the Negroes have freedom when they don't."

"Oh, Sammy." Lisbeth looked at her son, proud of his observation and insight, and torn about how to make sense of something for him that still confused her.

Sammy continued. "He left the room, but we all heard him yelling about the—you know, that word we don't use—'rabble-rousers' who were going to destroy his way of life. *I* got scared, and I couldn't even *see* him."

"Me too," Sadie chimed in. "He pretends to be nice, but he is a bad man."

Lisbeth's stomach dropped. She hadn't realized Sadie had heard Mr. Richards's fit of rage . . . or that she was listening in on this conversation.

"It was confusing and scary to be at Fair Oaks. We went to my old home full of excitement. Mr. Richards was nice, *to us.*" Lisbeth struggled to find the right words. "Now you understand more about why Poppa and I decided to live in Ohio, where we do our best to be respectful to everyone. Here children are taught to show kindness and respect to some people but not to others."

"Not to Negroes, you mean," Sammy replied.

"When can we go home?" Sadie asked. "I miss Poppa."

"I miss him too," Lisbeth sympathized. "We came to Virginia to care for Grandfather in his last days. There is no knowing how long we will be required to stay. Death comes in its own time. After the visit with Granny and Poppy, we will go back to Richmond, and we won't have to visit any plantations ever again."

———— ❧⊙℘ ————

Lisbeth was saddened at the toll the years and the conflict had taken on Mother and Father Johnson's dwelling. The cost of the war was apparent everywhere in Virginia, but her husband's childhood home was especially changed for the worse. This once impeccably maintained property had green paint peeling from the front door, and no marigolds surrounded the scraggy rosebushes anymore. Corn, a subsistence crop, grew in the surrounding fields instead of tobacco, which would have brought in income.

As soon as Lisbeth stopped the horse, the house's weathered door flew open. Mother and Father Johnson rushed out to greet them. It had been more than a year since the elderly couple had visited Ohio, but Sammy and Sadie didn't hold back from hugging their grandparents.

"You have both grown six inches since we saw you!" Mother Johnson exaggerated.

"Give us some sugar!" Father Johnson leaned over so Sadie could kiss his cheek.

Lisbeth smiled at the scene. After all the stress of Fair Oaks and Richmond, it was especially good to be here for a few days. Once again this family would be a sanctuary.

"This is your uncle Mitch," Father Johnson said, introducing the children to Matthew's brother.

Lisbeth hadn't seen him in years, and she'd never known him well. He looked like her husband though, so she had a tender space in her heart for him. He shook Sammy's hand and gave Sadie a sweet, if awkward, sideways hug.

"It's nice to see you, Sister," he said to Lisbeth. When he leaned in to kiss her cheek, he stepped on the edge of her shoe. He blushed and apologized a little too loudly.

"I'm so glad the children have a chance to meet you. We still hope we will get you to visit us someday soon." Lisbeth smiled at her brother-in-law.

Her in-laws greeted her, and after asking about her father they led the way up the rickety wooden stairs onto the porch and then into the house. In the doorway of the living room, Lisbeth remembered the moment that had changed her life forever. At twenty-one, hardly more than a sheltered child, she knew that she could not in good conscience marry Edward once she understood what kind of a man he was. She threw away tradition and everything her parents had planned when she proposed marriage to Matthew in this very home; she'd been so nervous she feared she might actually faint. He agreed to her bold question, and they began their new life in Ohio. She now shuddered to imagine how close she'd come to marrying Edward Cunningham. She would have had no Matthew, no Sammy, and no Sadie. That would have been a tragedy.

CHAPTER 12

JORDAN

Fair Oaks plantation, Virginia

"Mama, do you think he's going to kill Sarah? Should we go back?" Jordan rushed to keep up with her mother as they crashed their way through the woods toward Samuel.

"I think she safe so long as we stay away. We ain't gonna go back till we have Ella and Sophia. Then she gonna come with us," Mama replied without pausing.

"How are we going to find them?" Jordan asked.

"The Freedmen's Bureau ain't closed yet, right?" Mama turned her head so Jordan could hear her as she walked.

Jordan nodded.

"That how. We gonna go to Richmond and ask the folks at the bureau to ask the folks at the other bureaus until we figure out what happen to those little girls. Your brother gonna put his law schooling to use," Mama declared.

"Of course! I can't believe I didn't think of it." Jordan looked at her mother in admiration. "That's why you wanted to come now—before it closed."

"Jordan, you and Samuel book smarter than most folks, but that don' make you world smarter too. Don' ever forget that."

"Yes, Mama!"

Jordan heard the cock of a gun in the bushes. She froze, her heart hammering hard, and she tasted metal in her mouth.

"Samuel!" Mama yelled. "It jus' us."

Mama moved toward the sound. Jordan followed cautiously. Pushing through a bush, she saw her brother standing alone, holding a weapon in a shaky hand.

Samuel tipped his head back, let out a huge sigh, and said, "Thank you, Jesus!" His voice quavering with emotion, he continued. "That was the worst wait of my life. I never thought anything could be as worrisome as the night when Otis was born, but I was wrong!"

He pulled his mother and sister into a long, tight embrace.

"Did you hold your mustard seeds?" Mama asked Samuel after their hug.

He nodded with a smile. "I did, Mama."

"Did it give you a bit more faith?" Mama wondered.

Samuel shrugged and nodded with a lopsided smile. "Yes, it did. I don't understand why or how, but it did."

"You don' have to know how or why faith work—you jus' got to make sure you find some when you feelin' lost."

Jordan and Samuel exchanged a look—the "we both know her beliefs are superstitions, but we do love her" look.

Mama leaned in and whispered, as if there were someone else nearby listening, "I lef' a mustard seed in the quarters. That gonna give Sarah some of my faith when her own gets lost."

Early the next morning they set out for the half-day ride to Richmond. Jordan had wanted to just get going, but Mama insisted it was safer to travel by daylight. Jordan, as tense as Mama, rode facing backward to give warning if need be. Halfway through the journey Jordan became alarmed when the wagon stopped for no apparent reason. She scrambled around, looking for the cause. She didn't see anything blocking the way. She looked at Mama and then at Samuel. His head was slumped over. Worry started to rise, but then she heard a soft snore coming from his lips.

He'd fallen asleep with his hands still holding the reins. Sleepless nights had taken a toll on him. Mama roused him. He was embarrassed and insisted he could keep driving, but eventually he agreed to lie down in the wagon bed to sleep. Mama slid into the driver's seat, Jordan joined her up front, and they got moving toward Richmond again.

Just before they got to the Manchester Turnpike on the outskirts of the city, they woke Samuel up. Mama said he would draw less attention driving the cart than an old Negro woman. Jordan breathed to steady her nerves as they waited to pay the toll, but once Samuel handed over the money they were waved through.

Richmond wasn't as big as Cincinnati, more like Cleveland, but everything was packed in close. Samuel had read that the last census in 1860 counted nearly 38,000 people in Richmond, about one-third of them colored or Negro. Like most cities, it had grown significantly during the war, especially with freedmen.

The turnpike was a wide, smooth gravel road, unlike anything they had ever experienced. It took some coaxing, but eventually the horses accepted that they could move as fast as the other carts and wagons. Jordan was too distracted by the hustle and bustle around them to feel worried. Colored men, as well as White men, worked on steamships and barges on the James River to the south. Full wagons carried goods into and out of town; sometimes loads were so wide that Samuel was forced to stop or pull over to let them by. Single riders on horseback galloped past them in both directions.

"I had no idea it would be this crowded!" Samuel said.

"How are we going to find the bureau?" Jordan wondered. "Where are we going to stay?"

"Remember, we gonna find this church," Mama said, handing Jordan the paper from Pastor Duhart. "Pastor say they gonna set us up with everthin' we need."

"Clay at Adams," Jordan read out loud. She looked around. There was nothing to indicate which street was which. "How do we know what street is Clay, or Adams?"

"When I get off the turnpike, we can ask the first friendly colored person we see," Samuel said.

"The kindness of strangers," Mama lectured, "usually works out just fine."

"Oh my!" Jordan exclaimed as they were suddenly in the midst of charred ruins. Burned-out buildings lined the road; bricks and rubble were scattered around them. The fire that had ravaged these buildings must have been huge to burn so many blocks. In stark contrast, a white-columned building shone in the sunlight up the hill to the right. Jordan shuddered when it hit her that it was the capitol building of the Confederacy. Jefferson Davis had worked from that building. His "White House" was nearby. She was in the heart of the enemy. To the south stone pillars poked out of the churning water, showing where a bridge had once crossed the James River.

Some of the ruined buildings had workers clearing debris or making repairs, but mostly their remains stood alone and silent as a haunting reminder of the devastation that had been experienced by this city at the end of the war.

Jordan was utterly enamored with Miss Grace's boardinghouse. The pastor's wife, Nell, had brought them straight over to this street of newly built homes. The "row" homes were so close that they shared walls with one another. Jordan hadn't seen one White face since they arrived at this neighborhood, Jackson Ward. Miss Grace, born free in Richmond, rented out three well-furnished bedrooms to colored people who were passing through town or looking to relocate. Jordan expected to feel unsettled in this stranger's home, but Miss Grace lived up to her name and put them at ease.

After weeks of living out of a carpetbag, it was a welcome pleasure to unpack her clothing into a cherrywood wardrobe. Mama and Jordan worked side by side, settling into the room. Mama reached into her chemise and pulled out a fat wad of paper money. Jordan gasped loudly and watched her ma reach up high to tuck the money in the back of the wardrobe shelf.

When Mama saw the look of outrage on her face, she said, "For all the costs while we here."

"Where did you get that?" Jordan asked, energy swirling in her body.

"Been saving," was Mama's unsatisfactory explanation.

Jordan walked to the shelf and reached for the money. She expected Mama to protest, but she just watched Jordan count the bills. Sixty dollars! Mama must have saved for years to accumulate that much money.

"You had this when I was desperate to fund my tuition?" Jordan heard the heat in her own voice.

Mama replied, "We knowed you'd find the money on your own, and you did."

Jordan stared hard at her mother, silently signaling her hurt and confusion.

"Not everybod' has a pretty life handed to them with a bow," Mama said.

A bolt of anger flashed in Jordan. A constant refrain in her childhood was that she took for granted all that her parents had done to give her a life of freedom. Nothing she accomplished could ever exceed the challenge of escaping from slavery with a baby tied to her back.

"I worked hard, extremely hard, to be an excellent student," Jordan declared, striving to keep her voice calm. "You have no idea what it is like to be one of the few Negro students—and a woman— in college. Every single day I had to prove I belonged at Oberlin. In addition, I was forced to beg for the funds for my tuition."

"Church folks were proud to help you with a collection. And you got that nice grant from Oberlin College. Pops and I had faith you could figure it out—and you did," Mama said.

Jordan admonished, "You and Pops could have saved me from shame and humiliation. For what? Far-off 'family'?"

Mama pulled herself up. "They ain't 'far-off family' to me. You gonna forget 'bout us when you in New York? When Otis need somethin' in twenty years, you gonna ignore him?"

Jordan sucked in her breath, all the outrage flying out of her. How did Mama learn about her plan to move to New York? She stared at her mother, uncertain about what to say.

"I ain't stupid. I seen you making plans to leave us and go to the city," Mama said.

Jordan's heart hammered, and her hands got clammy. This wasn't how she wished to have this conversation. She calmed her gaze and finally said, "I guess both of us have been keeping secrets from each other."

"I was hopin' maybe you gonna change your mind after comin' here." Mama's eyes softened too. "You might see that we still got a fight of our own."

Mama looked so small and vulnerable as she spoke. Even through her anger, Jordan felt sorry for her mother. This whole trip might have been a ruse to keep Jordan close. Mama could be that manipulative. She did not understand that Jordan had to live her own life, free in her own way, separate from her parents.

"Mama, the right to vote *is* a fight for *me*—can't you see that my rights matter?" Jordan implored.

A knock at the door interrupted them. Samuel came to tell them Miss Grace and Mrs. Washington were waiting to chat on the front porch. Jordan followed her brother and her mother down the stairs, still ruminating on the conversation with her mother. She wondered if Samuel also knew about her plan . . . or Pops? Perhaps they all wanted to get Jordan to care about the suffering of the freedmen more than the cause of suffrage. She resented Mama for figuring out her plans, but she had a measure of relief that her secret was out. Now she wouldn't have to face breaking the news to them.

"Mrs. Washington says you looking for some little girls sold south," Miss Grace said to start the conversation.

Jordan nodded. "To North Carolina, we believe."

"What plantation they come from?"

"Fair Oaks, out by Charles City," Mama explained.

"Fair Oaks?" Miss Grace leaned back her head in thought. She looked at Mrs. Washington. "Didn't Emily come from Fair Oaks?"

Mrs. Washington replied, "Who?"

Miss Grace clarified, "Ari and Winnie Smith, their son William married an Emily. I believe she comes from Fair Oaks."

Mrs. Washington nodded in understanding. "That rings a bell."

"Skinny Emily?" Mama perked up. "She tall and yellow? Has about forty years?"

Miss Grace nodded. "Her husband's people live around the corner on Second."

"Well, well, well, if it ain't a small world," Mama said. "First we see Miss Lisbeth, and now I hear of Skinny Emily."

"Skinny Emily?" Jordan asked. "Who's that?"

"Lisbeth's maid after I was sent back out. She probably not skinny anymore." Mama laughed, then got a sad look in her eyes. "We weren't never too nice to her."

"I remember," Samuel concurred. "You all shunned her—like she was a ghost. I never understood why she got you all riled up."

Surprised, Jordan asked Samuel, "You knew her too?"

"Not really," Samuel replied. "She was in the house. Only Mama ever went between those worlds. And Lisbeth."

"You *never* went inside?" Jordan asked.

"Not once. Though it loomed large for all of us." Samuel thought for a moment, then shook his head. "That life is like a dream. Well, more like a nightmare."

"Massa was Emily's pa," Mama explained quietly. "She was brought in when her ma died. That's why folks weren't so kind to her."

Jordan's heart squeezed tight. Once again the harsh reality of slavery hit her like a physical blow—a horse kick to the stomach. She'd never known her mama to be cruel to anyone. She even prayed for people she was mad at, but she'd been unkind to an orphan?

"Emily moved here with them," Mrs. Washington explained.

"Who?" Jordan asked, afraid of the answer.

"Her massa and his family," Miss Grace replied.

Jordan was disgusted: the word *massa*, the idea that the man had fathered this Emily and then forced her to stay with him.

"How can you be so matter-of-fact about this story? It's horrible!" Jordan was embarrassed to feel tears pushing at her eyes.

Mama tilted her head. "Jordan, no need to tell me it's horrible. I lived it."

"Sorry, Mama. I just . . ." At a loss for words, Jordan took a deep breath. "The nastiness has so many layers, too many for me to understand."

"You right about that," Mama agreed. The others all nodded too.

"There are a few ways to go about finding those girls," Mrs. Washington said, handing Mama a newspaper. "You can make an ad like these—in the North Carolina colored paper."

Mama passed the paper to Samuel, who read out loud.

> EVANS GREEN desires to find his mother, Mrs. PHILLIS GREEN, whom he left in Virginia some years ago. She belonged to old 'Squire Cook, of Winchester, whose son was an attorney-at-law. Any information respecting her will be thankfully received. Address this paper.

He went on to the next ad, his voice quavering as he read.

> INFORMATION WANTED Of my children, Lewis, Lizzie, and Kate Mason, whom I last saw in Owensboro', Ky. They were then "owned" by David and John Hart; that is, the girls were;—but the boy was rather the "property" of Thomas Pointer. Any information will be gladly received by their sorrowing mother, Catharine Mason, at 1818 St., between Master and Thompson, Philada.

Jordan felt sick. Faces of imaginary children popped into her mind. She looked at the paper her brother was reading. The page was filled with these small advertisements.

"Does this actually work?" Jordan asked.

Miss Grace shrugged. "It works to make people feel like they are doing somethin' to find their people."

"How much does it cost to place an ad like this?" Samuel asked.

"Two dollars fifty cents for a month in the newspaper," Miss Grace replied.

Samuel, Jordan, and Mama all gasped. That was a lot of money, even for them.

"That's an expensive gamble," Samuel said.

"The *Christian Recorder* is less costly, fifty cents for a month," Mrs. Washington said. She gave Samuel some papers. "They get read out by the ministers on Sunday. We got a few families back together in our very own church."

Samuel looked over the papers in silence, and then he passed them to Jordan.

Mama said, "Read to me. Please."

Jordan cleared her throat and read the one on the top of the page.

INFORMATION WANTED Of my mother, Virginia Sheperd, also of my sisters, Mary, Louisa, Mandy and Caroline Sheperd; of my brother, William H. Sheperd: my uncle Paten Sheperd, and my aunt Dibsy Madison, all of whom belonged to Ben Sheperd. Also of my aunt Martha Young, who belonged to Henry Young. All lived in Prince Edward Co., Virginia. My mother and her four children were sold, at Prince Edward County Court House, to a slave trader named Sam Jenkins. Any information of the above named persons will be thankfully

received by Martha Sheperd. Address MARTHA
PARIS, Lebanon, St. Clair Co., Ill.

Ministers will please read this notice to their
congregations.

She scanned the pages. Post after post filled four sheets of paper.
Her heart ached, and her eyes stung.

Jordan looked at her mama. "They basically say the same thing.
Different names and places, but they are all folks wanting to find
their family. You read these?" she asked the two women. "Out loud
in worship?"

"Every week," Mrs. Washington confirmed. "It's a holy time, with
everybody hopin' that there might be a match—we all lean forward
and listen real careful. It's only happened twice, but oh my, what a
joy to have someone yell out in church 'cus they knowed the person
that made the notice." Her face looked filled with the joy that comes
from the Holy Spirit.

Jordan was stunned once again. The hope and resistance in the
face of the overwhelming pain and loss were striking—and touching.
She took a deep breath and sat back.

"What about the bureau?" Mama asked.

Mrs. Washington shrugged and nodded, an odd combination.

Miss Grace said, "None of us put much stock in the bureau, but
sometimes they come through. It's free, so it don't hurt to go down
there and give 'em the name of the folks you're looking for. It can't
harm, and it might help."

"And the orphanage," Mrs. Washington added. "You have to go
to there, 'cus your babies might just be up the street. We had a match
from there once, praise God!"

Miss Grace thought it would be a treat for Mama and Emily to catch up with each other after so many years, so she had arranged for Mama, Jordan, and Samuel to walk around the corner that evening for a visit at William's parents' house. Mama agreed with enthusiasm even though she said she'd not been close to this Emily before.

"Hello, Mattie." The light-skinned woman smiled shyly after welcoming them in. "This Samuel? And Jordan?" She shook her head slowly in disbelief and reached out her hand to greet them.

"Tell me all 'bout you!" Mama said when they all sat down. "All grown! Married lady with a son. You free!"

Emily snorted. "Mrs. Ann don't seem to share your thinking on that."

Mama giggled. "How the Wainwrights doin'? Is Massa Jack as awful as ever?"

"Jack just became the justice of the peace," Emily said. "He tryin' to get powerful."

Mama clicked her tongue and shook her head at this news. Jordan didn't fully understand what passed between the women, but she wasn't going to interrupt the flow of conversation with a question. It was too sweet to see Mama looking like a schoolgirl gossiping with a friend, even if she didn't sound like herself calling some White man *massa*.

Emily went on. "Mr. Wainwright is passing soon, so Miss Lisbeth is visiting to tend to him."

Mama looked at Jordan. "That explains why we saw her."

"You saw her in town?" Emily asked.

Mama shook her head. "At Fair Oaks. We went visitin' to Sarah."

Emily furrowed her brows. "I hope Mr. Richards didn't see you. Ever'body says he taking the end of the war extra bad. Some of the planters are getting on with the new way, but others . . . are still fighting the lost cause."

"He threw us out! I've never been so frightened in my life."

A little White boy ran through the door, followed by a tall colored man. The boy waved a baseball glove around and said, "Ma, Sammy says I can keep it!"

"Willie, you're being rude." Emily gestured toward the guests.

Emily introduced her son and husband to them. The boy only looked White, Jordan realized, which wasn't a surprise, given how light Emily and William both were. The men shook hands.

Jordan asked, "Did you get that glove from Sammy Johnson?"

Willie nodded, looking utterly bewildered.

"Sammy is quite the baseball fanatic and very fond of his glove," Jordan said. "He must be impressed with you."

"You know Sammy?" Willie asked, wonder filling his voice.

Jordan nodded and told him, "He's one of my students."

The boy gaped at her; incomprehension and doubt covered his face.

Jordan explained to him, "I'm a schoolteacher in Oberlin, though I mostly work with the younger students."

"I didn't think Negro ladies could be teachers," Willie replied.

"We can be, and now you know it." Jordan smiled.

"Are you a teacher too?" Willie looked at Samuel.

Samuel shook his head. "I studied law, not education. And I make furniture with my pops," he said.

William perked up at that information. "You heard about the new amendment? Number fourteen?"

"Of course," Samuel said, nodding.

"It say I can vote, right?" William asked.

"We believe so," Samuel replied, but then he went on. "There is no guarantee that states will respect that intention, but Virginia will not be admitted back into the Union until your new state constitution is approved, and it requires voting rights for all. However, many senators argue that we need a fifteenth amendment specifically laying out the right for Negro suffrage."

"Negro men's suffrage," Emily corrected.

Jordan looked at the woman with new respect. Perhaps she had a kindred spirit in this "Skinny Emily."

William ignored his wife's comment and asked Samuel, "Is it true it say that Confederate officers can never vote?"

"No, that's a false rumor," Samuel clarified. "They can vote, but people who engaged in insurrection or rebellion against the United States can't hold office at the state or federal level, and they won't get a pension for fighting in the war."

"And pay? Do that amendment require equal pay for the races?" William asked.

"I argue it does. Equal protection should mean equal pay, but I fear the federal government will be weak on enforcement unless there is a strong Republican majority," Samuel explained. "You're employed?"

William nodded. "At Tredegar."

"The munitions factory?" Samuel asked.

William nodded.

"You made the weapons for the Confederacy?" Samuel wondered, sounding as incredulous as Jordan felt. How could a colored man support the Confederate war effort?

William nodded. "I didn' thin' too hard about what they were used for. I tried to put in a small mistake so they wouldn't work quite right—a weak seam so it backfire or somethin.'"

Mama asked, "Ain't it closed now that the war over?"

William laughed and shook his head. "Now we making equipment for the railroads. We as busy as ever. I'm glad for a job, but it don't sit right to be paid so much less than the Whites, especially immigrants."

Jordan followed the conversation, but she didn't have much to add. This William seemed nice enough, but it was hard for her to understand why he and Emily stayed in a place like this with such limited opportunities for their family.

Jordan expected large, well-appointed offices, but the Freedmen's Bureau was a dingy room with hardly more than a desk. It practically sat in the shadow of the Virginia capitol building, the headquarters of the Confederacy not so long ago. Jordan reassured herself that the United States had won the war as they walked toward the ominous building.

A White man looked up from his work when they walked in. No one else was in the room. One wall of the bureau's office was covered with postings that explained the new right afforded to all Americans. Or at least American men.

"How can I help you?" he asked.

Samuel walked toward the man with his hand extended. "I'm Samuel Freedman."

The man rose and shook Samuel's hand. "How do you do? James Brooke."

"We'd like some assistance in finding a family member. We understand there is a register where she might be listed."

Mr. Brooke gestured to the chair, dug through his drawers, and pulled out a register. He acted as if Samuel were alone, insulting both Jordan and Mama. Jordan reminded herself that this wasn't the place to fight for respect.

"Well, Mr. . . ."

"Freedman. That should be easy for you to remember," Samuel joked.

Mr. Brooke furrowed his brow, laughing when he understood the connection. "Ah, yes! Well, Mr. Freedman, I will do what I can to reunite you with your loved one in the time I have allotted to me. However I want to caution you not to expect too much of this office."

Samuel nodded.

"We have been given notice that we are closing in two months. 'Our work here is done,' according to the federal government. Do you know how many are employed by the Freedmen's Bureau in

Virginia?" he asked, his voice charged with emotion. He looked at Samuel expectantly.

Samuel shook his head. Mama and Jordan did too, but the man wasn't paying them any attention.

"One hundred forty-three," he stated. "Do you know the population of Virginia?" Without waiting for a reply, he said, "Nearly one hundred fifty thousand reside in this fair state. One-third are freedmen. Most of the rest are Confederates determined to maintain their preferred order of things." The man sighed. "We have done some good, but it hardly seems enough most of the time." He picked up his pen. "Name?"

"Samuel Freedman," Samuel replied, clearly frustrated by the man's lack of attention.

"Not yours. Your relative's."

"Sophia and Ella."

"Last name?" the man asked without looking up.

"We have reason to believe they would use Brown."

"Last known location?" Mr. Brooke continued.

"North Carolina."

"Can you be more specific?" the man asked.

"Hope," Samuel replied.

"You hope you can be specific?" the man asked.

"No, sir," Samuel explained. "They were sold from Fair Oaks near Charles City to Hope Plantation in North Carolina. Senator Stone was the owner at the time."

"Age?" the man went on.

"Nine and twelve," Samuel replied.

The man sighed. "Now or then?"

"Now."

"When were they sold?" he asked.

"In 1864."

The man looked up, his lips pursed in concern. He sighed and said, "After emancipation." He shook his head slowly. "I moved here to be of service to a righteous goal, but I fear it is *our* cause that is lost." The man stared off into space and then asked, "Where are you from?"

"Ohio," Samuel said.

The man gave a wry smile. "How about that?" he declared. "Me too. Sixteenth Division."

Samuel said more than asked, "Then you saw the Battle of Shiloh."

The man nodded. "It was as bad as you've heard. You?"

Samuel replied, "Fifth Regiment United States Colored Troops."

"Then you've been to Virginia before," the man said. Apparently he was one of those who tracked where various troops fought.

"Yes, I have," Samuel replied. Jordan noticed Samuel didn't reveal that he had been born in Virginia, and she understood why. People treated you differently when they learned you were a slave, and he didn't bring it up casually, especially with White people.

Mr. Brooke got an intense look on his face and said, "After the war I wanted to make sure our fighting, and dying, was *for* something, so I signed up to work for the bureau. Don't make the same mistake I did and think you can make a difference here. There is nothing we can do to assure the liberties of the freedman. Go back to Ohio. When this office closes I am heading home to be of help there. My mother has sacrificed enough. My brother lost a leg. My father's nerves are shot. My mama needs me."

He stared at Samuel, waiting for a reply.

"I understand, sir. I'll take your advice under consideration, but for now, while you're still here and I'm still here, we'd appreciate anything you can do to reunite us with our nieces."

"Description," the man continued.

Samuel answered as best as he could. There was so little information to go on that Jordan had little hope Sophia and Ella would ever be found.

"Don' you have a list you can look on? See if you already knows about 'em?" Mama asked Mr. Brooke.

The man looked at her like he was surprised she could even talk. He clicked his tongue and pulled out a printed piece of paper.

"I don't suppose you can read?" the man asked.

"My sister and I are both well educated," Samuel replied. "She is a teacher. I am a lawyer."

"Hm," the man grunted. He spun the paper around until it faced Samuel. "Feel free to look this over then."

They did, but they didn't see any information that might lead them to Ella or Sophia. Before they left the office the man handed Mama a brochure entitled *Plain Counsels for Freedmen* by Clinton B. Fisk, assistant commissioner in the Freedmen's Bureau.

Mama passed the brochure to Jordan. She skimmed through it as they walked back to Miss Grace's. She kept reading it when they were sitting in the front room of the boardinghouse.

As she read Jordan grew more and more outraged, until finally she burst out, "Listen to this!"

I have a few words to say to you about your old master. It may be he was a very good master, or it may be he was not so good as he might have been, but that is all past now; he is your master no longer, and I earnestly advise you to live on good terms with him.

He has had a hard time of it, during the war, as well as yourselves. His wealth has melted away like wax before the fire. His near relatives, and in many cases his sons, have died on the field of battle, or have been crippled for life, and the Government will grant no pensions in their cases, because they fought not

under its flag. You have been made free against his
will, and all the money he paid for you might better
have been sunk in the bottom of the sea.

Jordan looked up from the pamphlet and said, "The freedmen
are supposed to feel compassion for their former masters because
they lost money?"

She shook her head and continued reading.

Now it is natural that he should feel sore; that he
should grieve over his loss; that he should be slow
to adapt himself to the new state of things; and
that he should be some years in putting off the airs
and manners of a master, just as you find it hard to
shake off the habit of slaves.

It is natural, too, that he should feel severe toward
you. It is true you did not, in your servitude, agitate the
questions of the day; you did not meddle with politics; you were neither Republican nor Democratic;
you did not bring the war; and he admits that you behaved all through the conflict in a very proper man-
ner. Still, whenever he sees you he can not but think
of the great change, and can not avoid blaming you
for it, although his better judgment tells him he ought
to praise, rather than blame you.

You must think of these things, and think kindly
of your old master. You have grown up with him,
it may be, on the same plantation. Do not fall out
now, but join your interests if you can, and live and
die together.

"Tsk, tsk, tsk." Mama clicked her tongue. "Join your interests! This man do not know what he talking about!"

> You want his money, or lands, and he wants your labor. He is not able to do without you, and you will, in most cases, find him as kind, honest, and liberal as other men. Indeed he has for you a kind of family affection, and in spite of this bad feeling, I have noticed, he desires you to do well in life. Be frank, then, with him, and treat him with respect.

> Do not think that, in order to be free, you must fall out with your old master, gather up your bundles and trudge off to a strange city. This is a great mistake. As a general rule you can be as free and as happy in your old home, for the present, as anywhere else in the world.

Jordan stopped reading and looked up in disbelief. "This is from the Freedmen's Bureau! How can they encourage the formerly enslaved to 'think kindly of' their former masters and 'live and die together'?"

Miss Grace laughed. "Those Northerners think they know something, but they don't. They're pretending this conflict is over so they can walk away feeling good about themselves. The planters may have surrendered to the United States government, but they aren't about to share respect or wealth with any of us. Not without a long fight."

CHAPTER 13

LISBETH

Charles City County, Virginia

Lisbeth and Mother Johnson were preparing the midday meal while Sammy and Sadie tended to the animals with Uncle Mitch and Poppy. The kitchen in this old farmhouse was very outdated. Lisbeth would no longer take her stove and pots for granted. She hadn't realized how much she'd missed the simple pleasure of cooking.

"What time is our guest arriving?" Lisbeth asked.

"Around noon," Mother Johnson explained. "Thank you for allowing Miss Thorpe to impinge on your visit. We rarely have even one guest, let alone two—not that you are guests. It was quite a surprise when our minister asked us to host her for a meal during her travels."

Lisbeth replied, "I think I shall find her interesting, and I am curious to learn more about the freedmen's schools. Besides, I think it will be good for Sammy to see that there are White people working on behalf of the emancipated slaves."

The older woman asked, "How has your visit been with your parents?"

To her surprise Lisbeth teared up at the question. She looked at her mother-in-law and said, "It's been . . ."—she searched for the right word—"challenging. I'm honored to care for my father at this time, but it is gloomy. My mother's attitude continues to confuse me. One day she is warm, and another she is hostile. She has no interest in knowing my children, which pains me. Julianne and Jack have taken a liking to Sadie, but I fear their influence conflicts with our values." Lisbeth's voice broke. "And Sammy seems to be very disappointed in me after seeing where I come from."

Mother Johnson patted her hand.

"I am managing, but I miss Matthew. And I don't know how much longer we will be away from him. But that's enough about me. Do you have any news from Michael or Maggie in California?"

"The letter from this week said they had a lovely crop of apricots that fetched a good price in San Francisco," Mother Johnson said. "Apparently the climate in Oakland is very suitable for the many kinds of fruit they are growing. They report that the community has changed in the two years they have been there; soon there will be ten thousand people living there."

"You must miss them," Lisbeth said.

"Aurelia and Emma have grown so much," Mother Johnson said. "We treasure their letters, but it is not the same as being together."

"I'm sorry all your grandchildren live far from you," Lisbeth said, imagining the pain of being so far from her own children.

"We can manage travel to Ohio, but . . ." Her voice tightened. "I fear we may never see Aurelia and Emma again."

Lisbeth's chest swelled in empathy.

Mother Johnson's eyes welled up. "California is so very far. They have encouraged us to resettle there, but we cannot imagine abandoning this home, our siblings, Mitch . . . visits with your family."

"The changes in our nation are tearing families apart," Lisbeth said.

Mother Johnson nodded, then mixed her biscuits in a sorrowful silence.

As Mother Johnson spoke gratitude to the Lord for these people and this food, Lisbeth strongly felt the blessing and the sorrow of this moment. Being with this part of the family was a rare treat. She wanted to savor it for herself and for her children, but she was acutely aware that it was going to be an all-too-brief visit.

Sadie held her left hand and Sammy her right. In front of her a huge stack of boiled corn and a plate of buttermilk biscuits were flanked by two roasted chickens. Father and Mother Johnson sat at the head and the foot. Mitch and Margaret Newbold Thorpe, the teacher from the freedmen's school in Williamsburg, sat on the other side of the table. Lisbeth was excited to get a firsthand account of Miss Thorpe's experience; however, the conversation soon took on a difficult tone.

Miss Thorpe said, "I am proud of the work I do here. It is my duty as a Christian to raise up the Negro as far as it is possible. They will never be the equal of Whites intellectually, but their hard work and cheery attitude make them earnest learners. I am grateful they are not in a position to be disheartened by comparison with White children, as Negroes' achievements can never equal the achievement of our race."

Sammy looked at Lisbeth, outrage in his eyes.

"You look like you have something to say to that, Sammy," Father Johnson said.

Sammy gave a quick nod.

"Go on," his grandfather prodded. "All voices are welcome at this table, even children's."

Bolstered by the encouragement, Sammy declared, "Henry is the best student in my class, and he's a full Negro."

The teacher replied, "You must be mistaken. Oftentimes mulattoes look like Negroes. But he must have some White blood in him."

Sadie spoke up without any hesitation. "Miss Jordan is Negro. She's so smart she attended Oberlin College."

"I fear you misunderstand me. I appreciate your sentiment and your enthusiastic support of the Negro race," Miss Thorpe explained. "I arrived at my post with the innocence of a child myself."

Lisbeth bristled on behalf of her children. She felt compelled to enter into the discussion with this condescending woman.

"Do you believe in Negro suffrage?" Lisbeth asked.

The woman shook her head slowly. "No longer. My time as a teacher in the freedmen's school has given me a clear understanding of Negro capacities. Blind idealism has been cut from my heart. My beliefs are grounded in the truth of experience. Negroes are not born with the capacity to understand the complexity of our electoral system.

"It is cruel to encourage them to pursue opportunities that are beyond their natural abilities. A cow cannot fly, and an eagle cannot produce milk," Miss Thorpe proclaimed.

"What about mulattoes?" Mitch asked.

Miss Thorpe replied, "Since I am speaking frankly among friends . . . the mulattoes will do best to form their own nation where they can rise to their own level of success, unencumbered by the Negroes, similar to Liberia, only perhaps in the Caribbean rather than Africa."

"Momma believes everyone should be able to vote, even women," Sadie declared.

All eyes turned to Lisbeth. Her pulse quickened in fear of condescension from around the table. She took a deep breath, hoping it would help her to sound calm.

"Matthew and I both advocate suffrage for all," Lisbeth said.

"Do you favor equality for the sexes?" Mitch asked. "You run the farm, and Matthew bears your next child?"

Laughter went around the table.

"I do work on the farm; Matthew does care for our children. We have different, but complementary roles. My desire and ability to vote will not make me less of a woman or him less of a man."

"We are just teasing you, Sister. You do not need to be so serious," Mitch replied. "We may not be quite as radical as you and Matthew, but we are loyal Republicans."

"Judge Underwood shares your thinking, as do I," Mother Johnson declared. "He argued vehemently for suffrage for women, as well as for Negro men."

"Who?" Sammy asked.

"John Underwood is the federal judge who presided over the Virginia Constitutional Convention earlier this year," Father Johnson explained.

Mitch inserted, "No Virginians will be voting in the upcoming presidential election—man, woman, Negro, or White."

"Why not?" Sammy asked.

"Your Congress won't admit us back into the Union until Virginia has a new constitution," Mother Johnson explained. "This spring, at the Constitutional Convention, one was drafted, but it has not been ratified yet. The current draft, the Underwood Constitution as we call it, enfranchises Negroes, but not women."

"Is there doubt that it will be ratified?" Lisbeth asked.

"There is controversy, of course. We can't seem to stop fighting." Mitch shook his head. He explained, "The most radical Reconstructionists wish for publicly funded education and voting rights to all people, including women, over the age of twenty-one, except for those who fought for the Confederacy. But those who fought for the Confederacy are not about to give up the franchise so easily."

Father Johnson said, "The current draft is a compromise. It includes public education and voting rights for all men, except Confederate officers."

"I cannot tell you how disappointed I was when I realized it was my suffrage that was negotiated away," Mother Johnson said.

"Granny, you almost got to *vote*?!" Sadie chimed in. Lisbeth had thought she was in her own world, not following this conversation at all.

"Who gets to decide?" Sammy piped up.

"Decide what?" Mitch asked.

"What the constitution will be," Sammy explained.

"We will vote on it soon," Mitch said.

"Will women get to vote that they won't get to vote?" Sammy asked.

The adults laughed. Sammy looked hurt. Lisbeth realized that he was making a valid argument. She had been following the news about the slow return of the Confederate states to the Union. It was confusing—and the process was instructive about the limitations of the US Constitution.

"Sammy, you are noticing a perplexing paradox about our democracy," Lisbeth said, siding with her son. "You are wondering who gets to vote about who gets to vote."

"Yes, why doesn't everyone get to vote?" Sammy asked, looking very confused.

Father Johnson said, "Many in the South believe it is each state's right to decide."

Sammy knew about the argument in theory, but living in Oberlin, he had never heard people who directly advocated for states' rights over federal rights.

"Sammy, I think you are suggesting that the federal Constitution applies to all people in the United States, but not everyone agrees with that," Mitch explained. "Many people argue that each state has the power to declare who is a citizen."

"What?" Sammy asked.

Mother Johnson replied, "Do not feel bad if you are baffled, Sammy. The men of our nation are so confused by these matters that we had a war to try to settle it."

"But rest assured, Son," Father Johnson said, "we agree with your belief that all adults should have the rights of citizenship. But we are in the minority around here."

Sammy looked comforted by his grandfather's proclamation, but still perplexed by the conversation. Sadie seemed to have stopped paying any attention to the adult conversation altogether. She sat humming a song to herself, so quietly that only Lisbeth could hear her.

"I encountered a very rude and angry portion of your community this year." Miss Thorpe drew the attention back to herself.

When all eyes were on her, she said, "The Ku Klux Klan paid a visit to one of my fellow teachers."

"Are you certain it was them?" Mitch asked.

"They wore the sheets they are so fond of and declared that they were the true Ku Klux Klan," she reported. "At first we thought the KKK would not hurt anyone, that it was only fun and a desire to frighten the Negroes from voting the Republican ticket, but now I know better."

Lisbeth looked at the children. Thankfully Sadie was still lost in her own imagination, but Sammy was listening to every word. Lisbeth had read an article about this KKK, so she explained to her son, "They are a new organization of White men determined to suppress Negro rights, and we are starting to believe they are not shy about using violence to achieve their goal."

Miss Thorpe said, "I witnessed their tactics for myself! They brought a poor missionary from his bed in his nightclothes and beat him. His wife stayed with him the whole time and brought him back nearly dead. I helped care for him, so I can vouch for it."

The horrified look on Sammy's face was an arrow to Lisbeth's heart. He was being unduly exposed to the brutality of life on this journey. She checked on Sadie, but her innocence was not disturbed.

Lisbeth turned her attention back to Sammy. She patted his arm and whispered in his ear, "I do not fear that we will be harmed by this Ku Klux Klan."

"But what about Miss Jordan and Mrs. Freedman?" he implored, panic in his eyes. "Are they safe?"

"Oh, Sammy. I believe so," Lisbeth said, offering a weak reassurance to her son. But she felt ill knowing the KKK most likely added to Mattie and Jordan's peril.

CHAPTER 14

JORDAN

Richmond, Virginia

"I caution you against high hopes for success." Mrs. Avery, the White Methodist woman who ran the orphanage, spoke plainly. "So many folks come here set on finding their kin. Most leave disappointed."

"Is there any chance we will find them?" Samuel asked.

"Of course. Some families are partially reunited. I have yet to meet a family that was fully brought together, though I imagine it happens. We are more than happy to have the contraband of all ages find a permanent home."

"*Contraband*," Jordan said, feeling disgusted. "What a cruel way to speak of children."

Mrs. Avery nodded with a tight, crooked smile. "It does seem a disservice, doesn't it? First you are called a slave. Then you are labeled contraband."

Jordan asked, "How can a child be considered a spoil of war?"

Samuel replied, "These boys and girls are hard workers. The United States government didn't want their energy to aid the cause of the Confederates, so they encouraged them to come up here."

Mama said, "Hopefully we all just gonna be people soon."

"Amen, Mama," Jordan said.

Mrs. Avery explained as they walked to the backyard, "I will gather all of the girls so you may question them."

"They are nine and twelve years old, so we only need to speak with girls in that age range," Jordan said.

Mama shook her head. "None of 'em knows how many years they have."

"Really?" Jordan asked.

"They ain't had anyone to track it for them," Mama explained. "There ain't such a thing as a calendar in the fields. They might a heard it a New Year, but they ain't told any number to go with the year."

It made sense once Mama explained it, but it was sad to imagine that these children didn't even know their own ages.

"I think we need to leave the questioning to Mama," Samuel said.

"All right," Jordan agreed, mostly because she didn't think it mattered, not because she understood what her brother was thinking.

The yard wasn't exactly depressing, but it wasn't lovely either. The hard-packed dirt was marked by a few puddles and muddy spots. There were benches around the edges and no greenery to speak of. Children kicked around balls and twirled ropes in circles around children jumping in rhythm while chanting. Jordan smiled at the children playing clapping games. Even in dreary circumstances, most children found a way to play.

A few of the girls looked like they were hardly out of diapers, but Mrs. Avery said some were so malnourished that their growth had been stunted, making nine-year-olds look like they had five years. She said there was no telling how old any of them were by the way they looked or spoke.

The children stopped playing and gathered around Mrs. Avery, gawking at the visitors. All of them were very thin, but they seemed healthy enough. They had hair of varying lengths and styles: some of them had bouncy braids, some had hair pulled back tight, and others wore it free in a big halo around their heads.

"Mrs. Mattie is looking for her family," Mrs. Avery explained to the girls. "We expect honest answers. If you are not certain you may say so. Only girls need reply."

Mama asked, "Was you called Sophia or Ella when you was little?"

Seven hands went up. One girl said, "I think I called Sophia, ma'am."

Mama told all of those girls to separate into a new group to the right.

"Anyone have a mama called Sarah?" she asked the remaining original group.

A few hands went up. "Me," came a shout.

Those girls were directed to join the group on the side. Mama asked a few more questions and then went over to the new group to narrow down the possibilities.

One of the girls who was left out of the questioning pulled at Jordan's skirt with her rail-thin arm. "You be smart to take me. I picks faster than anyone, and I knows how to clean."

Jordan was amused by the confidence this child exuded, and sad that the child so readily offered herself up for manual labor.

"We aren't looking for a worker," Jordan explained. "We are seeking out our nieces."

"You talk like a White lady," the girl declared.

Jordan laughed. "I suppose so. Where I live many colored people speak the way I do."

"You ain't colored! You a nigger like me," the child declared.

Jordan was dismayed to hear that word used so freely, especially out of the mouth of a colored child. Jordan took the opportunity to offer some education.

"And where I live we do not use that word," she explained firmly.

Ignoring Jordan's admonition, the girl asked, "How come you talk like that?"

"School," Jordan replied.

The girl's eyes got big, and her scratched-up hand covered her mouth. She said, "It a sin for a nigger to learn. Jesus gonna send you to hell."

"That is a lie," Jordan corrected the child, hoping the others around her were listening as well. "God wants all people to blossom into their full capacities. Whoever told you that simply wanted to keep you down for his own purposes—not God's purpose."

The girl looked at Jordan through narrowed eyes and asked, "Can you read and write?"

Jordan nodded.

"Show me!" the girl exclaimed.

Jordan laughed. She looked around for a stick to write in the dirt. "Normally I write with chalk on a board or pen on paper, but this will do. What is your name?"

"Tessie," the little girl proclaimed proudly. "After my great-grammy."

"Well, Tessie, this is what it looks like in writing," Jordan said, and scratched TESSIE into the dirt.

"How I know you ain't just saying so?" Tessie challenged.

Jordan smiled. This was a very clever person. She pointed to Samuel and said, "Ask my brother to read it, and he will say your name."

Tessie looked dubious. Jordan raised her eyebrows and nodded vigorously.

"His name is Samuel, and he is very kind. Go ask him," Jordan coaxed.

Tessie yelled, "Hey, Samuel. What this say?"

Samuel walked over and read out loud, "Tessie."

Tessie screamed and jumped up and down. She twirled around, waving her arms, and said to the girls around them, "You hear that? He say my name!"

The other girls smiled and nodded with her.

When she recovered her composure she demanded, "Do it again!"

Jordan agreed to the girl's command. "This time you tell Samuel what to write and then I will read it."

Jordan walked a few paces away. She watched her mother crouch down, chatting with a small group of girls. Mama was staring intently into the dark-brown eyes of one little girl. Jordan could not make out what she asked, but the little girl nodded in response.

Tessie tugged at Jordan's arm and brought her back. A circle of girls gathered with Samuel, leaving a space for Jordan and Tessie.

Jordan took in the words scratched into the earth. Her heart dropped, and tears pushed at the back of her eyes. She cleared her throat and read out loud, "Take me with you."

"That right!" Tessie yelled, excitement in her voice. "That what I whispered in that nigger's ear!"

"I can make one of those," a quiet young voice said.

"You lying!" another girl replied.

Jordan looked the child over. She was dressed in the same brown muslin tunic as the others. Her hair was pulled into one messy braid, with bits of hair springing out at the sides.

"Mama," Jordan said across the space. Her mama didn't respond. Louder, Jordan yelled, "Mama!"

Her mother looked up at her. Jordan waved her over. When Mama was next to her, Jordan pointed and said, "Look . . . at her necklace."

Mama walked up to the little girl. Her eyes were dark and round, and her skin matched Mama's. She was so tiny it seemed impossible that she could be nine years old, let alone twelve.

"Do you know where you got that shell around your neck?" Mama asked.

The little girl grabbed it with her dusty hand and shook her head back and forth, causing her braid to bounce. "It mine, I swear. I ain't taken it from no one." Tears filled her eyes.

Mama reached under her bodice and pulled out an identical shell. "Look," Mama said gently. "I gots one too."

The little girl's eyes went big. A wave of emotion passed through Jordan. Could this be Ella or Sophia?

"My mama gave me mines," Mama said, calm in voice, though Jordan imagined she was excited to see the shell. "You get yours from your mama?"

The girl shrugged, then nodded. "Maybe."

Jordan crouched down low. "What do they call you, honey?"

She shrugged again.

"You don't have a name?" Jordan smiled. She projected calm on the outside, but she was anxious to hear the child's answer.

"Sallie. The soldiers say I Sallie," the little girl said so quietly that Jordan had to lean in to hear her. "I called May before the soldiers came."

"Do you remember what your mama call you?" Mama asked.

She shook her head a little from side to side.

"But you can write?" Jordan asked gently, wanting to sound encouraging without scaring the child.

"I know one," Sallie/May replied.

"One word?" Jordan coaxed.

The child shrugged.

"Show me." Jordan smiled.

Samuel handed over the stick. The little girl gripped it at the top. When she pushed down, the wood snapped in two. The girl froze, and her eyes got round with alarm.

"It's fine," Jordan reassured her. "Just use that little bit; it's easier that way."

Slowly the girl drew a line from top to bottom. She made a vertical line across the top, the middle, and then the bottom. A chill ran down Jordan's back.

"That an *E*?" Mama asked. "Like for Emmanuel?"

Samuel nodded. "Yes. And for Ella too."

"My mama learned me that," the child said. "I remember that about before."

"Did you got a sister too?" Mama asked, her voice betraying a little excitement. "And a granny?"

The girl nodded. The courtyard had gone quiet. Everyone had gathered around them, listening intently and not speaking a word.

"Did you and your sister leave your mama together?" Samuel asked.

The girl nodded.

"Was your sister older?" Samuel asked.

"She bigger than me if that what you mean."

Mama asked, "You 'member a river?"

The girl shook her head. "No, ma'am."

Mama stared hard at the little girl. Jordan could see how little Sallie/May favored Cousin Sarah a bit, but it was impossible to be certain of anything because Sarah was so weathered. Jordan studied Mama, trying to see what she was thinking. It was hard to read the older woman's face.

The child added, "There was a willow tree. I 'member that."

Mama's shoulders dropped in relief, and her lips tugged up into a bittersweet smile. She nodded confidently. She'd made up her mind.

Mama said, "I 'member the willow tree too." She opened her arms, ready to hug the little girl, but the child didn't move forward into the offered embrace.

Mama rubbed the girl's arms held stiff at her side and said, "I think you my grandniece. We gonna help you find your mama."

Eyes grown big, Sallie/May/Ella said, "Thank you, ma'am."

Jordan asked, "Is your sister here too?"

Sallie/May/Ella shrugged.

"I can be her sister," Tessie declared.

Mrs. Avery spoke up. "Sallie came to us from North Carolina. Tessie came to us from Tennessee."

"North Carolina!" Mama said.

Samuel nodded and said, "Mrs. Avery, that confirms our suspicion. Our niece was living in North Carolina."

"You takin' her 'stead of me?" Tessie challenged.

Jordan's stomach sank. She'd been so focused on Sallie/May/Ella that she'd forgotten about Tessie. "I'm sorry. Really I am. We believe she's our family."

"I be good if you take me too. Promise!" Tessie pleaded with her eyes as well as her words.

Jordan felt sick. With the right care this precocious and earnest girl would blossom; without it she would wither. Jordan looked at her mama, hoping she had a good answer.

Mama said, "You family gonna find you, I bet."

Tessie shook her head. "They all dead," she explained. Then she suddenly put on a happy expression. Her voice took on a casual, almost defiant tone. "Don' you worry. They loves me here, right, Mrs. Avery? You say I the most helpful girl of all."

Mrs. Avery nodded, gave a tender smile to the resilient child, and said, "Indeed. I do not know how I would manage without you."

Then she looked at Mama. "You may take Sallie right now. I just need your contact information and your assurance that you will not use her as a servant."

Jordan was stunned. "You need nothing besides our word?"

"We have no capacity to research families," Mrs. Avery explained. "Some days it's a wonder that we have enough to feed each of these children."

They filled out a paper with their temporary and permanent addresses and were free to go.

Jordan asked, "Does she have any belongings to fetch before we leave?"

"You may keep the dress she is wearing and the shoes," Mrs. Avery replied.

"There's nothing else?" Jordan asked, looking between the woman and the girl.

They both shook their heads. Jordan's heart felt like an anchor was weighing it down. Nothing. How could this child have nothing besides the clothes on her back and a necklace?

Jordan smiled at Sallie, imagining she'd be excited to be leaving. But the girl's face didn't show any emotion as they left the building. Jordan glanced back to see Tessie watching intently from a window, her brown nose pushed hard against the glass. Jordan's heart was pained at the sight. She vowed she would return with a gift for Tessie before they left, bringing something to these orphans who had nothing.

"What would you like us to call you?" Jordan asked the little girl as they walked back to Miss Grace's boardinghouse.

"You cans call me what you like," the child replied.

Mama, looking indignant, spoke up. "Your name is important. It the first thing anybod' discover about you."

The child shrugged. She looked overwhelmed at the offer.

Jordan kept it light. "I think you have three lovely choices: Ella, May, or Sallie."

"You say my mama gave me Ella?" the girl asked.

"We believe so," Samuel replied. "We aren't certain our cousin is your mama, but we have good reason to think she might be."

"You ain't really sure," she said wistfully. "Whatever I picks might jus' be for a little while anyways."

Jordan felt bad for the little girl. She wanted to offer reassurance that they were her family, but they couldn't be certain until Sarah met her. Jordan did not want to think about what would happen to the child if Sarah said they were wrong. Bringing her back to the children's home would be unbearably cruel. Jordan pushed the thought out of her mind and decided to cross that bridge if it came to that.

Mama said, "You pick a name for yourself, and it can be yours in your heart for always, no matter what other folks call you."

They walked in silence for a while. Jordan offered her hand to the child while they crossed a street, but the little girl just looked confused.

Jordan explained, "When I'm walking with children, I usually hold their hands as we cross the street to keep them safe."

The child put out her scratched-up hand. Jordan wrapped her fingers around it. The girl didn't grip hers in return, but she looked up at Jordan with a small, sweet smile. On the other side of the road, Jordan didn't let go, and the child didn't pull away. They walked along, close to each other in silence.

"Ella," the girl suddenly announced. "Even if I ain't who you think, I gonna be Ella. It a name given by a mama. Maybe she not my mama, but a mama picked it out for somebody."

"That sounds real nice, Ella," Mama said with a nod and gentle smile.

Jordan offered a silent prayer: *Please, God, for both of them, let this little girl be Cousin Sarah's missing daughter.*

A large brown horse trotted past with a White man in the saddle, holding the reins and scanning the scene. Jordan's heart sped up. It was strange to see a White face in this part of town. She'd quickly learned that there were neighborhoods that were White, areas that were colored, and a few places where they mixed. She knew it was best to avoid White people when they were here. He came to a sudden stop a few steps ahead. Her instinct was to turn around and walk quickly the other way, but she held herself in check.

"Mama, shall we go back?" Jordan whispered.

Before Mama could answer the man turned to look at them. He bellowed down from his horse, "You, boy. Why ain't you working?"

"We jus' visitin' relations, suh," Mama said. "He work back home."

The man swung down from his horse. He sauntered up to them, staring hard at Samuel. Jordan put a protective arm around Ella and moved them both in close to Mama.

The man glared at Mama with his bright-blue eyes. "I ain't talking to you now. Am I?"

"No, suh," Mama said, head bowed over. "Sorry, suh."

"Let me see your hands," the man said to Samuel.

Samuel looked at Mama, fear in his eyes. She nodded and gestured with her eyebrows. Jordan could feel the tension in her mama's body. Her brother put his hands out, his fingers trembling.

The man scoffed. Then he looked each of them up and down slowly. Jordan's legs shook, and her chest got tight.

Looking at Samuel, the man said, "I'm taking you in for vagrancy. And theft."

"What!" Jordan exclaimed without thinking. "You can't do that!"

The man glared at Jordan. "Yes, I can."

"We will go to the justice of the peace," she countered.

"Shush!" Mama hissed at her.

"You listen to your mama. She understands respectin' the law!" The man looked Mama up and down slowly, a challenging smile on his face.

He leaned in and smirked at Jordan. Then slowly he drawled out, "I am the justice of the peace. There is nothing you can do to stop me."

Jordan's heart rose up into her throat. The man grabbed Samuel and spun him around. He pulled Samuel's arms hard behind his back. Jordan was utterly helpless. She dug her fingers hard into Mama's arm.

While the man roughly lashed his hands together, Samuel leaned toward her and whispered into her ear, "Find Lisbeth! Tell her what's happened to me."

Confused, but knowing not to speak, Jordan just nodded.

Samuel stared at her, despair in his brown eyes, and whispered, "Tell Nora and Otis that I love them. Always."

"You will tell them yourself!" Jordan said.

The justice of the peace hissed at her, "Shut up or I'll round you up too!" Then suddenly he shoved her hard in the sternum. The wind flew from her chest. She grunted and fell backward, jerking Mama and Ella with her. She nearly pulled them to the ground, but she found her footing.

Panting to get her breath back, Jordan saw Mama reach into her pocket, pull something out, and press it into Samuel's palm. His hand closed up tight, but not before one of the mustard seeds bounced to the ground.

Jordan looked up, watching in horror as the evil man tugged on the rope and dragged her brother away. Samuel resisted, but it did him no good. The man swung up onto his saddle and tied the rope to the horn. Her brother turned to stare back at them, his dark-brown eyes filled with such anguish and desperation. Jordan stifled a scream of protest.

Samuel watched them until the momentum of the horse forced him to turn around. Jordan watched his awkward figure get smaller and smaller until he was dragged around a corner and gone from their sight.

She exhaled and looked around in disbelief. Their worst nightmare had just come true: Samuel had been captured. Confused and disoriented, Jordan felt panic start to rise. She looked over for comfort, but Mama looked as terrified as Jordan felt. Samuel was gone, just gone, and the horrid White man had said there was nothing they could do to get him back.

CHAPTER 15

LISBETH

Richmond, Virginia

"Momma, can I just eat supper in the kitchen?" Sammy implored, his hazel eyes open wide.

Lisbeth shook her head. The children were tired after spending half of the day traveling back to Richmond. Lisbeth would have preferred an informal meal as well, but her mother had declared they would have supper as a family.

"So Grandmother Wainwright just decides for everyone when and where we eat?" he asked.

Lisbeth nodded firmly.

"In their home, we will do what she asks." She looked at her son sharply. "I expect you to be a good example for your sister."

Sammy acquiesced. "I will."

"Put your glove away, and wash your hands," Lisbeth instructed.

Sammy's face fell. "I don't have my glove."

Lisbeth sighed and then scolded, "Did you misplace it?"

"No." Sammy shook his head slowly. Then he said, "I gave it to Willie."

He looked at Lisbeth, waiting for a reaction. She gave him a small smile.

"You're not sore, are you?" Sammy asked.

"No. That was very kind of you," Lisbeth said. "It is your glove. You may do what you like with it."

"When I bought mine, Mr. Evans said he could teach me how to make them if I wanted. If I help him I bet he'd let me work for him in exchange for a new one."

"I think you are right about that," Lisbeth agreed.

"Willie was *so* excited, Momma." Sammy beamed. "You'd think I'd given him a hundred dollars!"

Love for her son welled up in Lisbeth. It was sweet to see him so very excited at another person's happiness. She tousled his head, gave him a sideways squeeze, and said, "Wash up! Supper is waiting."

———— ❧◦❧ ————

Jack arrived at the table after the food had already been served onto plates.

"Miss Sadie," Jack declared, "you look very lovely this evening."

"Thank you, Uncle Jack." Sadie beamed at him.

"You are late," Mother scolded.

"It was a busy day—many arrests at the Tredegar."

"What happened?" Sammy asked.

"Vagrants," Jack replied.

"They are a growing problem," Julianne said. "We spoke of it at the Ladies Memorial Association last week."

"Vagrants?" Lisbeth asked, concerned at the tone the conversation was taking. She'd hoped for a quick supper without conflict and a calm evening.

"Those living idly or unwilling to work at the prevailing wage," Jack replied. "I'm sorry to say that William was caught up with the nigger agitators. I could not show him preference, even though this will cause Emily distress."

Lisbeth nearly gasped. She reached under the table and took her children's hands. This meal was turning as unpleasant as possible.

"The law is the law," Julianne reassured him. "You are bound to uphold it, even when it causes you distress."

"I don't understand," Sammy said, pain in his voice.

Jack said, "Our law is very simple. Regardless of race, men who do not work to support themselves and their families will be arrested and leased out for the best wage we can procure. My job is to enforce the laws."

"But William has a job," Sammy countered.

"He was agitating for pay equal to what the White men receive, which is absolutely unrealistic, and he understands that fact. He did not return to work when he was warned," Jack explained. "He knew the consequences of his choice."

"He has to go to jail?" Lisbeth asked, concerned about Emily and Willie, as well as William. "For how long?"

"Three months," Jack replied.

Lisbeth was grateful that at least it wasn't for very long.

"But his family needs him," Sammy declared.

"He will be put on a work detail. Expenses will be taken from his pay, and the rest will be forwarded to his family," Jack said.

"That is how we are taking care of the freedmen who believe they are entitled to be kept without working," Julianne explained. "Their numbers have been growing and growing without end. It has only worsened since the end of the conflict. It is dreadful."

"They are indolent and disrespectful," Mother added. "These laws help them to fulfill their place in society and contribute to their own well-being."

"But—" Sammy started to argue.

"Samuel, stop. Enough questions," Mother said. "Julianne, please tell us about your association meeting."

Lisbeth surreptitiously glanced over at Sammy. She saw he was blinking back tears. Lisbeth breathed in deeply to quash the sense of dread rising in her belly.

Julianne explained, "We have finally agreed on a project. We are going to focus upon Gettysburg for the moment. Our fund-raising effort will go toward getting our fallen heroes reinterred in the Hollywood Cemetery, as well as to create a memorial to their sacrifice in the public square."

Lisbeth barely heard her sister-in-law's words. She had wanted her children to understand more about the world she had come from, but she hadn't counted on Sammy coming to care for a child who was so directly affected by the nastiness. Lisbeth hadn't imagined her children would be hurt by being here and that she would be powerless to protect them. She patted her son's leg, hoping to provide some comfort. But he jerked his thigh away at her touch.

Her son looked at her with contempt and disappointment. Lisbeth suspected he wanted her to come to William's rescue in some way, but she did not have the experience or power to challenge the legal system in Virginia. Simply staying here until the end of her father's life was challenging enough for her.

––––––– ❧⟋☙ –––––––

Late that evening, while her children were asleep in bed, Lisbeth was startled to hear a light tap at the door. She opened it to find Emily on the other side. Clearly she had been crying. Lisbeth took her hand and pulled her into the room.

"Emily, I'm so sorry to hear about William," Lisbeth whispered.

"Thank you, ma'am," she replied. "It's been a blow. We're praying for him."

"He'll be back in three months; you can be grateful for that," Lisbeth reassured her.

Emily gave her a harsh look, then closed her eyes and shook her head.

"I don't mean to be dismissive, Emily. It's just, on a positive note, three months is not so very long," Lisbeth said calmly, wanting to sound supportive and kind.

"They don't come back," Emily whispered through a tight throat.

Instantly alarmed by Emily's tone, Lisbeth questioned, "What do you mean?"

"They been arresting men for almost two years now using this law. Hardly any of the men that get put on work detail are released after three months. After they plant or harvest around here, they're moved south to work on roads . . . and we don't hear from them again."

Fury passed through Lisbeth. "Emily, that's just wrong! You have to speak with a judge. I will help you."

Emily shook her head. "Miss Lisbeth, you mean well, but you really have no idea what you're talking about. It's the judges that are ordering the men to go to work in the South. They say it's for 'running away.'"

Lisbeth heard Emily's words, but they didn't make any sense. She stared at Emily, trying to formulate a question or response.

Emily continued. "I didn't come here for help with William. I came to ask you about Willie."

"Willie?"

"When you go back to Ohio, will you take him, please?" Emily said, her voice high and tight.

"We would love to have him visit with us," Lisbeth replied. And she meant it; it would have been sweet for both of their sons. "But I do not intend to return anytime soon, so I don't know how we would manage to get him home again."

Emily shook her head. "No . . ." She cleared her throat and squeaked out, "To keep."

"What!" Lisbeth exclaimed.

"Don't answer right away," Emily rushed to say. "Just think about it, please. My Willie is so light he can pass for White."

Lisbeth's blood went cold as it dawned on her what Emily was asking. Emily could not possibly wish to send Willie away permanently. He would be devastated to lose all that was familiar to him.

One of the children stirred in the bed, drawing her attention away from Emily. Lisbeth watched Sammy roll over under the covers. She and Emily waited quietly until he settled again. Lisbeth turned back to Emily and took a deep breath.

"Please think about taking him into your family," Emily whispered. "He is your blood, your half nephew. Slavery may be over, but he is going to have a better life in the White world."

"You can't mean this," Lisbeth said, forgetting to keep her voice quiet. "You love him too much to part with him."

"I love him so much that I want what's best for him, no matter how much it hurts me," Emily replied, her eyes moist.

Lisbeth's head spun with the implications of what Emily was asking. "Both of you come with us!" she whispered fiercely. "We will help you settle in Ohio."

Emily shook her head. "I've given this a lot of thought. If I came, then . . ." Her voice broke. "Then he'd . . . still be colored."

Lisbeth felt sick; her throat tightened, and bile lurched into the back of her mouth, burning and acrid. She swallowed hard.

Emily pleaded, "He's a good boy. You know that. Sammy would be a good big brother to him."

"Oh, Emily, I—" Tears burned at the back of her eyes, threatening to spill over. She blinked hard, not wanting to be more emotional than Emily.

Interrupting, Emily said, "I don't want an answer now. Just think about it. We have money saved. I can send all of it with him . . . and send more later."

Emily turned away without waiting for a reply. Lisbeth's head swirled. She felt trapped. Abandoning Willie felt as untenable as taking him in. Only the most appalling conditions would cause her to choose to live separately from her children. It was a measure of Emily's desperation that she was willing to do so.

The woman paused at the doorway before walking out. "They took Samuel too."

Lisbeth was confused. She looked at Sammy, asleep in the bed. "My son?"

"No." Emily shook her head. "Mattie's Samuel. He got rounded up today too."

Lisbeth's knees went weak. She collapsed onto the bed.

A small wry smile passed over Emily's face. "Like I said, it's not really over," she reiterated. "Mattie came by this afternoon and asked me to tell you to meet her at the Ebenezer Baptist Church on Leigh between Judah and Saint Peter. She's waiting for you there, right now."

And then Emily vanished. Lisbeth stared at the white door, so overwhelmed that she could not move. Her arms and legs were too heavy. But her heart pounded with urgency. She was torn, wanting to go to Mattie immediately, but also scared.

If Jack found out that she had gone to a Negro church or that she was still in touch with Mattie, he might lash out at her, make things more tense in this home—and perhaps worse for Mattie as well.

But Mattie had never once asked for Lisbeth's help. Lisbeth owed her everything. And she might be of true assistance to Samuel.

"Momma?" Sammy's sleepy voice cut through Lisbeth's confused and terrified thoughts. She tamped down her internal storm and slid closer to her son, sitting on the edge of the bed.

"Yes, Sammy?" Lisbeth said, hoping he hadn't heard the conversation that had passed between her and Emily.

"Are you going to help Mrs. Freedman?" Sammy asked.

He had been awake! Lisbeth's chest tightened, and her head nearly burst. Sammy was asking her to act. She stared at her son; longing covered his face. The desire to make Sammy proud overwhelmed her. This was a chance to show him how to live morally with deeds, not just words. Lisbeth nodded.

"I'm going to see if I can do anything for her, though I don't know that I can be of any actual help. Can you take care of Sadie if she wakes up?" Lisbeth asked.

Sammy nodded.

"Find Miss Emily if you need any help," she instructed him.

He nodded again. "Is Willie going to be my brother now?"

A chill traveled down Lisbeth's spine. She took a deep breath, exhaling slowly before she spoke. "Oh, Sammy. I . . . I don't know. We will have to think about it very carefully."

"Miss Emily says he's not safe here. We have to take him," Sammy pleaded.

Lisbeth felt torn and overwhelmed. "It's a big decision," she explained. "I'm not prepared to make it without a lot of thought. Poppa—"

Sammy interrupted, "Poppa will agree if you say it is the right thing to do. Write to him."

"Sammy, I know you care for Willie. So do I, but a third child? It's not a simple choice to make."

"Momma, I promise I'll take care of him. I'll walk him to school and help him with his chores and his schoolwork—"

"Sammy," Lisbeth interrupted. "I promise I will think about it. But tonight I need to go speak with Mrs. Freedman. And you need to go back to sleep. Good night."

"Good night, Momma," Sammy said, not sounding like he was ready to go back to sleep anytime soon.

CHAPTER 16

JORDAN

Richmond, Virginia

"Mama, we can't just let him take Samuel!" Jordan screeched.

"Hush!" Mama rebuked. "We gonna calmly walk to Miss Grace's house so we don' make things any worse than they already are."

Jordan took in a shaky breath and worked to steady her racing heart. She looked at the little girl next to her. Ella stood still, staring off into space, detached from what had just happened. Jordan followed her mama down the street. Anger and frustration built in her with every step, but she didn't yell or scream until they got inside.

As soon as the door to the living room closed, Jordan burst into tears and shouted, "Mama what are we gonna do?"

"You sit right there with Ella," Mama directed her. "I'm gonna find Miss Grace."

"We shouldn't have come," Jordan reprimanded her mother. "This whole trip was a mistake. You knew something just like this could happen, and now Samuel is gone!"

Mama's face grew tight and hard. Her caramel-brown eyes gestured that Jordan should be mindful of Ella. Jordan got the silent message to act calm.

Changing her tone, Jordan said quietly, "Mama, I'm so scared."

"Me too, baby." Mama rubbed Jordan's arm and left to get help.

The two women came back into the room, and Miss Grace explained, "They rounded up lots of men today. It's harvest time, so they need workers for the tobacco fields."

"Samuel's a lawyer! He doesn't know how to work the fields!" Jordan said, outrage burning in her. "He's going to die out there."

Mama turned her head and stared at Jordan. She looked and sounded incredulous as she stated, "Jordan, this ain't good, but you screamin' ain't gonna help him. Your brother worked the fields when he was a boy. He survived it then. He gonna survive it now. I ain't worried about a few days. We got to worry about the years."

Jordan flushed. She'd once again forgotten the distance between her own childhood and her brother's.

Mama looked back at Miss Grace. "Where is my boy?"

"They being held at the auction house until they leased out," Miss Grace said.

"Auction house?" Jordan asked, confused.

"Slave auction house," Miss Grace explained. "Where they use to hold slaves before the auctions. Now they use it to hold prisoners waiting to be leased out. Same difference to them."

Auction house? Leased out? Jordan could not believe what she was hearing.

Mama asked, "How we get him freed?"

Freed. That word burned in Jordan's soul. How could Samuel not be free? The war was over; slavery was over, yet her brother was being held in an auction house, waiting to be leased to work in the fields of a Southern plantation.

Miss Grace shook her head with a tsk and replied, "There's not much hope of having him released early. I heard that a White man can get someone back if he say he's his worker. The Freedmen's Bureau supposed to have the power to make things right, but they don't. There's too many people doing too much wrong for them to keep up. And they packing up and leaving, so no one takes them serious."

"We need to send word to yo' father—fast," Mama said to Jordan.

"You want to put Pops in harm's way too," Jordan challenged.

Ignoring Jordan's outburst, Miss Grace chimed in, "Send a telegram. They're expensive, but it's guaranteed to get there by tomorrow morning."

Mama nodded.

"The fewer the words the less it costs," Miss Grace explained.

Mama suggested, "How about: *Samuel captured. Come now.*"

Getting the message that she needed to act more maturely, Jordan took a deep breath to calm herself. She was going to be helpful, not emotional. Jordan said, "That's great, Mama. Do you want me to go to the telegraph office?"

Mama considered for a bit. Then she said, "We gonna go together. First there, and then back to the Freedmen's Bureau."

"All right," Jordan said.

"Then we gonna find Lisbeth Johnson like your brother say," Mama continued.

Jordan's stomach danced. "You want us to go to the White part of town?"

Mama nodded.

"How can she help Samuel?" Jordan asked, working to keep her voice calm and respectful.

"That was her brother that took him," Mama said.

Jordan's sucked in her breath. "Are you sure?"

Mama explained, "As soon as I saw him I think his eyes look like I knowed him from before. When your brother whispered to find Lisbeth, I 'membered who he is," Mama said.

"He can set Samuel free?" Jordan asked, hope stirring in her.

"If'n he wants to," Mama said with a nod.

Then Mama turned her attention to the other woman. "Miss Grace, we thin' we may have found one of the girls we lookin' for. Can you watch over her while we goes out?"

Miss Grace nodded. "I would love the company of a little one. I don't get enough of 'em in my life."

Jordan looked for Ella. In the chaos she'd been forgotten. She was curled up small on the ground, wedged between the sofa and the wall. The poor thing looked like her mind was lost in another world. Jordan slid down to the end of the couch and patted Ella's shoulder. The girl startled and looked up at her. Jordan took her hand and gently pulled her toward the sofa. The girl looked wary, but she rose off the floor and sat down cautiously.

"Have you ever sat on a sofa?" Jordan asked, once again aware of the divide between her own life and this child's experiences.

Ella shook her head. The girl rubbed her dry hands on the dark-green fabric. A small smile tugged at the edges of her mouth.

"This is velvet, the nicest covering around. Some people get dresses made out of it," Jordan explained, nodding her head and widening her eyes to confirm this surprising truth to this little girl.

Jordan continued. "Great-Auntie Mattie and I are going to go out. This is Miss Grace. She will take real good care of you."

The girl's head dropped, and her shoulders rounded. Looking defeated, she said, "You leavin' me here."

"Just for a little while," Jordan replied. "We'll be back. I promise."

"You jus' gets to come and go wherever you like?" Ella asked.

Jordan sighed and considered the question. It was one more poignant reminder of the vast gap between the life she might have lived and the one she had. Before this trip she would have said yes without hesitation. But now she said, "Not everywhere, but many places."

The little girl nodded as if she agreed, but her eyebrows knit together in doubt.

"We're going to get Mr. Samuel free," Jordan explained.

Ella shook her head and stared off into space. Her eyes took on a vacant quality, as if her mind were no longer in the room. Jordan found the behavior unsettling.

"I'll see you in a few hours," Jordan said gently, but the girl did not reply.

The telegraph and post office was their first stop. Mama and Jordan stood at the wooden counter watching the clerk work at his desk. No one else was in the office, so it was glaringly obvious that the White man was ignoring them. Jordan's anger rose as the time stretched out. She stared hard at the man bent over the desk, hoping he could sense her energy.

Finally he stood up and sauntered over to the counter without actually looking at them.

"Good afternoon, suh," Mama said in her most obsequious voice.

Jordan felt the bile churn in her stomach. This man deserved to be yelled at for his rudeness, and yet her mother was talking to him like he were a king.

The man grunted.

"We be wantin' to send a telegraphy, suh," Mama said, sounding even less educated than usual. "If'n that all righ'. I gots the money right here." Mama pulled out a small stack of US Treasury notes.

The man's face changed subtly, but still he didn't say anything to them. He pulled out a ledger and said, "That'll be twenty cents a word. Ten-word minimum."

"I unerstan', suh," Mama replied.

Jordan flushed with embarrassment on her mother's behalf. It took all her will to constrain herself from berating them both.

"Cans it say, *Samuel captured. Come now, please.*"

Contempt dripped from his voice as he said, "That's only *five* words."

"Yes, suh. We gonna pay for ten but jus' send the five."

Jordan was close to bursting out of her skin and desperately wanted to step outside before she said anything she would later regret, but she would not allow this man and his attitude to force her to leave Mama's side. She turned slightly away from the counter and closed her eyes. While taking a steadying breath, Jordan recited to herself a line from Psalm 23: *"Though I walk through the valley of the shadow of death, I will fear no evil: for Thou art with me."*

She opened her eyes to see the man taking all of Mama's money from her hand. Jordan cleared her throat. The man looked at her sideways. He peeled off three bills and handed Mama the rest back. Mama smiled politely and nodded.

Jordan's heart hammered. She probably should have just let it go, but she was too outraged to stand by while this man cheated her mother.

"Excuse me, sir," Jordan said. "Did I misunderstand you? Isn't the price *two* dollars?" She smiled demurely.

The man grunted and placed a one-dollar treasury bill on the counter. Salmon Chase, former secretary of the Treasury, stared up at her from the paper. The man turned around and went back to his desk. Mama started to leave.

"Please address the telegram to Emmanuel Freedman, Oberlin, Ohio," Jordan said, hoping she sounded calmer than she felt.

The man looked at her full on, a simmering rage in his eyes. "You tellin' me how to do my job?"

Jordan took a shaky breath. "No, sir. My mama forgot to let you know where to send it." Then she added, "She's not smart enough to know about something as complicated as a telegram."

"And you are?" he challenged.

"Oh, no, sir. I could never know what you know, sir," Jordan said. Just a few days ago she would not have believed she could stoop so low, but now she understood what she would do in service of freeing Samuel. The man grunted and returned to his desk. Jordan wanted to see him send the telegram, but there was no point in staying in the office. She had no way of confirming that he would do what they asked. They'd just paid half a month of Pops's earnings that might be for nothing.

<hr />

Mr. Brooke immediately recognized them when they walked into the Freedmen's Bureau, giving Jordan hope that he would work on their behalf. The room was as quiet as it had been when they were here a couple of days ago.

"Where's the young man . . . um, Mr. Freedman?" Mr. Brooke asked, sounding proud of himself that he remembered.

Mama looked at Jordan, wordlessly encouraging her to do the talking in here.

"My brother has been wrongly captured by the justice of the peace. He has not broken any laws."

Mr. Brooke's face fell. "Oh, that is a shame. He was such a nice young man. And a fellow Ohioan too."

"Can you offer us any assistance for securing his release?" Jordan asked.

"Well, now, as much as it pains me, there is little I can do," Mr. Brooke said.

Annoyed at Mr. Brooke's proclaimed impotence, Jordan simply stared at him.

"Is he still in Richmond?" the man asked.

Feeling a slight shimmer of hope that Mr. Brooke had jurisdiction, Jordan explained, "We believe he is at the auction house."

"Isn't that a shame!" Mr. Brooke looked incredulous. "The auction house. That is just adding insult to injury."

Jordan stared at Mr. Brooke, waiting for him to take action. When he just looked at her she said, "Can you secure my brother's freedom from this injustice?"

"I can make a request that a federal marshal investigate," he replied.

"Thank you!" Jordan exclaimed, a mixture of gratitude and annoyance surging in her. This man's kind but ineffective outrage would do nothing to help Samuel; he needed to take some action.

Mr. Brooke took out a notebook. He added *Samuel Freedman* at the bottom of a long list. Jordan noted that he remembered both her brother's first and last names.

"His charges?" the man asked.

"Vagrancy," Jordan replied.

"Oh, that is a shame," Mr. Brooke said again. "It will be difficult for him to disprove that since he is not employed in the state of Virginia, is he?"

"No, sir," Jordan said. "He is not."

"Such a shame," the man repeated, looking truly pained.

Fury welled up in Jordan. She'd never felt so helpless and angry in her life. Something she'd never before felt built inside her: the urge to punch this White man. She clenched her fists hard and shook them. Mama grabbed her forearm and turned her away from Mr. Brooke.

"We thank you for anythin' you can do for our Samuel," Mama said. "We gonna come back tomorrow to see what you find out."

After they'd crossed the threshold, Jordan said, "Mama, I don't know how you can be so calm with those men!"

"I gots years of practice, Jordan," Mama said. "Years and years."

Jordan sighed, though she really wanted to scream.

"Pray, honey," Mama said. "You tell God all about how you feelin'. But don' let none of those men see that they gettin' to you."

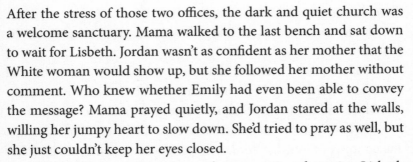

After the stress of those two offices, the dark and quiet church was a welcome sanctuary. Mama walked to the last bench and sat down to wait for Lisbeth. Jordan wasn't as confident as her mother that the White woman would show up, but she followed her mother without comment. Who knew whether Emily had even been able to convey the message? Mama prayed quietly, and Jordan stared at the walls, willing her jumpy heart to slow down. She'd tried to pray as well, but she just couldn't keep her eyes closed.

"Mattie?" a tentative voice said, interrupting the quiet. Lisbeth Johnson was standing over them.

A slow smile spread over Mama's face. She stood up and hugged the White woman, long and hard. Mama took her two smooth, pale hands between her own and looked right into her eyes and said, "Thank you for coming, Lisbeth."

"Of course, Mattie," Lisbeth replied. She looked scared and young. "I'm glad you asked me for help."

"Come sit." Mama pointed to the bench. Jordan slid over to make room. Lisbeth took her hand. It was smooth and cold.

"I'm so sorry about Samuel," Lisbeth said to Jordan.

Jordan's chin started to quiver, and her eyes burned. She didn't want to cry, so she bit her lip. Lisbeth nodded at her with a tight smile, but didn't say anything else. She turned back to Mama. The two women leaned in close, their shoulders touching.

"Your brother took him," Mama said, her voice high and tight. "Can you talk to him?"

Lisbeth's shoulders dropped. She bit her lip. Jordan thought she looked scared, but eventually the woman nodded.

"I'll do it, Mattie, though I don't believe he will listen to me." Lisbeth rushed out an excuse. "He is still so very angry that I married Matthew. But of course I will speak to him. I will call upon his vanity. Perhaps that will save Samuel from . . ."

Lisbeth stopped speaking. A tear pushed out of the corner of her eye. Jordan was touched that Lisbeth seemed to care so much, but like Mama said, strong feelings were of no help to Samuel. Her assurance that she would speak to her brother was something, but she did not sound confident in her ability to sway her own brother.

Mama reached out her hands. "Let's ask for our Lord's blessing." Lisbeth offered her hand to Jordan. Jordan clasped the outstretched hands, completing the circle. Mama's was warm and cozy and Lisbeth's cold as snow.

"Dear God," Mama prayed. "We're yo' humble servants. Thank you for listening to us. We ask you to keep us strong. Keep our Samuel safe, and return him to us. Provide a safe path to my Emmanuel as he journeys to us. And please, dear Lord, open up Massa Jack's heart to yo' love, 'cus we know he needs it."

The Holy Spirit shot like a lightning bolt through Mama's and Lisbeth's hands into Jordan's soul. For a fleeting instant, she was filled with hope, love, and calm. She hadn't felt a moment of peace since that man, Lisbeth's brother, had stopped his horse. Hour after hour, moment by moment, she'd been stifling panic. For just a moment she felt the kind of faith Mama was always talking about but Jordan rarely glimpsed. The feeling was gone quickly, but the echo of it left her with a measure of courage and strength. Somehow, they would get through this together.

She looked at Mama, then at Lisbeth. They smiled and nodded wordlessly. Perhaps they'd felt the Holy Spirit as well. Their eyes sparkled with unshed tears too.

CHAPTER 17

LISBETH

Richmond, Virginia

Lisbeth tossed and turned in bed that night, rehearsing what she wanted to say to Jack in the morning. She imagined the joy on Mattie's face if she returned with good news. She wouldn't let herself think too hard about disappointing her. Lisbeth knew that to be successful she had to ask Jack in such a way that she did not insult or accuse, and that playing to his vanity was going to be the best route to success.

Over breakfast she gauged his mood. He read the newspaper to himself, but he had greeted her cheerfully enough that she decided to take her chance this morning. After he left the table she waited fifteen minutes and then went to his office.

Lisbeth screwed up her courage and tapped on the door.

"Come in," his resonant voice shouted.

Her legs were weak as she approached her brother sitting behind the desk, the one Father had used in Fair Oaks. It brought back a mixture of childhood fear and sentiment.

"Jack, how are you?" Lisbeth asked, perhaps too sweetly.

"What do you want?" he replied briskly.

Lisbeth used her most flattering voice, putting aside her pride for Mattie. "I understand that as the justice of the peace, you have quite a bit of authority over prisoners?"

"How'd you learn that?" he inquired.

"Mother tells me about your work. She's so proud of what you do for Richmond," Lisbeth fawned.

Jack looked at her stony faced. Lisbeth gave him a forced, tight smile.

"What do you want from me, Elizabeth?" Jack growled.

"One of my acquaintances from Ohio was arrested this week."

Jack stared at her, wordlessly daring her to go on.

Lisbeth cleared her throat. "I wonder if you have the power to have him released."

"I do," he replied. "I have power over all of the prisoners in Richmond."

Lisbeth nodded slightly and swallowed. Her heart was pounding fiercely. "I realize this is a very large favor."

Jack scowled. "*You* want a favor? From me?"

"I would not ask if it were not important." Lisbeth hoped she sounded calm.

"Important—to you!" Jack scoffed. "You betrayed our whole family. *You* ruined us, and you ask me to take on your concern."

"I have no right to expect anything from you, but I beg of you." Lisbeth worked to keep her voice even. "Anything I can do for you I will. Please."

A small smile turned up Jack's mouth. If it gave him pleasure to see her plead, she didn't care. She'd gladly appear weak to secure Samuel's release.

"Who?" Jack demanded.

"Pardon me?" Lisbeth asked.

"Who would you like me to release?"

Lisbeth exhaled in relief. Her skin tingled with hope. "Oh, thank you!" she exclaimed. "I am so grateful for your kindness."

"Write the name, and I will consider your request," Jack growled, sliding a piece of paper to Lisbeth. "No promises."

Grateful for this change of spirit, she wrote *Samuel Freedman* and handed the paper to Jack. He opened it slowly and snorted when he read it.

"The moment you walked in that door, I knew what you wanted from me," Jack said. "You think it was an accident that I rounded him up? You believe I am an utter fool."

Jack's eyes burned with fury. Lisbeth's heart pounded fiercely.

"I know exactly who he is, and I knew the moment *he* arrived in Richmond. If Samuel hadn't been a successful runaway, you never would have gotten the idea that you could just up and leave. *That* family ruined my life. This is *my* payback to *you*, Elizabeth." Jack drew out each word.

Lisbeth's throat tightened, the taste of metal filled her mouth, and moisture sprang from her pores.

"*You* taught him to read." Jack glared at her, venom in his blue eyes. "It took me a while, but when I finally figured that out it all made sense to me. That was the beginning of the end for us. And now he *comes* to Richmond saying he's a goddamned lawyer." Jack's face was red, and he spit as he said, "A nigger lawyer? Not in *my* town!"

Lisbeth's ears buzzed from the fierce beating of her heart.

Jack's voice went quiet. "His life is over, and there is nothing, absolutely nothing, you can do to save him. You will have to live with that knowledge for the rest of your life."

"Please, Jack," Lisbeth implored, tears in her eyes. She didn't care how pathetic she looked. "It is my fault, not his. He had absolutely nothing to do with my choice to marry Matthew."

"The tables are turned," Jack hissed with a smirk. "I have the power to make a decision that affects you, and there is *nothing* you can do about it."

Lisbeth bit her lip, willing herself not to cry.

"*Out!*" Jack bellowed, and pointed. "Get out of my sight before I round up your precious Mattie too! I would have done so already, but there's no market for leasing out old women."

Before she made it to the door, Jack spoke again, taunting her even more. "Sister, would you like to know whom I've leased him to?"

Lisbeth froze in place, her heartbeat hammering so hard the sound filled up her ears and she could hardly hear her brother's words.

"Edward Cunningham!" Jack gloated in triumph. "God has provided me with the sweetest revenge."

Lisbeth rushed out of the study. She climbed up the stairs, her legs shaky, praying she would not pass anyone. Quickly she closed and locked the door to the bedroom. Shame poured through her body like black tar. She was so naïve! Samuel's situation was far more dire than she had understood, and *she* was to blame for his fate. Samuel's arrest had been intentional.

She sank onto the bed, tears streaming down her face and regret filling every pore. She felt desperate and alone. Lisbeth longed for her husband. The urgent desire for Matthew's counsel and his comfort was a physical pressure. She imagined his face, the comfort of his embrace, and reassured herself that she would be with him again soon.

After the tears of frustration and anger stopped, she was left with a burning desire to get Samuel freed. She refused to surrender easily to Jack, and she was not going to face Mattie without some hope for securing Samuel's release. Her mind swirled with ideas until she finally came up with a possible plan, but first she had to ask her husband.

> *Dearest Matthew,*
>
> *As always the children and I miss you, and home, terribly. We look forward to being together soon.*
>
> *I have some disturbing news, which leads me to make a request. I can hardly believe it, but Samuel Freedman has been convicted for the crime of vagrancy—by my own brother! He has been sentenced to laboring for three months, but we fear that the sentence will be extended or that he may be worked to death, which is the sad fate of too many freedmen at this time.*
>
> *My attempt to convince Jack to release Samuel was unsuccessful. The Freedmen's Bureau is unable to provide us with any assistance besides assurances they will look into the situation. My understanding is they do not have the staff to adequately remedy this injustice. I cannot live with myself if I do not do something more.*
>
> *I do not want to put your family at risk, but I wish to ask your brother Mitch to intervene on Samuel's behalf. Please tell me as soon as possible if my thinking is amiss.*
>
> *Your loving wife,*
> *Lisbeth*

Lisbeth wiped her eyes and studied her warped reflection in the mirror. It wouldn't be immediately apparent that she had been so upset. She found her children playing in the yard and invited each of them to write a note to their father. Sadie's letter was as sweet as she expected.

> *Poppa,*
> *I miss you very much and look forward to being home soon. Please greet all of the animals for me, most especially Brownie. Tell her she is my favorite cow (but don't tell the other cows since that is not kind).*
> > *Your daughter,*
> > *Sadie*

Sammy wrote furiously.

He handed his letter to Lisbeth when he was finished and asked, "Is this good?"

Lisbeth could feel her son's intense focus on her as she read his letter. Her emotions rose to a high peak once again as she read.

> *Poppa,*
> *You would be proud at how helpful I am being to Momma. I mind Sadie whenever she asks, and am cooperative at all times. Johnny loves his glove. Please do not be angry with me for giving my glove to my new friend, Willie. Momma says I can work to earn a new one. He has so little, and it made him very happy. His poppa was arrested for nothing. I don't understand how that can happen in America. It's not fair, but nobody but us cares.*
> > *Willie's mother wants him to live with us in Ohio so he will be safe. Momma and I think that is a good*

idea. You will like Willie very much too. Please write
back with your answer.
  I hope to see you soon.
  Your son,
  Sammy

When she finished reading the note she nodded at Sammy and assured him it was fine. She'd become so occupied with Mattie and Samuel that she'd pushed aside Emily's request, but of course Sammy was most concerned about Willie. She wrote a postscript on her letter.

PS Emily has requested that we take Willie in,
permanently. She believes his opportunities will be
severely limited if he continues to live with her. I will
have to make a decision before we leave. Please share
your thoughts with me.

She enclosed the three notes in an envelope and sealed it. It would be hard to wait for his reply, but there was nothing else to do for now.

CHAPTER 18

JORDAN

Richmond, Virginia

Jordan was exhausted, but sleep wouldn't come. They had put Ella between them in the upstairs bedroom, but the girl hadn't settled down until she climbed out of the bed and curled up on the floor without so much as a blanket. Jordan envied the slumbering child. Each time Jordan closed her eyes, the vision of Samuel being dragged away popped into her mind's eye, causing despair to well up in her, filling her with equal measures of rage and sorrow. It was impossible to sleep with a racing heart.

She kept imagining the horrified look on her father's face when he received the telegram. Then she would picture Nora's tears when Pops informed her that her husband was being held captive. Jordan worried about her father making that journey on his own, but even more she hoped he wouldn't be foolish enough to have Nora and Otis come as well.

The more she thought about her family in Ohio, the more riled up she became. Finally her chest became so tight she felt as if she were suffocating. In a panic she sat up. Her breath was so jerky she couldn't take in any air. Mama sat up next to her; apparently she'd been awake too. Mama put one hand on Jordan's back and took her hand in the other.

"Breathe in deep and slow, baby," Mama said.

Jordan tried, but her lungs were too clenched.

"Take your time," Mama encouraged her.

Jordan looked at her mother. How could she be so calm?

"Take care of yo' breathing," Mama said. "You can do that right now to help yo' brother."

Jordan closed her eyes to concentrate on her own body. She felt her mother's hand on her back. She dropped her shoulders, and suddenly her lungs had space. Jordan took in a little air. There was room for more, so she kept inhaling, slowly filling her lungs. She leaned back as she exhaled. A tingle passed through her as much-needed oxygen filled her body.

"That's right," Mama soothed. "You doing it."

A few breaths later Jordan slowly lifted her eyelids.

"When that fear start risin' in you, you got to hand it over to God—especially in the night. When you can' *do*, you got to pray."

Jordan gave a little nod, grateful for her mama's calm presence. It had been years since she'd needed Mama because she was scared, but Mama was a great comfort now, just as she had been when Jordan was a child.

"Ready for some prayer?" Mama asked.

Jordan still could not speak, so she nodded. Perhaps the Holy Spirit would fill her again as it had in the church with Lisbeth.

"Dear God, it me, Mattie . . . and Jordan too. Please watch over our Samuel. Keep him safe from lasting harm to his body and soul. God guide us to help him best. And, Lord"—Mama's voice broke in the middle of the prayer—"please get him to be free again. Amen."

"Amen," Jordan echoed.

"Don' you feel better?" Mama asked.

Jordan nodded. She was calmer, but it felt like a tenuous peace. Fear and panic were still fluttering around the periphery of her heart.

"All the time I ask God, 'Keep him safe; set him free,'" Mama said. "It just running in my mind always. You do the same," she instructed. "And rub one of yo' mustard seeds. It gonna make you feel better and help yo' brother too."

Jordan rolled the seeds between her fingers and prayed in her head. *God, keep Samuel safe and set him free. Keep him safe. Set him free. Please keep him safe and set him free.*

Jordan exhaled with a sigh, nodded, and gave her mother a small smile. Fear and panic edged out a little further, suddenly replaced by exhaustion. Jordan slipped under the covers, and the tension in her body melted into the mattress. She turned to her side and closed her eyes. Mama rubbed her back and sang. Jordan's silent prayer for her brother mixed with the words of the familiar lullaby, providing comfort though nothing had really changed for any of them, until she finally fell asleep.

In the morning Jordan was anxious to make the rounds at the offices they had visited the day before, but Mama insisted that it was too soon and that they needed to do some good in the world first, starting with Ella.

Miss Grace pulled out the washtub in the laundry room. Jordan only needed to boil one pot of water to bring the bath to a nice temperature. Ella watched the preparations with a mixture of fear and interest on her face.

"It's ready," Jordan told the child.

Ella didn't make a move.

"You may get in," Jordan instructed.

Ella looked confused. Had she really never had a bath before? Jordan didn't think that was true, because Mama was always going on about the blessing of a warm-water bath in contrast to the cold ones from before.

Jordan explained, "This is just a bath, to get you clean. You've had baths before, right?"

Ella nodded. Then she pointed to her chest and asked, wonder in her voice, "I going first?"

"Yes." Jordan smiled. She was amused by the look of surprise on Ella's face. "Is this the first time you've bathed in clean water?" she asked.

Ella bit her lip and nodded.

"Then today is a special day for you. Go on . . . hop in," she encouraged.

Ella shook her head a little; fear overtook her wonder.

"What's the matter?" Jordan asked.

Ella pointed at the soap.

"Are you scared of the soap?" Jordan asked.

Ella nodded as she shivered by the tub.

"Do you think it will burn your skin?"

"Yes, ma'am," Ella replied.

Jordan picked up the soap and rubbed it between her hands under the water. She smeared the creamy liquid onto the tender skin over her pulse and waited a moment to see if it stung.

"This soap does not contain lye. It doesn't hurt me," Jordan declared, "so it won't hurt you."

"You sure?" Ella asked.

"See for yourself." Jordan put a dab on the girl's arm. "If you don't like how it feels, we can just use a washcloth."

The girl stared at her arm, waiting for the burn that didn't come. She climbed into the bathwater, gripping the sides of the tub carefully as she sat down. Her shoulders dropped as the soothing water surrounded her. A small smile tugged at the corners of her mouth. Jordan took vicarious pleasure in Ella's enjoyment.

"Is the soap to your satisfaction?" Jordan asked.

Ella looked confused.

"Do you like it enough to use it?" Jordan clarified.

Ella nodded, took the bar from Jordan, and started washing up. Jordan was sad to see all the cuts and scratches that marked up the little girl's arms and legs. Some still had scabs, others had healed over, and a few looked like they were going to leave marks for life.

"What kind of work did you do? Before the soldiers brought you here?" Jordan asked.

"I picked cotton. I ain't too fast, but I ain't too slow either," Ella said.

Jordan nodded, but she didn't have a response. She wanted to reassure Ella that her cotton-picking days were behind her, but she did not want to make a statement that might not be true. As much as she had come to care for this little girl, the child's future was uncertain.

Miss Grace came in with a jar in one hand and said, "Rub a little of this in your hair when you've finished washing it. This is guaranteed to make your hair softer and easier to comb out."

"What is it?" Jordan asked.

She replied, "Mrs. Jefferson from church sells this magic elixir. She won't tell us what's in it, but we love it."

Neither Jordan nor Ella had ever seen anything like it. Mama and Jordan pressed flaxseeds for oil to soften their hair, but she'd never seen a hair cream for sale.

"And here's a dress for you, Ella," Miss Grace said, holding up a hanger in her right hand.

The little girl's brown eyes got big with excitement when she saw the brown striped dress with a high collar and pleated skirt.

"It's beautiful, Ella," Jordan said. "You will look like a queen when we are done."

After Ella got out of the bath, Jordan combed through her hair and plaited it into twelve little braids. They rubbed oil into her skin, making it smooth with a light shine. Jordan brought her to the mirror upstairs to see the outcome of her transformation. Ella stood in front of her own reflection; Jordan stood behind her. The girl looked at the image before her and then looked around at Jordan, and then back again.

"Have you ever seen yourself in a mirror before?" Jordan asked.

Ella bit her lip and shook her head. Jordan gave Ella's arms a little squeeze. There were so many little pleasures in life that Jordan took for granted that this child had never experienced.

"You will get used to all these changes soon enough," Jordan reassured the little girl with a smile. As soon as the words were out of her mouth, she regretted them. This child might not be her cousin. Or she was her cousin, but Sarah would bring her to live back in the quarters at Fair Oaks. That shack didn't have a full-length mirror or hair cream. This child's fate was uncertain—and it wasn't in Jordan's hands. Perhaps it was cruel to be exposing her to these luxuries in life. All this might be lost to her in a few days.

When they came into the living room, Mama and Miss Grace clapped approval for Ella's new look.

"You look like a princess," Mama declared.

"Thank you, Auntie!" the girl said, beaming at the two women.

Ella looked proud and confident. Jordan was stunned at the transformation in the little girl. It felt good to show this child that she deserved to be showered with praise and treated with respect. It might only be temporary right now, but Jordan hoped it would give Ella something to aspire to forever.

———— ❧ ————

"Would you like to come with us this time?" Jordan asked Ella. She kept her voice light for the child. She didn't want her worry for Samuel to cloud Ella's day. First they were going to visit the Freedmen's Bureau to see if Mr. Brooke had made any progress on securing Samuel's release. After that they would attempt to bring Samuel some food at the auction house. Miss Grace said that the prisoners often went hungry, which only served to increase Jordan's concern.

Ella nodded vigorously. She and Mama had considered leaving Ella behind again, but it felt unkind to continue abandoning her, though Miss Grace was happy to have Ella remain with her. They decided it would be good to expose her to more of the world, though it might be uncomfortable at times. In truth, in her short life this child had experienced much more cruelty and indifference than Jordan ever had.

Mr. Brooke was as unhelpful as he had been the day before. He had no news or plan, but was "awfully sorry." Jordan didn't see the point in even coming to the Freedmen's Bureau, but when they left Mama said that she would see him tomorrow.

It took less than ten minutes to walk the half mile downhill to the auction house. Jordan felt protective of Ella as they approached the ominous building. She steeled herself for a miserable sight, but she wasn't prepared for the awful smell that assaulted her nose. The stench from bodily waste made it difficult to even inhale once they were within a few yards of the building. Jordan felt ill at the horrid conditions her brother was being held in.

Mama marched up to the line of women at a high window with metal bars across it but no glass. Jordan saw just the very top of a head through the opening, with a brown hand reaching through it. The old woman at the front of the line had her arm raised up high, touching what she could of the prisoner. After a few minutes those two moved away from the window, and the next woman, rail thin with a baby on her hip, moved forward and yelled a name into the building. Moments later she walked away, stony faced, without having spoken to anyone.

"Her man musta been taken away," the round woman ahead of them in line said to no one in particular, shaking her head.

They waited as six more women made it to the front of the line, called out a name, and were rewarded with a short visit—or walked away disappointed.

"Give me one of yo' mustard seeds, quick!" Mama pushed Jordan. Jordan shrugged.

"You don't have 'em?" Mama looked disappointed.

"Sorry, Mama. I left them at Miss Grace's."

Mama pressed one of her small seeds into Jordan's hand.

"Put some love and faith into it, quick! Your brother need some to get through this," Mama explained.

Jordan did as she was told. Holding the tiny kernel, she breathed in love and faith, then exhaled them into the mustard seed. Maybe this seed would give Samuel a bit of the peace she'd felt in the church that he could carry with him.

When it was their turn at the front of the line, Mama yelled out, "Samuel Freedman."

Mama raised her hands over her head, holding the seeds between her pointer finger and thumb. Jordan's heart beat fiercely in her chest. *Please let him be here.* The waiting felt interminable. She looked at Mama, who just stared forward, her face set, her fingers just over the opening. Suddenly Samuel's familiar fingers appeared, grimy with dirt. Mama passed their small gifts to his hand.

"Thanks for comin', Mama," he said, sounding despondent.

"Jordan here too," Mama said. "And Ella."

Jordan was sick. Samuel's shiny forehead was barely visible over the disgusting brick wall. She desperately wished she could offer him reassurance, but she didn't have any confidence they would secure his release. Instead of false promises, she greeted him.

"Hi, Samuel." Jordan's voice cracked. "You're going to laugh, but I've been praying for you."

"We brought you food." Mama reached down for the package of food and squeezed it to him through the bars. They'd included more than he would need so he could share, but Jordan wondered if they'd just complicated the situation for him. Too soon the next woman in line became restless—signaling to them to move on.

"We gotta go now, Samuel," Mama said. "But we gonna come back ever' day. And we gonna do what we can to get you free."

"'K, Mama," was all Samuel said. "I love you."

"Goodbye," Jordan said, and her voice broke. She didn't trust herself to say anything more, fearing she would sob uncontrollably, not knowing when or if she would ever see her brother again. She held it in until they had walked away from the line of women. Was she the only one who felt the pain of this so strongly?

Tears poured down her face. She looked at Ella, who once again looked like she was gone from this world. Then she looked at her mama. The shine in her eyes showed that she was sad too, but the hold of her jaw told Jordan that she wasn't going to show it to the world. Mama, and all these women, had a stoicism that Jordan had yet to learn.

They walked back up Main Street, past people going about their lives as if the world made sense. Jordan forced herself to say her prayer. *God, keep him safe; set him free,* over and over again until the tears stopped flowing. She wiped her face and walked on.

A few blocks later Mama suddenly stopped and declared, "We gonna plant a bit of love so we can get some hope."

"I can use some hope, Mama." Jordan paused. "But it's hard to imagine finding any."

"We gonna buy some supplies, and you gonna go to the orphanage and teach the future."

Mama stared at Jordan, expectant. Jordan didn't *feel* up to being with children after that depressing experience. She wished only to have a nap. But Mama was right—she desperately needed some hope right now. Jordan saw why Mama put her faith in small acts. They were fighting against something so big and ugly that she felt helpless. But all that ugliness couldn't stop her from teaching a child.

"Ella, would you like to learn all the letters in your name?"

The little girl nodded vigorously.

They walked on, past the stores, until they got to the black part of town. On Clay, not far from the orphan home, they found a store that had several slates and chalk.

Mrs. Avery welcomed them warmly and ushered them to the courtyard in the back. Right away Jordan spotted Tessie directing a circle of young children. When the girl saw Jordan her shoulders jumped and her eyes got big in surprise and excitement, but then she put on an indifferent air and strutted over.

"You came back?"

Jordan nodded. "Yes, I did."

"D'you 'member me?" the lanky girl asked.

Jordan nodded again. "Yes, I do."

"What's my name?"

"Tessie!" Jordan replied. "*T-e-s-s-i-e.* I brought some slates and chalk so I can teach you the letters in your own name."

Tessie looked wary. "Did Mrs. Avery say it all right?"

Once again Jordan nodded.

"You shore Jesus ain't going to send me to hell for writin' my own name?" Tessie demanded.

"Let the wise hear and increase in learning," Jordan quoted as a counterargument.

"That from the Bible?"

"Yes," Jordan said. "When you learn more you can read it there for yourself."

Looking convinced, Tessie nodded and ran off to the group of young children. She shepherded them toward Jordan and directed them to sit in rows on the ground for their first lesson.

Jordan smiled at Mama. She felt better already. Jordan took Ella's hand and led her to a spot on the ground. She returned to the front of the group and started at the beginning with the alphabet. Though she had never taught in an outdoor classroom before, she jumped right in.

"T-e-s-s-i-e," the girl spelled out. "Tessie!"

"That's right," Jordan replied. "You are a very clever girl. You learned that in one lesson! Tomorrow we will work on forming your letters."

Tessie nodded and ran off to wash for supper.

Mrs. Avery walked up and asked, "You plan to return?"

Jordan had said that without thought. Swept up in the moment, she'd just spoken out. She looked at her mama with a silent question.

Mama nodded and said, "I thin' teaching these children a good use of our time. Don' you agree?"

Jordan did. "They were very enthusiastic learners."

"They responded to you. Perhaps because you are Negro," Mrs. Avery speculated. "You can give them inspiration that our White teachers cannot."

Jordan felt her heart tug at the truth of Mrs. Avery's words. She offered these children something no White teacher could possibly do:

proof of their race's capacities. As much as she felt satisfaction with her work that afternoon, she did not want that responsibility.

"While we are in Richmond, I would be pleased to offer lessons each afternoon," Jordan replied.

Mrs. Avery responded with a tight smile. "Whatever you can offer these children will be a welcome gift."

———— ❧⚮☙ ————

Mama, Ella, and Jordan walked back to Miss Grace's home from the orphanage. With each step Jordan grew more unsettled once again.

"Let's turn here," Jordan suggested, to avoid facing the corner where Samuel was dragged away. Mama turned without a word, but Jordan could tell that she was also thinking about Samuel.

Jordan took her mama's hand and squeezed.

"They can take away my son, but they can' take away my faith," Mama announced.

Jordan said, on the verge of tears, "I feel so helpless."

"That what they want you to believe," Mama declared.

Jordan looked at her mother, a question in her eyes.

"Getting you to lose your hope the biggest weapon they gots. So our best weapon is to hold on to hope, however we can."

Their lives were being destroyed, and Jordan feared they were powerless to stop them—despite the fact that they had won the war! Hope was far from her fury-filled heart.

"You make it sound easy," Jordan said, emotion building in her chest.

"I got a lot more practice than you livin' in hope in the face of evil," Mama replied. "I ain't saying it easy. I just saying it the mos' powerful weapon we got. So you keep going back to that orphanage. It gonna give you a bit of hope doing somethin' to put some good in the world."

"Teaching children to read is nothing, just a little drop of water in a huge desert of mean."

"That' all most of us get—being a little drop of water. A few folks get to do somethin' big like Mr. Lincoln an' the Emancipation Proclamation. God givin' you a chance to help a child know they own name. It a little somethin', but it gonna matter to that one. We don' get to pick how *big* our good gets to be, but each of us picks if we gonna do some good right where we are."

Jordan bit her lip and nodded.

She must have looked unconvinced, because Mama went on. "If enough people put their drop of water in the same place, then we can make a flower bloom . . . right in the middle of the desert."

Jordan sighed. She wanted to believe like Mama, but doubt still reigned in her.

Mama's eyes welled up. "Never, in a million years, would my mama have imagined that she could read the Lord's words hersel'. And now you, her granddaughter, is a *teacher*—you went to college!"

Jordan's flesh rose at her mama's awe.

"You know why?" Mama asked. "You know who we gots to thank for our blessings?"

"Cousin Sarah?" Jordan whispered through a tight throat.

"Mm-hmm." Mama nodded. "And so many others."

Jordan listened attentively.

"Pops's pa filled his head with stories of freedom," Mama explained. "Yo' grandpoppy never made it, but he planted that seed in yo' pops. I wouldn't a thought to run, but when I tied mysel' to him—and he and Samuel made a good life that was waiting for us . . . after you was born, I just had to, no matter how scared I was."

Mama went on. "An' those people, the ones we never met and ain't ever gonna meet, who were called by God to make somethin' that ain' ever been before—*a college* for everyone that let a Negro woman learn. That' a miracle, baby. A miracle that blessed yo' life!"

A huge chill swept through Jordan at the truth of her mother's words.

"The Sower casts his seeds wherever he goes. Mos' of the seeds ain't gonna take root and blossom—but some will. You a sower today, baby. You cast seeds of knowledge to those chil'ren. You ain't gonna know how or where or if they gonna blossom, but you did God's work today—you sowed some seeds."

Awe and gratitude chased out the last bit of doubt in her heart, joining with the ever-present fear and sorrow she held for Samuel. Mama was right; her life was a miracle that she owed to God and to so many people. At the same time it was enraging that Samuel had been arrested. Somehow she had to hold both complicated and contradictory truths at once. Jordan hugged her mama long and hard.

"Thank you," Jordan whispered into her mama's ear as they separated. Then she took Mama's hand in her left and Ella's in her right, and they moved forward, together.

CHAPTER 19

LISBETH

Richmond, Virginia

Keeping to the routines was excruciating, but necessary. Lisbeth went through the days in a fog, avoiding Jack as much as possible, but she was required to take her meals with him. Each time she looked at him she felt he was taunting her.

Father slowly moved toward his final transition, sleeping nearly all day and all night. Lisbeth often sat with him, but she found it wearying to spend the entire day by his bedside. She had hoped that the frank conversation she had shared with Mother would open up a lasting affection between them, but it had not. Neither had spoken of it again. Mother's attitude seemed to be more affected by the drops than anything Lisbeth said or did.

Julianne's kind attention to Sadie was jarring to Lisbeth. Every afternoon her daughter had a new hairstyle courtesy of her aunt. Lisbeth wondered what the two of them spoke about during their time together and hoped Julianne wasn't an undue influence on Sadie, but she did not wish to stir up any curiosity or trouble, so she did not challenge the routine.

She checked the mail the moment it arrived, but there was still no letter from Matthew. More than a week had passed since she'd written to her husband, and she was beginning to fear that her letter had not arrived. It was difficult to manage with no information. She'd decided that if she did not get a letter tomorrow, she would send him a telegram.

She was pulled out of her thoughts by the sound of the chime at the door.

"Are you expecting a guest?" Lisbeth asked her mother, who was sitting with her in the parlor.

Mother shook her head but said nothing. She was in one of her quiet moods.

A few moments later Emily opened the door and said, "Mr. Matthew, ma'ams."

Lisbeth was confused. Then she saw her husband, and her heart leaped like a wild rabbit. She rushed to him, not giving her mother a thought.

"I cannot believe you are here!" she exclaimed.

"I decided to surprise you, and the children," Matthew replied.

He wrapped his arms around her, lifting her off the ground and back down again, then held her in a long embrace. Lisbeth relaxed into his body, burrowing her cheek into his chest, and got the comfort that came only from him. She had missed him so much.

Interrupting their reunion, Mother chastised, "You did not notify us that you were coming!"

They broke apart, though Lisbeth kept her arm looped through his.

"My apologies, Mother Wainwright," Matthew said graciously. "A friend was making the journey, and I joined him on the spur of the moment. I did not even have time to post a note."

"You expect to stay here?" Mother Wainwright asked, sounding incredulous.

Lisbeth's heart dropped. Would her mother really be so cruel as to deny her husband a roof?

"For the night, if you will allow," he replied, his tone calm and charming. "I would like to visit my parents with Lisbeth and the children in the morning, if she can be spared for a few days."

"I think it unlikely that *Elizabeth* will be concerned with my feelings. However, though my husband is coming toward the end of his life, there is no reason to believe it will be in the next few days."

Mother swept out of the room without giving Lisbeth a chance to reply to her harsh comments. Lisbeth didn't care. Matthew was here. She hugged him again.

"It is really you?" Lisbeth smiled at her husband. "I'm so relieved. Who did you come with?"

Matthew pulled her down to the couch and whispered, "Emmanuel came to free Samuel. I offered to join him to see if I could be of assistance. I'm prepared to testify that Samuel is employed by me and therefore not a vagrant."

"So you got my letter?"

"No. Emmanuel received a telegram. Pastor Duhart realized that a White man might be vital to success, and knowing our history, he asked me to accompany Emmanuel."

A shiver passed through Lisbeth. "Oh, Matthew! Thank you so very much."

"You know that will be the end of it, for you and your family?" Matthew stared at her intently with his hazel eyes.

Lisbeth sighed. She teared up, but nodded. "I had hoped so much for reconciliation, but there is none to be had for me here," Lisbeth explained. "Instead this journey has helped me see so clearly that I made the right choice . . . to leave." She smiled at Matthew. "I did not doubt it before; truly I did not. Asking to be your wife was the best decision of my life." She squeezed her husband's hand. He smiled at her. Lisbeth continued. "But before this visit I had not realized that Mother, Father, and Jack are not my family anymore. As sad as I am to know it, we have no bonds of affection or trust."

"So you are at peace with this decision?"

Lisbeth nodded. "An ugly truth is preferable to a beautiful lie. I am certain that I wish to help Mattie and Samuel however we may. Do we have a plan?"

"In the morning we will go to my parents. Emmanuel will meet us there with Mattie and Jordan. I hope he will have learned where Samuel is leased out."

"I know where Samuel is," Lisbeth told her husband.

"Where?"

"White Pines. Edward Cunningham has him harvesting the tobacco fields."

"Will we return to see Grandmother and Grandfather Wainwright before we go home?" Sadie asked as they were packing up in their bedroom.

Lisbeth wrestled with what to tell her daughter. She wanted Sadie to understand this was a forever goodbye, but she did not want the six-year-old to ruin their plans. She decided to tell her but keep her close until they left.

"Can you keep a secret?" she asked Sadie. "A very important secret?"

The little girl nodded earnestly.

"We are going to help free Miss Jordan's brother. We won't come back here afterward. So, no, you won't see Grandmother and Grandfather Wainwright again. But we can't tell them, because it needs to be a secret that we are helping Mr. Freedman. When you say goodbye to them, in your heart you will know it is forever, but you can't say that to them."

"Forever?"

Lisbeth's eyes welled up. She nodded. "Forever. We won't be visiting them, or Uncle Jack, or Aunt Julianne, or Cousin Johnny again."

"And they won't visit us?"

"No."

The little girl took in the information. The twitch in her left eye revealed to Lisbeth that she was holding back emotion, just like Lisbeth.

Finally Sadie said, "I'm sad that I won't see Uncle Jack and Auntie Julianne again, but not sad about Grandmother Wainwright or Cousin Johnny. Is that bad?"

Mixed emotions swirled in Lisbeth too. "No, it's not wrong that you feel that way. Your aunt and uncle have been very sweet to you. I understand why you will miss them. Johnny and Grandmother Wainwright have not earned your affection." Lisbeth went on. "However, it would be wrong to *tell* any of them."

"I know that, Momma!" Sadie declared. The girl got quiet. Her hand flew to the locket around her neck. She stared at Lisbeth with glassy eyes, then asked, "It wouldn't be right for me to keep it, would it? Will you take it off?"

Lisbeth's heart broke for her daughter. Sadie was right. The girl turned around, and Lisbeth undid the clasp on the locket. Sadie kissed the metal, whispered goodbye to it, and left it on the bureau.

"Does Sammy know?" Sadie asked.

"That we are leaving forever?" Lisbeth asked.

Sadie nodded, her blue eyes wide and her eyebrows curved in an arc. She looked so earnest it unsettled Lisbeth. This journey was proving even more complicated than she had ever expected.

"I will tell him what I have just told you. And of course Poppa is aware of our plan," Lisbeth replied. "There are no secrets in our family."

"Is that why Poppa came?" her child asked. "To help Mr. Freedman?"

"Yes," Lisbeth said. "You are a clever little girl."

"I'm not little," Sadie declared. "I'm six!"

CHAPTER 20

JORDAN

Charles City County, Virginia

Jordan felt ill as they left Richmond and journeyed back toward Fair Oaks. Sitting in the back of the wagon, she felt her stomach lurch with every rock and rut in the road. It didn't help that she was so sleep deprived, having tossed and turned all night long with her mind jumping around like a frog every time she started to drift off. She'd been glad to see her father, but terrified for him as well. She feared he would be taken away just like Samuel. *Brave. Be as brave as Mama,* she told herself, but her heart wouldn't comply.

They were heading to Sadie's grandparents' house—the Johnsons, not the Wainwrights. Apparently Matthew Johnson's parents would be sympathetic to their cause. Pops said this family might help them get Samuel released—or at least their house would be a safe location from which to act. Lisbeth and her family were meeting them there, and they would make a plan to retrieve Sarah as well as Samuel.

If she felt like this setting out, she could only imagine how scared she'd be as they got closer. She did her best to hide her anxiety, especially from little Ella, who was lost in her own world, staring off into the woods as the wagon bumped along. Mama and Pops sat in the front. Having Pops along should have been soothing, but it just made Jordan worry more. In Ohio neither of her parents had ever seemed fragile, but down here she felt enormously protective of both of them—and powerless to keep them safe. She reached into her pocket, hoping the tiny mustard seeds would transfer a bit of faith to her.

A few hours later they pulled up to a farmhouse in need of a good paint job. Jordan hung back in the wagon with Ella while Pops and Mama approached the three White folks who came out to greet them. The older two had mostly gray hair and the wrinkles that showed they'd worked outside for most of their lives. They were most likely Matthew's parents. The younger man looked enough like Matthew that she assumed he was his brother, but he could be a field hand.

"Can I help you?" the older man said, looking wary. Jordan strained to hear the conversation without staring.

Pops spoke up, keeping it light and respectful. "Mr. Matthew invited us, sir."

The man replied, "You must be confused; he doesn't live here."

"We know him from Oberlin," Mama said. She sounded nervous.

The folks nodded, but looked perplexed.

"Matthew and I drove together from Ohio to Virginia," Pops explained.

"Oh," the woman said, sounding excited. She looked around. "Where is he?"

"He and Lisbeth are driving they own wagon with the children," Pops said. "We thought they'd be here by now. They musta got held up."

"Well then," Matthew's father said, smiling, "it'll be nice to see them, and you are more than welcome." He stuck out his hand and said, "Mitchel Johnson."

The two men shook hands as Pops said his name back.

"This is my wife, Mary Alice, and my oldest son, Mitch," Matthew's father said.

"This my wife, Mattie Freedman."

Mrs. Johnson exclaimed, "Lisbeth's Mattie?"

Mama nodded.

"Oh my. It is a pleasure to meet you!" Mrs. Johnson grinned and said warmly, "She speaks of you so dearly. Please, come inside to wait."

The old woman looked at Jordan in the wagon, smiled, and waved her over. She and Ella joined the group. Mrs. Johnson greeted them warmly, but Ella shrank into herself when the woman put out her hand to introduce herself.

"Sorry," Jordan said, embarrassed at the girl's poor manners.

"It is not a problem, truly. I was reserved as a child, so I understand."

"Would you like some nice cool lemonade?" Mrs. Johnson asked Ella and Jordan when they were settled into the living room.

The child stared down at the worn rug. Jordan couldn't tell if she was being stubborn or if she was frightened.

Jordan replied for them both. "That would be lovely, thank you."

While Mrs. Johnson was out of the room, Jordan whispered to Ella, "Say thank you when she gives you the drink."

"I too scared," Ella whispered back.

"Of what?"

"The White lady," Ella said.

"How come?" Jordan asked.

"They mean."

"Not every one of them," Jordan explained.

The little girl eyed her dubiously. "Ever' one I ever met."

The girl dropped her head down again. Mrs. Johnson had returned. Jordan's impulse was to challenge Ella, to inform her she was wrong and teach her a new way of thinking, but she decided patience would serve them both better. The little girl would learn better that some White folks were kind by seeing it rather than by being told it was true.

Jordan whispered to the girl, "Have you even been in a White person's house?"

The girl shook her head quickly. Jordan saw that her hand was actually shaking. Jordan felt a surge of sympathy. Ella was so terrified.

"You're okay. Just stick by me," Jordan reassured the girl. "I know this is a lot of change for you, but you'll get used to it. And I promise you, not all White people are mean."

It wasn't long before they heard a wagon pull up. Mr. and Mrs. Johnson rushed outside to greet Lisbeth, Matthew, and the kids. Jordan watched the reunion from the front porch with Ella by her side.

Jordan leaned over to Ella. "Do you see how Mr. Johnson keeps wiping his eye? He is so happy he is crying!"

Ella looked at Mr. Johnson, then at Jordan with wonder on her face.

"Who that little White girl?" Ella asked.

"Sadie. She's six years old, which means you have to be kind to her since she is younger than you. Her brother, Sammy, is nine, same as you. The parents are Mr. and Mrs. Johnson. It's confusing with Matthew's parents, since they have the same last names."

"How come they gots two names?" Ella asked.

Jordan was confused by the question, but then she remembered that most slaves only had a first name.

She explained the tradition to the child. "We each have a family name and our individual name. My family name is Freedman. My parents picked it when they escaped from Virginia. We are Emmanuel, Mattie, Samuel, and Jordan Freedman."

The little girl nodded. "Do my mama have a family name?"

Jordan considered. "We aren't certain. We think it might be Brown, but you can ask her yourself."

"If she do, that gonna be my name too?" the girl asked. "If she my mama?"

"Yes," Jordan replied. She ached for the little girl waiting to find out if she belonged.

"We really gonna find her?"

"That's one reason we traveled here, to have Cousin Sarah meet you."

"Do I have a pa?"

Jordan's heart dropped like a sack of grain. Talking with this child was like walking too close to an empty pit. She shrugged and shook her head.

The little girl bit her lip so hard Jordan was afraid she would make it bleed. To distract Ella Jordan asked, "Would you like to go meet Sadie?"

The child stopped chewing on her mouth, but she looked more alarmed than enthusiastic.

"She is very nice," Jordan reassured her. "One of my most friendly and helpful students."

Ella nodded but still looked wary. They joined the group just as Mama and Pops were greeting Lisbeth and Matthew. Pops shook the man's hand and clapped him on the back.

"Bless you for comin' with Emmanuel," Mama said to Matthew.

"I'm happy to be here, Mattie." Matthew smiled at Mama.

Lisbeth gave Mama a big hug and said, "I'm sorry we have to do this at all, Mattie. We are going to do whatever we can to help you get your Samuel free."

Mama nodded, her mouth pressed tight. That word was a spear to Jordan's heart. Her brother wasn't *free*. Before this trip, she'd believed that justice always moved forward, but now she knew better. There were terrible people determined to keep her people down. Jordan had to agree with her parents: the fight for colored rights wasn't over, and it was just as important as women's suffrage.

Sadie ran over, shouting, "Hello, Miss Jordan!"

"It's nice to see you, Sadie," Jordan said. "This is Ella. Ella, this is Sadie."

"I'm six years old," Sadie informed Ella. "How old are you?"

"Nine," Jordan mouthed to Ella, and held up nine fingers, though the girl couldn't count. She was stating that fact as if this child were Cousin Sarah's daughter, but for all they knew she was a seven-year-old born in North Carolina rather than a nine-year-old born in Virginia.

"Nine?" Ella said aloud to Sadie, sounding more like she was asking a question than stating a fact. Sadie looked up in thought and put up one, two, three fingers.

"You are three years older than me!" Sadie said.

Ella nodded, but Jordan wasn't sure it meant as much to her as it did to Sadie.

They all squeezed into the living room. Jordan and Ella hung back at the edges, expecting to watch more than contribute to the conversation. Sadie stayed close by, clearly having decided that she and Ella were going to be best friends now. Ella looked both flattered by and scared of the attention.

"Prayer. We gotta start with a prayer." Mama waved Jordan and the little girls over. "Ever'body come close and take a hand!" Then she looked at Emmanuel and nodded pointedly.

Jordan moved forward and took Lisbeth's hand. She reached her left hand out to Ella. The girl looked confused, but she wrapped her fingers around her palm. Sadie grabbed Ella's other hand, and she was all set.

Jordan looked at the chain of connection around the room. This was an odd mishmash of people, of various ages and hues. Some were her closest people, her parents, and others were barely more than strangers to her. These were the people who were going to do their best to set things right for Samuel. Was this grace, an unearned gift, that brought them together, or was this the result of her mama's scheming? Whatever it was, Jordan was grateful.

"God," Pops prayed, "we in need of your blessing. Guide us, and open the hearts and minds o' Samuel's captors. Release our son from his bondage if that your will, as you have released so many others from captivity. Amen."

*Amen*s echoed around the room. A calm settled into Jordan, and she joined in with an *amen* of her own.

Matthew leaned in and told the Johnsons what they knew of Samuel's situation. Mrs. Johnson shook her head slowly the whole time he was speaking. Jordan couldn't quite read her mood. She suspected that Mrs. Johnson was sympathetic to their cause but concerned about getting caught up in a dangerous situation.

"Are you certain that he is at White Pines?" Mr. Johnson asked.

Lisbeth shrugged. "I only have Jack's word for it. He may have only been taunting me, but it seemed genuine."

Mitch let out a large sigh and shook his head. "Edward Cunningham will be difficult. He has a severe case of soldier's heart.

He went mad after you broke off your engagement to him and you two got married"—he gestured to Lisbeth and Matthew—"but he is even less stable since the war. We must be extremely careful."

Jordan's interest perked up at that information: Lisbeth had nearly married the man who was working Samuel? She made a note to ask Mama about that.

Pops spoke up. "I been thinkin' about the best ways to free my son. I think we say Matthew here brought me and Samuel to harvest for you folks."

"We tell this to Edward?" Mr. Johnson asked.

"No, jus' talk to his overseer," Pops replied.

"With this in yo' pocket, he gonna listen to you," Mama said, pulling out the stack of cash.

Everybody in the room rustled at the sight of so much money. Now Jordan was grateful, rather than angry, that Mama and Pops had squirreled away that cash. It could save her Samuel.

Mitch said, "Money like that has a way of getting a man's attention."

"All right then," Matthew said. "How about Mitch, Emmanuel, and I go early tomorrow and have a talk with the overseer of White Pines?" he suggested.

"I'm coming too," Lisbeth said, looking fiercely determined.

"No, Lisbeth," Matthew said. "You stay here with the children."

"It wasn't a question, Matthew," Lisbeth declared. "I am coming as well."

No one spoke. Tension filled the room. Jordan looked between their faces. She cheered Lisbeth on inside her head. Her husband looked like he wanted to continue the debate, but he just let out a sigh and nodded.

"Emmanuel, Mitch, *Lisbeth*, and I will head to White Pines in the morning," Matthew said.

"And me, Jordan, and Ella are gonna go get Sarah," Mama declared.

All eyes turned to Mama. Jordan was startled to hear her own name. She'd been so caught up in thinking about Samuel that for the moment she'd stopped thinking about the plan she'd made with Mama to persuade Cousin Sarah to meet Ella.

Casually Pops said, "You wait for me to get back, so's I can go with you."

Mama shook her head decisively and said, "We gonna go in quietly and leave quietly. We don' need a fight. Besides, if'n we do it while you gettin' Samuel, we can get out of this county before the end of the day—maybe before noon."

Now Pops looked like Matthew had a few minutes before—concerned, but resigned to his wife's plan.

Ella and Jordan were sitting in the back of the wagon in the same stand of trees on the Fair Oaks plantation that Samuel had waited in so many weeks ago. Mama had left them here and sneaked over to Cousin Sarah's. Jordan had been hesitant to let her mother go alone, but eventually she agreed with the wisdom of her mama's plan. Mama going to the quarters by herself would be much less conspicuous than the three of them.

Jordan had a new appreciation for the torment that Samuel had gone through the night they left him here. It hadn't been more than half an hour since Mama left, and Jordan was ready to jump out of her skin with worry.

"What gonna happen if she ain't my mama?" Ella asked in a pitiful voice.

Jordan's stomach flipped. She'd wondered that very question herself and had yet to come up with an acceptable answer.

Returning Ella to the orphanage would be cruel beyond measure. Jordan would be haunted by the memory of the girl for the rest of her life if they abandoned Ella to an unknown fate. Mama wasn't enthusiastic about taking in an orphan, and Jordan didn't feel ready for that responsibility. She was hesitant to change her plans for her future, to give up on her dream of working for suffrage, but she could not let herself rule it out either.

As promised, Jordan had returned to teach at the orphanage every day since Samuel's capture. It was the highlight of each day, giving her hope and purpose. The children had taken up a special place in her heart, especially Tessie.

Though she'd initially dismissed Mrs. Avery's suggestion that she take a teaching position in the freedmen's school, Jordan found herself conjuring lesson plans for this setting. These children needed different instruction than the children in Oberlin. Pride in their race's history and instruction in morality would be equally as important in lifting up these children as mathematics and reading. If it turned out Ella was not her cousin, she might decide to stay in Richmond to teach and watch over this child. To her surprise she was not entirely disappointed at the possibility, though she very much hoped Ella was Sarah's daughter.

Hopefully the prospect of meeting her youngest daughter would entice Cousin Sarah into the woods and convince her this child was one of the ones she was waiting for. If so, they fervently prayed that Ella alone would persuade their cousin to leave with them. Even though that would mean leaving Virginia without knowing Sophia's fate, their possibilities in life would be so much better. There were too many ifs buzzing around in the air like bees ready to sting.

Ella gazed at Jordan, longing in her eyes, waiting for a reply. Jordan cleared her throat. She longed to offer reassurance to the child, but she could not lie or offer false hopes.

"You gonna take me back, huh?" Ella nodded slowly. The little girl curled her legs up to her chest, wrapped her arms around her shins, and rested her head on her knees. Curled up into a ball, she rocked herself slowly.

"I honestly do not know," Jordan said, her voice husky. She put a hand on the small of Ella's back as a slight measure of comfort and support, but the girl's shoulder tensed up, and she twisted away from Jordan's touch. There was no solace to be had right now.

Shame filled Jordan. She wanted the very best for this sweet, shy, and pained child, but she could not commit to being her family, so she deflected the responsibility.

"My mama will know the right thing to do," Jordan said. "She'll make sure you have a good place to be."

Ella looked up, stared at Jordan with doubt in her eyes, shrugged, and hid her face back on her curled-up knees.

Jordan sat close to Ella, not quite touching, offering silent companionship, the waiting interminable. After a few minutes Jordan asked, "Want to do some letters?"

The little girl's head, still resting on her knees, shook so intensely her braids bounced around.

"How about some counting?" Jordan coaxed.

Her braids shook again.

Jordan offered, "Little Sally Walker?"

There was no response. That was better than a no. Jordan didn't push. Instead, she clapped out the rhythm on her hands and lap, slapping into the empty air in front of her. Ella turned her head ever so slightly and watched out of the sides of her eyes. Jordan added a quiet hum. Ella lifted her head off her knees. Still humming and clapping, Jordan scooted to the right and twisted to the left, giving enough space to orient the air slapping toward Ella. The girl accepted the unspoken invitation and clapped along, starting the words at the beginning of the next verse. Jordan sang along with her.

Little Sally Walker, sitting in a saucer,
Rise, Sally, rise, wipe your weeping eyes;
Put your hands on your hips, and let your
    backbone slip.
Shake it to the east; shake it to the west.
Shake it to the one that you love the best.

The pair was still playing clapping games when they heard a rustle in the bushes. Jordan's pulse quickened, and her mouth went dry. She saw fear mirrored in the little girl's eyes. Jordan nodded in recognition of their shared feelings and took a calming breath to set an example, and they both looked at the bushes, waiting for what was to come.

"It us," Mama called out before Jordan could see them.

Ella looked at Jordan, alarm in her eyes. Feeling protective, Jordan put an arm around the girl.

Mama broke through the shrubs first. Sarah rushed close behind, her dark-brown eyes big in excitement, or maybe fear. Cousin Sarah stopped walking the instant her eyes landed on Ella. She froze three feet away, staring at the child. Jordan looked back and forth between the girl and the woman. Anxiety covered both faces. Neither moved.

Suddenly Sarah collapsed to her knees. Loud sobs poured out of her, tears streamed down her cheeks, and her shoulders shook up and down. Jordan had only seen crying like that at a funeral.

Ella turned to Jordan. "Why she crying?"

Uncertain what it meant, Jordan shook her head slowly as she said, "I don't know."

Sarah cried out, "My baby! You my baby." Sarah raised her arms and motioned with her hands.

A chill ran down Jordan's arms; relief surged through her. Jordan beamed at Ella. "She recognizes you!"

Ella looked confused.

Jordan clarified, "She says she *is* your mama!"

"Really?" Ella asked.

Jordan nodded and directed her. "Go. Give her a hug."

Ella looked scared. Jordan gently took the little girl's hand and slowly walked with her the three paces that separated her from her mother. Jordan knelt in front of Sarah. Ella followed suit. Jordan took Ella's small hand and placed it in Sarah's.

Tears streamed down Sarah's face. She held Ella's fingers in one hand and stroked her cheek with the other. She fingered the shell that hung around Ella's neck. It was so beautiful to watch that Jordan teared up too.

"You my baby, my baby girl. I missed you so."

Jordan stood up. Mama stood by her and wrapped an arm around Jordan's back. Jordan rested her arm across her mama's shoulder and hugged her close.

"You really my mama?" Ella asked, wonder on her face.

"Really!" Sarah nodded. "I know those eyes from anywhere!"

A small smile tugged at the girl's mouth. Fear and pride, a strange combination, mixed in her expression. Ella nodded. At first it was a small nod. Then it grew bigger as she seemed to understand. Eventually a huge grin split her face.

Ella looked at Jordan and Mama; wonder shone from her eyes. "You right. We found her!"

With a tender smile and moist eyes, Mama said, "Yes, we did."

Cousin Sarah didn't hesitate for a moment. She left everything and everyone behind and climbed into the back of the wagon with Ella. Jordan wished she could see her face as they drove away. It was way too personal to ask how it felt to be leaving. Jordan imagined it would be a whole mixture of emotions: relief to be reunited with Ella and sorrow to be left with questions about Sophia, and there had to be fear and anger too.

Sarah and Ella sat close to each other in the back of the wagon. Jordan drove the wagon with Mama sitting next to her. They were quiet in the front, eavesdropping on the chatter from the back. Mama chuckled at the little girl's giggles. Jordan's spirits soared.

"Somebody comin'!" Ella declared, ending the joyful moment. A shot of adrenaline coursed through Jordan. In the sudden silence, Jordan heard the creak of the wagon and the clap of the horses' hooves. Mama turned around and sucked in her breath.

"It look like Massa Richards," Cousin Sarah said.

"Is he alone?" Jordan asked, her heart fluttering like a trapped moth.

"Uh-huh," Mama replied.

That was only the smallest relief.

"Should I stop?" Jordan asked.

"Not unless he say so," Mama instructed.

Jordan kept her shaky hands tight on the reins. It was hard to hear over the beating of her heart, but soon the sound of galloping filled her ears.

"Stop right now!" an angry voice yelled.

It was hard to pull the reins with sweaty hands, but Jordan managed to slow the horses to a standstill.

The man rode up along the right side of the wagon atop his dark-chestnut stallion until he was eye to eye with Mama. His face was the brightest red Jordan had ever seen, and his eyes burned with fury.

"I told you to stop interfering with my business!" he bellowed, inches away from Mama's face, leaning toward her. Jordan pulled away from him, but Mama didn't flinch.

Without breaking eye contact with Mama, he yelled, "Sarah, get out of that wagon. *Now!*"

The wagon jostled as Sarah started to get up. Mama's arm shot out, stopping Sarah from climbing out of the wagon.

"No, suh," came Sarah's voice, quavering but clear.

Mr. Richards's head whipped around. His eyes bulging hard, he screamed at Sarah. "I am going to whip you within an inch of your life!" Spit flew from his mouth. "This is my home. I am the massa here. You will do as I say, *now*. Or you will pay!"

Sarah shook visibly, but she didn't move. Mama kept holding one arm; Ella clung to the other one, her face burrowed into it.

Mr. Richards turned his gaze back to Mama. "Sarah was content with her place until you showed up!"

Mama stared back at the man. Jordan shook all over, and her chest tightened up. She started to pant. She flashed on the image of Samuel being dragged away. Was this man going to grab her mama?

In an instant the cane was over his head, ready to strike.

Without thinking Jordan put her arm into the path of the stick, protecting Mama from the blow. The cane crashed onto her forearm. Jordan heard a loud crack and felt something give way. A stabbing pain shot through her arm, radiating out until it filled her entire body.

Mama grabbed the stick and twisted hard, forcing it from the raging maniac's grip. The bottom tip of the cane twirled around, smashing him in the face. He cried out and jerked back, falling off the horse. His body hit the ground with a thud, and Jordan heard the sound of the air getting knocked out of him. Her lungs clamped down in empathy, making it hard to take in air.

Mama leaned over the side of the wagon and yelled, "We protecting what ours, and not *yours*."

Jordan couldn't see the man, but she heard him whimpering from below.

"Don' you never strike my daughter again," Mama hissed to the ground. "Or I'm gonna kill you!" She looked like she meant it.

She raised the cane over her head and smashed it on the wagon rail. The carved stick split in half, with one side flying into the wagon bed. Ella and Sarah cried out and dodged it as it sailed past them. Mama threw the eagle-topped half of the cane into the bed of the wagon.

"Drive on," Mama told Jordan.

Jordan stared at her mama without making a move. Scared that he was truly injured yet hoping that he was no longer a danger, Jordan leaned over to get a glimpse of the man on the ground. Pain shot through her.

Blocking her way, Mama commanded, "Drive on!"

"Is he . . . ?" Jordan asked between shallow breaths.

"He don' matter! It between him and God right now," Mama declared. "Get goin.'"

Mama reached over, flicked the straps in Jordan's hand, and called out to get the horses moving. Jordan, jerked around by the sudden movement of the wagon, fell over onto Mama, but despite the pain in her arm, she held on to the reins. Mama pushed her upright, holding her steady with her strong arms. Jordan's heart was still pounding, and her head was too light. It took all her will to focus on the road in front of her.

Ella's young voice reported from the back, "He still down."

Jordan listened for the sound of pursuit, but the thrumming in her ears made it hard to hear.

"He ain' even sat up yet," Ella declared.

Jordan worked to take a deep breath; slow and jerky, she managed to force her lungs open a bit more. She swallowed hard and looked over at her mama, trying to make sense of what had just happened. Was it over—or was more to come?

"Still down. Maybe he dead!" Ella wondered.

"I don' think he dead, but he gonna be down for a while," Mama replied, sounding confident.

When she was finally able to speak, Jordan said, "Mama, you were so brave!"

Mama smiled wryly. "I been plottin' against men like him my whole life."

"Is he going to come after you?" Jordan asked. "Should I cut into the forest—to hide?" Protecting her mother was foremost on her mind.

"He ain't nothing but a coward and a bully. He the kind of man who gonna go back and say that he fell off his horse taking a jump. He ain't never gonna tell a soul a woman, a Negro woman, bested him," Mama said confidently. Then she whispered conspiratorially, "But go fast as you can just to be safe."

Jordan laughed weakly. "I sure hope you're right." She couldn't tell if Mama was just pretending to be so certain, but she stayed on the dirt road as her mother suggested.

Ella reported again. "The horse gone 'way, but that man still lyin' on the ground."

With that news, Jordan breathed a sigh of relief. Mr. Richards was a long way from help by foot, especially with injuries. They were safe. She looked over at Mama and smiled.

"You were right! Looks like he can't come after us."

"I shore hope Emmanuel and Lisbeth have as good a luck as us," Mama said.

"Me too, Mama," Jordan agreed.

"I'm gonna pray for them," Mama explained, and then she got quiet.

As the adrenaline slowly left Jordan's body, she felt the pain in her arm. The intensity grew with every bump in the road. Sweat beaded at her temples and her forehead, dripping into her eyes. The road became blurry, and her lids grew so heavy that she worked to keep them up. It took all her concentration to stay sitting upright. She felt the horses slow down, but her wrists didn't have the strength to flick the leather straps in her hands.

Mama stopped praying, looked at her, and said, "Jordan, stop the wagon."

Jordan tried to lift her arms to pull back, but they wouldn't move. Mama took the leather straps from her hand and tugged back on them until the horses came to a standstill. Surrendering to her body's demands, Jordan slumped over with her eyes closed, barely aware of whispering. Mama came around to her side and carefully guided her off the driver's bench. Gentle arms led Jordan to the back and helped her lie down in the wagon bed. Jordan heard but couldn't follow Mama's whispers.

"Baby, this gonna hurt a moment, but it gonna help you heal faster," Mama said loudly enough for Jordan to hear.

"Ahh!" Jordan screamed in pain. Mama was pulling on her arm. Jordan tried to take in a breath, but her lungs wouldn't work. Someone held her hand. She squeezed it hard, hard, hard, wanting to push the pain away. And then it was over.

"You gonna be fine, baby. You rest, and we gonna get us to the Johnsons." Mama kissed her forehead.

Through blurry eyes Jordan saw her arm was in a splint. Ella sat at her side, and the other two climbed into the front and got them going again. As she was surrendering to her dreams, Jordan heard them speaking.

"You know how to drive a wagon?" Sarah said in wonder.

"I shore do. You gonna learn how too," Mama replied confidently. Jordan smiled. Her mama deserved to be pleased; she had saved them from a bully, had set Jordan's arm, and was taking them where they needed to go. Despite the agony of her arm Jordan was so grateful— and so proud of her mama.

CHAPTER 21

LISBETH

Charles City County, Virginia

Lisbeth's heart sped up as they came to the fields. If any of the workers noticed them arriving in their wagon, they didn't show it. No heads turned; no one stood up straight to get a better look. The brown-skinned men continued slicing leaves off the tall tobacco plants, perhaps twenty people in all. Two White men sat on horses, patrolling the workers. Lisbeth felt sick at the sight of the whips on their saddles. This was a scene that was supposed to be history. One of the overseers rode toward them as Matthew brought their wagon to a stop.

Lisbeth exhaled loudly and gave Matthew's arm a squeeze. She whispered, "Good luck!"

The man climbed down from his horse, meeting Matthew and his brother Mitch on the ground. Emmanuel stayed in the back of the wagon. Lisbeth could hear his quiet breathing from behind her. She felt ready to jump out of her skin and could only imagine how much more worked up Emmanuel felt. His son was out there, being held captive. If he could contain his emotions, she was obliged to exude calm on the outside no matter how she felt on the inside. She forced herself to take steady breaths.

"Mitch." The man nodded and shook her brother-in-law's hand.

"Jesse." Mitch returned the courtesy. "This is my brother Matthew."

"How can I help you?" Jesse looked bored rather than hostile.

Mitch said to the man in the tan hat, "I've come for my laborer."

"What?" the man asked.

"You have one of my workers, and I want him back," Mitch said plainly to the overseer.

"What makes him *your* worker?" the man replied, sounding less bored, but still not hostile. "I have a lease on each one of these men."

"My brother here brought him from Ohio to harvest my crops," Mitch explained, pointing to Matthew. "They stopped in Richmond to visit kin, and he got rounded up for vagrancy. I need him to work on my farm."

"Take it up with the sheriff, not me," the man replied.

Lisbeth's attention moved between the conversation and the sweaty workers in the fields. Her eyes traveled from man to man, scanning for Samuel's lithe silhouette. One seemed familiar, and she stared at him hard, willing him to turn his head up. When he did, she sucked in her breath. It looked like William—Emily's husband.

Without turning around, Lisbeth said quietly, "Emmanuel, do you see Samuel?"

Emmanuel whispered back, "He in the middle of the middle."

Lisbeth concentrated on the figures in the middle until she saw Samuel. She nodded, though no one was looking at her.

"I believe I see William out there," she said. "To our left on the end. Do you agree?"

"I don' know him," Emmanuel reminded her, "so I can' say."

"Of course," Lisbeth said. She wasn't thinking clearly. She whispered, "Well, I believe it is him. I'll be right back."

She climbed down from the wagon, counting as she walked to Matthew—one . . . two . . . three—up to seven until she was by her husband's side. Lisbeth tugged on his arm to get his attention. He looked at her with a question in his eyes. She motioned with her head for him to speak with her in private. They stepped away from the two men negotiating for Samuel's release.

"I believe William is here," she whispered urgently. "We have to get him as well!"

"Who?" Matthew asked.

"Emily's husband," Lisbeth replied.

Matthew looked confused.

"The boy Sammy gave his glove to?" Lisbeth said, waiting for recognition in Matthew's eyes. When it came, she said, "His father!"

"Oh!" Matthew suddenly understood.

He nodded and walked to his brother. Lisbeth hoped Mitch would be savvy enough to go along with this change without argument. She stood close by to listen to their conversation, working to make herself unobtrusive. Matthew interrupted the two men.

"We need William too," he said, and pointed to the fields.

Mitch looked confused, as if he was about to ask a question.

Matthew quickly explained, "I brought three workers from Ohio with me: Samuel, William, and Emmanuel. Two just up and disappeared. I'd heard that Samuel was here, but lost track of William. Guess he got caught up in the same sweep."

"Why would you bring in workers from Ohio?" the overseer asked, his voice raised. "That don't make any sense!"

"You know how hard it is to find laborers these days. You think the sheriff is gonna lease them to us?" Mitch said. "We all gotta be creative these days."

"We paid sixteen dollars for them two," Jesse said. "I can't just take a loss like that."

Matthew scratched his head. "My wife's brother is the justice of the peace in Richmond; he sent me here," Matthew lied. He pulled the wad of money out of his pocket and counted it out. "Here's eight for Samuel, and eight more for William, plus twenty for your trouble."

Matthew stared at the man while slowly waving the US Treasury bills between his pointer finger and thumb. It was more than this man's monthly wages. The man scrunched his eyes and rubbed his cheek. A slow smile spread over his face, and he reached for the money.

"You shoulda led with that," the man said. "It's all about business, right. Take 'em. What do I care? I'll just ride the other niggers harder. The young one got roughed up a bit. He ain't used to hard work, but we showed him his place."

Samuel was injured! Lisbeth's insides felt hollowed out. Had they really secured his release? She slowly walked back to the wagon, working to appear calmer than she felt. At the wagon, she paused by the front.

Without being obvious she whispered to Emmanuel, "He says we can take them back with us!"

Emmanuel let out a long sigh. He bowed his head, and his lips moved in a silent prayer. Empathy crashed through Lisbeth. This experience felt unbearable to her; she could only imagine how overwhelmed and helpless Emmanuel must feel, having to sit in this wagon and watch while two White men negotiated money for his son's release. She burned with shame and rage.

Climbing onto the wagon seat, Lisbeth watched Matthew move into the rows of tobacco plants. It struck her that he had never met William. What if he walked up to the wrong man? She couldn't see them in the midst of the tall plants. She telegraphed a silent message to her husband: *Samuel knows William. Samuel knows William. Go to him first.* She forced herself to sit calmly, gazing out over the scene.

She saw Matthew's hat in the area where Samuel was harvesting. She let out her breath. Samuel would be able to find William. Lisbeth couldn't read Samuel's face from this distance, but after a brief reunion, the two of them walked toward the end of the field where William was picking.

William startled at their approach. He was hesitating. This was taking too long. She glanced at Jesse, the overseer. He was still chatting with Mitch, oblivious to the undercurrent. The other overseer was not. He'd turned his horse in their direction and was staring at the three men.

Lisbeth telegraphed another silent message: *They're safe people, William. You'll be safe if you come with us. I promise. Please come.*

The other overseer leaned forward to signal his horse to move. William noticed, looked at Samuel, and nodded. They walked back toward the wagon. William and Samuel were limping, their heads bowed down. They didn't look at either overseer or the other entrapped men as they trudged away. As they drew close to the wagon, Lisbeth caught a glance of Samuel's face. She gasped at the sight.

One of his eyes was swollen shut; a hot red line crossed the lid. Tiny slices marked the skin on his hands, some still bleeding. Lisbeth felt physically ill. She squeezed her hand hard and resisted the urge to react or look directly at him or William.

Matthew had stopped to chat with Mitch and the overseer. Lisbeth stared at them. She saw her husband throw back his head, laughing. A large grin on his face, Matthew shook hands with Jesse and waved to the other man on the horse in the fields. When he turned away from the overseers, his face fell flat and his eyes were hard.

As he climbed next to Lisbeth in the wagon, he quietly said, "May God forgive me for laughing at such sin."

Mitch, sitting to Lisbeth's right, said, "Brother, I pray God will forgive us for more than that; otherwise, heaven will be empty of White men."

A powerful, painful spirit hung in the air between the two men. Lisbeth studied Mitch. A touch of the madness and sorrow Mary's brother lived with was in her brother-in-law's eyes too. She searched her husband's face. If she was honest with herself, it was there as well. On the surface, he was calm and resolute, but underneath so much more was buried. Matthew nodded in shared understanding of his brother's words.

Lisbeth and Matthew usually pretended that the battlefield hadn't changed him, but in this moment she knew that was a lie. Throughout the United States, so many families believed the conflict was behind them, but it wasn't. In homes, cities, and states the war raged on— inside of those who had fought it. For all of them the certain line between good and evil had permanently blurred. They'd battled and lost, no matter the specific outcome of each skirmish. There was no winning when success meant you had destroyed another American— someone's son, husband, or father.

Matthew got the wagon moving. Lisbeth returned her attention to the fields, her heart full of emotion. She watched the tall plants jerk back and forth as the leased laborers cut tobacco leaves. Brown hands wiped sweat off brows between slices. One young man looked up and stared at her. He was hardly older than Sammy. The intensity in his dark-brown eyes pierced her soul. He mouthed, "Pray for me." Pain shot through Lisbeth like a physical arrow. She bit her lip hard to keep from yelling out.

She'd believed this was over, that slavery had been ended, but now she knew another truth. That boy's desperate brown eyes would startle her awake in the night. She was abandoning him, all of these boys and men, to this unjust fate. They'd succeeded in their mission to rescue Samuel and William, but that meant nothing to the ones they were leaving behind. She'd have to live with that for the rest of her life.

A tear running down her cheek, she closed her eyes and prayed, "God, please show mercy for these men and reunite them with their loved ones." It was a small act that felt completely inadequate for the horror of this situation. "And please forgive me for not doing more."

She squeezed her eyes tight and took a long, jerky breath to calm herself. She shook her head to clear it of any unpleasant thoughts, because this was no time for severe emotion. When she opened her eyes a rider was coming from the direction of the big house. Her pulse quickened, and she wiped her cheek dry.

"That's Edward!" she whispered to Matthew. "I am certain of it."

Her belief was confirmed when the rider came closer. Even though Edward's dark hair was mostly gray and he had gained considerable weight, Lisbeth immediately recognized his angry eyes.

"I hear someone is interfering with my plantation," Edward shouted as he pulled up next to Mitch, his chestnut-brown horse stomping in place. Peering around her brother-in-law, Edward startled when he saw Lisbeth framed between the two men.

His hard, cold eyes bore into Lisbeth. "You!"

Terror filled Lisbeth's body. Her heart pounded, and her mouth went dry. She slid her arm through Matthew's and pressed closer to him.

Lisbeth's mind flashed to the last time she'd seen this awful person, a man she'd believed she felt true affection for. But in truth she had only felt enamored with the idea of him. He had been furious when she came to White Pines to return his gifts and inform him that she had married Matthew. At the time, she'd feared he would hurt her, but she escaped without any lasting scars. Ending her engagement to him had been the most difficult, and best, decision of her life.

"We made a business deal with your overseer," Matthew said. "We don't mean you any harm."

Edward laughed. "Well, now we both know you are simply lying—because you have done nothing but harm me!"

Lisbeth pleaded, "Please, Edward, leave us be."

Edward's gaze narrowed at her. "Leave *you* be. Once again you come to my home, disturb my peace, and demand that I leave you be!" he scoffed. Madness showed in his eyes. "You do not belong here. What would possibly make you return?"

She had the urge to shout, *Something you don't understand at all: love and compassion.* Instead she calmly replied, "Family. We made a promise to our family. And we are keeping it."

Edward continued glaring at her. Lisbeth poked Matthew's pocket. He looked at her, and she nodded. He reached in to pull out the thick stack of money. That got Edward's attention.

Matthew counted out five bills. Lisbeth's heart raced to be giving away so much of Mattie's hard-earned savings. But the hungry look in Edward's eye told her that money was still all that mattered to him. Matthew passed the bills to Mitch.

"This should more than make up for your trouble, Edward," Mitch said as he held out the money. "Let's just make this business. Nothing personal."

Edward looked at the money, at Mitch, and then back at the bills. He glanced at Lisbeth, hatred in his eyes.

"You are not worth the trouble," Edward said. He grabbed the money and yelled, looking at all of them, "None of you are worth anything to me!"

Lisbeth turned her head toward Matthew and whispered, "Please, just move on."

Her husband flicked the reins, and the wagon lurched forward, startling Edward's nervous horse sideways. Lisbeth gazed ahead, feigning calm and ignoring the hatred of the man she'd nearly married. To steady her pulse she slowly took deep breaths in, and then she said a silent prayer of gratitude that this plantation was not her home.

CHAPTER 22

JORDAN

Charles City County, Virginia

Mama's scream woke Jordan. Heart hammering and the blood rushing from her limbs, Jordan scrambled to sit up. Pain shot from her arm through her whole body, forcing her to freeze despite her urgency. She rolled to her side and pushed up, being careful to protect her injured arm. She looked around, disoriented and confused. Mama was sprinting away from the wagon. Samuel stood ten feet away.

Jordan sighed with relief. They were back at the Johnsons'; Mama had screamed in delight.

Her mama reached Samuel and kissed him like he were a little boy. Ella scampered over Jordan to get a better look at the scene on that side of the wagon. Jordan's heart lurched as her emotions spun from terror to joy. Samuel was back, Ella was her cousin, and Sarah had left Fair Oaks. The pain of her arm was a small price to pay for the joy of this day.

Samuel accepted Mama's attention until she hugged him too enthusiastically. Mama pulled back. Jordan got a good look at his beaten face and gasped, her emotional compass spinning again.

"Oh, my baby! What did those monsters do to you?" Distress filled the older woman's voice.

"Mama, don't you think about it," Samuel reassured her weakly. "I'm back now. Let's just forget what happened."

Mama's face got hard. "I ain't never gonna forget . . . about any of it."

Taking Samuel's hands in her own, Mama studied them, turning them over to look at both sides. She gently touched the cuts with the tip of her finger. She looked up at her son's face, cupped his cheek gingerly, and shuddered.

Tears in her eyes, Mama said, "I shouldn' have asked you to come with me." Her voice cracked. "These hands ain't s'pose to look like this again."

The joy Jordan had been filled with moments before slipped away. She clenched her jaw in outrage for Samuel. Fury and sorrow caused tears to well up. It was so unjust. She felt like hitting something.

Jordan had never seen her mother look so defeated. Her heart twisted for her mama's pain and her own inability to protect either her mother or her brother.

Mama said, "Sorry ain't enough, but that's all I got."

Samuel just gazed at Mama, blinking, then bowed his head. Jordan held her breath, longing to hear Samuel reassure their mother that he was fine, but he only stared at the ground. After a long delay he shook his head like he was shaking off a memory.

Samuel looked up and gazed at the scene. He saw the wagon and slowly asked, "You got Cousin Sarah?"

"Uh-huh." Mama nodded.

"And?" Samuel asked.

"Ella her girl."

A wistful look on his face, Samuel smiled and nodded. "Today *is* a good day, Mama. No amount of hate can take that from us. We did God's work, coming here."

"Thank you, Son," Mama said, looking relieved. Samuel wrapped his arms around Mama, offering a gesture of reconciliation, but Jordan noticed he did not give her any reassurance that he was fine.

Cousin Sarah walked up to them, and Mama reintroduced Sarah to Samuel. Jordan was startled to remember that they hadn't yet met on this trip. It had been nineteen years since Samuel and Sarah had seen one another. Sarah and Ella felt like family to her now; it was hard to believe she didn't care about them a few weeks ago.

The battered screen door flew open. Pops walked out of the house carrying a pitcher, followed by Lisbeth holding a stack of cups. He stopped suddenly when he saw Mama talking to Samuel. He tipped his head back, eyes closed, and his lips moved as if he were praising God. Jordan was moved by the intensity of his emotion. He sure did love Mama.

Lisbeth, having left the cups on the little table on the porch, walked to Pops and wordlessly took the container from his hands. She patted his arm, and they shared a small smile. Pops walked down the stairs and wrapped his arms around Samuel and Mama. Lisbeth hung back on the porch, watching Mama's reunion with Pops, while Jordan watched her family from the wagon. Ella had joined them too. She stood close, watching the adults speak to one another.

Mama pointed to the wagon, and Pops made eye contact with Jordan. It was suddenly too much. All her held-back emotion burst through. Tears welled up in her eyes and spilled down her cheeks. As Pops walked over to her she took a shaky breath.

"Baby girl, we all okay. No need to cry, now," Pops soothed. He climbed up next to her in the wagon and hugged her gently while she let the tears flow.

She pulled back from the embrace and looked at her father. "Is . . . is Samuel all right?" Jordan asked.

"He gonna be jus' fine," Pops said. "I hear you saved your Mama."

Jordan shrugged with a shy smile.

Pops kissed her cheek. "This broke your arm?" Pops held up the top half of the walking stick. Jordan nodded.

"I've never seen Mama so fierce," Jordan said. "She slammed it down so hard it split right in two."

"Mattie a strong one when it's called for," her father confirmed with a nod.

Pops's calloused fingers rubbed the small metal eagle. Mama, Samuel, Sarah, and Ella came to the side of the wagon. Pops passed the stick to her brother.

"Look what yo' mama done in one whack," Pops said.

"Wow, Mama," Samuel said in admiration. "This is a thick stick."

"Big sticks need to be broke!" Mama said.

"Whatcha gonna do with it?" Pops asked.

Mama looked at Sarah, a question in her eyes. Their cousin shook her head with a shiver and replied, "I don' know what to do with such evil."

Sarah touched the beak of the eagle that had killed her mother for protecting Ella and Sophia from a cruel and hateful act. Jordan's heart welled up again. The joy and the pain were nearly too much to hold at once. Way deep in her soul she felt the gift of having her family reunited, but too many people didn't share that blessing.

Sarah looked around the circle. She swallowed hard. "Thank all you all for findin' my Ella. And comin' for me . . ." Her voice broke.

Jordan's mind flashed to a missing little girl. How could Cousin Sarah ever be fully at peace when Sophia was alone in the world with no one to care for her? Jordan looked from face to face, waiting for someone else to say the words of reassurance that filled her head. When none were offered, she screwed up her courage and said, "Cousin Sarah, we aren't going to forget about Sophia. We'll keep writing, searching, and asking until we find her too."

Or find out her fate, Jordan thought, but did not say out loud. Cousin Sarah smiled tenderly at her and took Ella's hand.

She said, "We gonna have a new life to welcome her to when we do find her."

Mama said, "Ella, you gonna love Oberlin. You gonna get to go to school, and our Jordan gonna be one of your teachers!"

Jordan's heart skipped a beat. It was time to be honest with herself . . . and her family.

Gently she said, "Mama, I'm not going back to Oberlin with you." Jordan blinked back the tears that were once again pushing against her eyeballs.

Mama sucked in her breath. "After all this?" She shook her head, looking hurt. "You still gonna go to New York?"

Jordan's throat was tight. "No, Mama," Jordan said. "I have to stay in Richmond . . . to teach at the freedmen's school. God's calling me to help the children from the orphanage get a hand up. I'm going to be a sower, right here."

Mama's shoulders dropped, and a tight, sad smile crossed her face. "It ain't so safe, you know?"

"You didn't teach me to be safe," Jordan replied. "You taught me to be brave." Jordan looked over, scared to see her father's reaction.

Pops said, "Anythin' I can say to change yo' mind?"

Jordan shook her head, tears seeping out the sides of her eyes.

"You are *just* like Mama," Samuel confirmed. "Once you set your mind to something, you make it happen."

Everyone laughed.

"I'll write letters every week," Jordan said. "I promise."

"That gonna be real nice," Mama replied. Then she whispered fiercely, "You leave at the first sign of trouble! You hear me?"

"Yes, Mama. I will." Jordan laughed through her tears.

"An' you tell any suitors that this ain't really home," Mama said, teasing, but not.

Jordan nodded. "Don't worry, Mama. When it's time for me to have babies, I know where I belong . . . with you at my side."

CHAPTER 23

LISBETH

Charles City County, Virginia

Lisbeth's heart nearly burst with pride and joy when Mattie marched up to her on the porch. The older woman pulled her into a long, tight embrace. Mattie pulled back and looked intently into Lisbeth's eyes.

"Thank you, Lisbeth." Mattie's warm hand cupped Lisbeth's face in affection. "You saved my son."

Lisbeth had finally made a substantial payment on the enormous debt she owed her beloved Mattie. Lisbeth beamed at her.

"All that's best in me came from you," Lisbeth said, choking up.

Mattie smiled and gave her another sweet hug.

"When I think . . ." Lisbeth shook her head. "I was *so* close to having that life. So much cruelty and fear would have been inside me, if you hadn't taught me otherwise. Thank you for giving me my life."

"You always had a good heart, Lisbeth. I taught you to trust it." Mattie continued. "And thank you for givin' me *my* life!"

Confused, Lisbeth asked, "What do you mean?"

"I always say Sarah wrote our ticket to freedom, so we owe her everythin'. But you's the one who started the teachin'." Mattie nodded, looking straight at Lisbeth.

Lisbeth's mind whirled. She'd never considered her impact on Mattie's life, only Mattie's influence on her. She smiled at Mattie, nodded, and squeezed her hand.

"I guess we are both fortunate that God brought us together."

"Yes indeedy," Mattie replied. "Blessed indeed."

Mattie sat down on the love seat and pulled Lisbeth down next to her. She patted Lisbeth's leg. Lisbeth slipped her arm through Mattie's, savoring a closeness she hadn't experienced in years.

Lisbeth watched Sadie lead Jordan up the front stairs to the porch, more enthusiastic than careful. Fortunately Emmanuel was supporting the injured young woman on the other side. Sadie directed Jordan to the wooden chair next to Lisbeth and then poured a glass of water for her favorite teacher. Lisbeth watched, touched by her daughter's desire to be helpful and caring. Jordan smiled at Lisbeth and mouthed a thank-you. Lisbeth wasn't sure what the thanks was for, but she nodded nonetheless.

Emmanuel placed something on the little table and said, "Here yo' prize." Then he walked away to manage the horses. Sammy ran up to Emmanuel, offering to be of assistance. Lisbeth was touched at Emmanuel's enthusiastic appreciation of the idea.

"Whoa!" Sadie squealed. "That's Mr. Richards's . . . from his grandpa! It's broken."

"He struck me with it," Jordan explained.

"I knew he was a bad man!" Sadie said, sounding outraged, but also proud that she was a good judge of character.

Jordan continued. "My mama snatched the cane away from him and snapped it in two."

Lisbeth was impressed. Sadie's eyes got big. She looked at Mattie with a little fear and a lot of respect in her eyes.

"I had to protect my baby!" Mattie told Sadie.

Sadie laughed. "She's not a baby."

"She ain't *a* baby anymore," Mattie replied, "but she always gonna be my baby."

"Can I hold it?" Sadie asked.

Mattie picked up the top half of the cane and handed it to Lisbeth's daughter. The little girl held it in one hand and rubbed the eagle with the other. She looked at Lisbeth in disbelief.

"Mr. Richards said the eagle represents the liberty of being American. He didn't mean us though, did he?" Sadie said.

"Why you say that, Miss Sadie?" Mattie asked.

Sadie thought for a moment, then said, "Well, ma'am, I don't think he believes my momma should get to vote or you should be free. How can you have the liberty of America if you can't vote or you aren't free?"

"You a wise little girl." Mattie chuckled. "I see my Jordan been yo' teacher!"

Sadie beamed and exclaimed, "My faaavorite teacher!"

"I wonder how old it is," Jordan said, still examining the cane.

"He said it was made in 1788," Lisbeth replied.

Jordan nodded. "The year the Constitution was adopted." The young woman went quiet, then said, "Eighty years old."

"That's old!" Sadie sounded impressed. "Don't you think so, Momma?"

Lisbeth nodded. "Older than all of us, even Granny and Poppy."

"In eighty years I'll be eighty-six," Sadie said. Her eyes rolled up in thought. "That will be in the nineteen hundreds! I think everyone will have liberty by then. Don't you think so, Momma? Miss Jordan?"

Lisbeth's heart hurt for her optimistic and confident daughter. Lisbeth looked to Jordan, hoping she had a good answer, but she too seemed to be searching for the right words to say to Sadie.

"Yes indeed!" Mattie interjected. "With little girls like you sayin' it should be so, ever'body gonna get liberty someday soon."

"My brother's speaking up too!" Sadie said.

The three women laughed. Lisbeth was grateful for Mattie's enthusiastic encouragement of Sadie's naïve beliefs. Someday she'd have to explain to her daughter that it would be a long road, perhaps a very long road, to true liberty for all. But Lisbeth was glad that for today her daughter could hold on to her belief in a better future.

Sarah and Ella joined their circle. Sadie crossed over to the little girl and asked if she knew the clapping game Little Sally Walker. Ella looked at Jordan and smiled.

"She does," Jordan explained to Sadie. "I taught her that recently, but she is very good already."

"My momma taught me," Sadie said.

"Guess who I learned it from?" Lisbeth asked her daughter.

Sadie shook her head from side to side. Lisbeth pointed to Sarah. Sadie's mouth dropped in exaggerated surprise. Lisbeth nodded her head, her eyebrows pulled up in affirmation.

"Really?" Sadie asked.

Lisbeth smiled and nodded. "Do you remember that, Mattie? Sarah?"

Sarah furrowed her eyebrows together and shook her head no.

"Sometimes I went to the quarters with Mattie. On one of those visits, when I was about six, Mattie asked you to teach me that game. I balked, but she insisted I 'learn something new, Lisbeth,'" Lisbeth said, imitating Mattie. "It was my favorite game for years. I played it with Mary whenever we had the chance, but don't think I ever got to be as fast as you!"

"I kinda 'member that now that you tell the story," Sarah said. "That was a lifetime ago." She got a faraway look in her eyes.

Ella stared at her mother, the woman she hadn't been close to for so many years.

Sarah noticed and smiled at the child. Then she asked her daughter, "You and me?"

Ella nodded shyly. She put up her hands. Sarah started the chant slowly, and they moved their hands in rhythm to the words. Sadie joined in. Lisbeth started to shush her, to give Ella and Sarah their time together, but Jordan chanted along with them, so she let Sadie continue chanting. Soon Mattie joined in, and finally Lisbeth as well. The six of them, mothers and daughters, chanted faster and faster until hands faltered, and laughter broke out.

"Feels good to laugh together," Mattie said.

"It sure does," Lisbeth agreed.

"Are you certain you will be safe?" Matthew asked his parents, concern filling his voice.

Lisbeth sat with her husband, her in-laws, William, and the Freedmans on the front porch. They were squeezing in a quick meal before leaving. The crowd of people ate picnic style, scattered around outside after filling their plates with food inside. Mother Johnson smiled at her son, nodded, and said, "We won't be intimidated by men who cling to power using violence."

"This is our home," Poppy replied. "It can seem as if we are alone, but many of our fellow Virginians are glad for the outcome of the war. It has been decided that we are *one* nation. The ballot box has to be more powerful than bullets."

Lisbeth appreciated the sentiment her in-laws were expressing in theory, but still she feared for their well-being.

"But will you be safe?" Matthew asked again.

"We did not leave during the war," Poppy reminded him. "We are not leaving now. So many have sacrificed more than we have."

Mother Johnson took Matthew's hand, looked into his eyes, and said, "You made your choice. We have made ours. I hope you will accept ours, as we have accepted yours."

Matthew stared at his mother, clearly torn, his face showing a mixture of sorrow and fear. Like Matthew, Lisbeth would prefer to have his parents be close and safe, but it was neither Lisbeth's nor Matthew's decision. They'd had this very same conversation many times over the years. Her husband exhaled slowly and nodded in consent.

"If you change your mind, there is always a place for you with us," Matthew said.

Lisbeth inserted, "And Mitch too, of course."

Matthew's parents nodded back at them, their eyes shining, obviously touched by their offer.

"We are blessed to know that we have a safe sanctuary, should we need it," Mother Johnson said.

Father Johnson cleared his throat and said, "Thank you, Son. Now let's see about getting you all home safely."

Nods went around the circle. The conversation was over—for now.

Emmanuel spoke up. "Matthew, you drive a wagon with all the women and children. Samuel, William and I gonna go get Emily and

Willie and meet you in Washington. William says you gonna be safe there waiting for us, right?"

"Washington don' take any stock in Virginia lawmen; that's for sure," William replied. "We all be safe if we can cross into DC."

Matthew sighed. "I can't say I like being left out, but that seems like a wise plan."

Lisbeth looked over at Mattie. The older woman was shaking her head. She looked as doubtful as Lisbeth felt.

"I have given this much thought," Lisbeth said, clearing her throat and pulling out her courage. "William, I understand you wish to get Emily and Willie, but it will be safer, for all of us, if *I* do it."

The men startled and stared at her, doubt covering their faces. Matthew started to speak an objection.

Lisbeth raised a hand to quiet him. "Please hear me out," she insisted. "We can all travel together to Richmond. You will remain hidden in the public square park while I go *alone* to my parents' home, which is only a few blocks away. I will act as if I have returned to nurse my father, and say that Matthew and the children have remained at his parents' for a few days. Late in the night, after everyone is asleep, I will wake up Emily and Willie. We can leave quietly in the dark without raising any suspicions."

Matthew challenged, "Lisbeth, is it wise to put yourself at risk? What if Jack learns that we came for William and Samuel?"

"I do not believe that Edward will be racing off to another county to publicly share his humiliation with Jack or anyone else. You paid him well. He cares more for money and his pride," Lisbeth said. "We will be gone from Richmond before the sun rises."

Emmanuel looked as if he was going to say something, when Mattie spoke up. "That sounds like a real wise plan, Lisbeth."

Grateful to have an ally, Lisbeth smiled at Mattie. Tension rose in the circle.

Lisbeth looked at Matthew, but her message was for all of the men. "Of course it will be hard for you to hide in a park and wait, but this will be the simplest way to get Emily and Willie without detection, confrontation, or violence."

Doubt wrestled with agreement in Matthew's eyes. Lisbeth looked around at the faces. "Do not let your pride put Emily and Willie, or any of us, at risk," she declared. "Getting all of us to Ohio without further injury is our goal, correct?"

"Mm-hmm," Mattie agreed.

The two of them stared down the men, until Matthew finally nodded.

"You're right," he said. "Our chances to get everyone out of Virginia safely will be greater if you get Emily and Willie." He exhaled heavily, then said, "We'll wait in the park, but if you get detained, I'm coming to get you."

Lisbeth nodded.

"You up for this?" William asked Lisbeth.

"Absolutely!" Lisbeth said with a smile. She displayed an easy confidence, but she was also scared. This *was* the best way to move forward—but she was going to be unsettled until they were all in the wagons, driving away from Richmond.

"Elizabeth, I am so glad you have returned," Mother gushed, opening her arms for an embrace. Recognizing the sentimental mood that came from laudanum, Lisbeth leaned in to kiss her on the cheek. Mother grabbed Lisbeth's hand and pulled her down next to her on the davenport.

Mother looked directly at Lisbeth, her eyes welling up. "Your father has taken on the death rattle," the older woman said. "The end is soon, likely tonight. I'm so relieved you are here to be with him."

Sadness welled up in Lisbeth. Her throat tightened, and she swallowed hard. She was surprised that she was still concerned for the well-being of her parents. It was going to be harder than she had imagined to walk away from them again tonight—this time for good—without so much as a goodbye.

"I have made a decision," Mother said, sounding eager, "to accept your offer to live with you after your father's affairs are settled."

Lisbeth's stomach flipped.

"While you were away I realized that despite all you have done to me, I find you comforting, as only a daughter can be."

Lisbeth felt nauseous. For years she'd longed to have her mother come to Ohio. Now she was willing, just when Lisbeth was going to commit a final act of betrayal—abandoning her mother without explanation. It was unforgivable. What kind of daughter was she? But then she thought of her family, and Mattie and William waiting at the public square. Her own brother had intentionally arrested William and Samuel. Mother would never understand why she had worked for their release. Lisbeth nodded to her mother, pretending to agree with her plan.

"Go sit with your father. You will be a comfort to him. Even if his mind is not aware of your presence, his soul will be," Mother commanded. "I will send Emily with a tray when she has finished making supper."

Walking up the stairs, Lisbeth realized her mother was so selfish that she hadn't even noticed that Matthew, Sadie, and Sammy were not with her.

Father had changed dramatically. It was hard to believe they had left Richmond only yesterday morning. His eyes were sunken into his head, and his arms were abnormally thin. With each jerky breath his lungs gurgled disturbingly loud. A sickening smell of decay filled the room, despite the open window. Lisbeth took shallow breaths through her mouth to avoid the stench.

She sat down in the chair next to her father and took his hand; it was cold and flaccid.

"It's Lisbeth, Father." She cleared her throat. "Elizabeth. I'm being brave again. Though I'm not so sure you would approve this time, but I've made my choice."

Lisbeth studied her father, hoping for some sign of awareness, but nothing changed on his face. She'd have to just imagine that he'd approve, though his blessing was not something she used to make choices.

She reached for the book sitting on the marble-topped side table and resumed reading out loud, despite the distractingly loud sounds coming from her father. She'd made it through two more chapters of *A Tale of Two Cities* when Emily walked in with a tray. Lisbeth's heart leaped. She stood to take the tray from Emily and set it down. Then she leaned in so close their shoulders touched.

Lisbeth whispered, "Please stay calm."

Emily's eyes went wide with terror. "You have news of William?"

Lisbeth nodded and quietly confirmed, "Yes, good news."

Emily's hand flew to her mouth. It was shaking. Her gaze bored into Lisbeth.

Lisbeth's eyes darted to her father to confirm that he was not aware of their conversation.

"We lied about the reason for our visit to Matthew's parents." Lisbeth continued in hushed tones. "We went to secure Samuel's release. We found William as well, and he has been freed."

Emily gasped, and her eyes welled up with tears. "Truly?"

Lisbeth nodded.

Emily closed her eyes and tilted her head back. "Thank you, Lord." She took a slow, steady breath, her eyes still closed.

Lisbeth took Emily's hands and watched the jerky movements under her lids.

Emily slowly opened her eyes. "I thought I would never see my husband again." She shook her head as if to clear it. "Thank you! Lisbeth, I . . . don't know what to say."

Lisbeth smiled at Emily. Her gratitude was palpable.

"Where is he?" Emily asked.

"We believe he will continue to be targeted," Lisbeth explained. "I've come back to get you and Willie."

Emily looked confused.

"We are all going to Oberlin," Lisbeth whispered. "Tonight."

The door opened, startling Lisbeth and Emily. Mother walked in, wiping her eyes on a handkerchief.

Quickly Lisbeth said, "Thank you, Emily. That is all," and signaled with her eyes. Lisbeth hoped Emily got the unspoken message to pack up and be ready to leave in the night. They wouldn't have a chance to speak again before it was time to escape.

Emily left, and Mother settled into the chair on the other side of the bed.

"I've informed your brother that I will be leaving with you," Mother said with a sigh. "He was quite upset, but I must take care of my own needs. He can attend to your father's affairs and manage disposing of the household goods to pay the debts," she explained.

Lisbeth's mind and spirits reeled. Mother studied her face. Lisbeth took a long, slow breath, struggling to appear calm so as not to raise any suspicions.

"You think me callous, but I am not. I am sensible," Mother practically shouted, trying to be heard over the sounds of the dying man's jerky breaths. "Your father and I had a practical marriage. I am fond of him, and I will miss him, but I will not wallow in sentimentality."

Mother's red-rimmed eyes betrayed the struggle within her. Suddenly it was quiet. Lisbeth and Mother looked at the man in the bed. Lisbeth's heart squeezed tight. Had Father just taken his last breath? She placed her hand on his chest, sending him a blessing on his way. His head lurched back, and he took in another loud breath. It was not over yet.

Agitated by the disturbing sound that filled the room again, Lisbeth closed her eyes and took in a deep, slow breath while asking

God to help her stay calm and strong. When she opened her eyes, Mother was no longer in the chair. She stood by the door, her hand on the knob, ready to leave.

"I cannot bear this," Mother explained, her lips pursed tight. "I hoped we could face this together, but I do not have the strength. I will wait downstairs; please inform me when he has taken his last breath."

Lisbeth stared at the woman who had borne her, anger, annoyance, and pity churning inside her. Her mother was a coward, running away from her own husband's death.

"Goodbye, Mother," Lisbeth said, sounding too formal even to herself. Her mother looked at her strangely. Her eyebrows drew together; she pinched her lips and shook her head.

"Good night, Elizabeth," Mother said, and left Lisbeth alone with her dying father.

———————— ❧ ☙ ————————

Restless and impatient, Lisbeth sat at her father's side. She tried reading out loud, but soon gave up on that because his breathing was so loud that she had to shout to be heard over it, which was not soothing for either of them.

She held his ice-cold hand and hummed what she hoped was his favorite hymn. Partway through the second verse, he was suddenly silent. She stared at his chest. Was that his last breath? At once sad and relieved, she slowly counted: one, two, three, four.

His chest jerked, and the loud gurgles of the death rattle filled the room again. Lisbeth sighed and sat back. As much as she wanted it to be, it wasn't over yet.

Lisbeth heard the clock declaring a new hour. Ten. She did not have much more time before she must leave. *Dear God, please have him pass over soon,* she prayed. It would be much easier to leave if he had taken his final breath.

When the clock struck eleven the thought of placing a pillow over his mouth to help the process along crossed her mind, but she decided against it. It wasn't her place to decide such matters; he was in God's hands. She continued to hum, watch, and pray.

Eventually the clock struck midnight, and she needed to leave even though her father was still alive. Despite the distance between them, it was a painful choice. He was entirely unaware of her presence, but she knew that she was abandoning her father to be alone in his last hours.

She looked at the dying man. Lisbeth put a hand over his heart and whispered, "God, please judge this man with mercy, and if you see fit, invite him into your circle." Then she leaned over and kissed her father's ice-cold cheek. It wouldn't be long now.

"Goodbye, Father," she said, swallowing hard.

She stood up to leave, taking the Bible and the *Tale of Two Cities* from his bedside table. Lisbeth slowly opened the door and listened carefully. As she had hoped, the house was quiet and dark. She went to her room to grab her carpetbag. After putting the books in it, she tiptoed down the stairs, startling at every creak or sound.

At the bottom of the stairs, she froze at the open parlor door. Mother was sitting in the dark, in Father's chair. Lisbeth's mind spun an excuse.

"He's resting comfortably. I need some water," Lisbeth explained in hushed tones, hoping the quiver in her voice would be attributed to unshed tears rather than fear. She kept the bag hidden behind her body.

Her mother made no response. Slowly Lisbeth stepped closer to the old chair and saw Mother's lids were down; she was fast asleep. Lisbeth snorted, somewhat amused. She scanned the room. *Goodbye,* she thought.

Lisbeth continued down the hallway, through the kitchen, to the door in the back. She didn't knock, but slowly turned the knob.

Emily and Willie were sitting on the bed, dressed and ready to travel, packed bags at their feet, fear on their faces. Lisbeth sighed in relief. She smiled at Willie, hoping to offer a small reassurance to the scared boy, and placed her finger to her lips to ask him to be silent. Lisbeth gestured with her hand for them to come. She jumped and froze when she heard the click of a knob, but it was only Emily closing the door to their room. Very quietly, they escaped through the back door.

Though the night was warm, Lisbeth shivered. Every one of her senses was on high alert, and she looked around to see if they were being followed along the empty street. Emily and Willie held hands right behind her without speaking. A lantern might have betrayed them, so she had not brought one, but the moon was just bright enough to light their way for the two-block journey to the public square's park.

They crossed Monroe Street. One more block to the public square. After crossing Henry Street she pointed to the direction they would walk to get to the stand of trees where the wagons and people were waiting. They walked on the dirt path through the deserted park, Lisbeth gaining confidence with each step.

She heard the sound of a gun being cocked, and her heart exploded. She froze and felt Emily stop beside her. The two women spun around, Emily pulling Willie behind them.

Jack was pointing a gun straight at her heart. Adrenaline shot through Lisbeth's body.

"I can't think of one reason not to shoot you right now," her brother slurred in a drunken state. He swayed a bit; his eyes were bloodshot, his cheeks flushed red.

Lisbeth's chest clenched so hard she felt like she was being stabbed. Emily grabbed her arm. Lisbeth's eyes were riveted to the weapon. Matthew, Sammy, and Sadie flashed into her mind. Her children would be devastated! Her mind raced for words, anything that might stop her brother.

"Sadie! You care for her, you do," Lisbeth implored, staring desperately into her brother's eyes. "Please don't make her motherless, Jack. I beg of you."

Jack's eyebrows drew together just a touch—her words had penetrated.

Suddenly Jack jerked over sideways, falling to the ground. Lisbeth gasped and lunged backward. The gun flew from his hand and bounced twice on the earth. He didn't even reach for it; instead his arm stayed strangely close to his side. She noticed a rope pulling tight around his middle, Samuel holding the other end of it. Emmanuel rushed out of the darkness and kicked the firearm far away from Jack.

Lisbeth's knees collapsed. Emily caught her before she hit the ground hard. Lisbeth's head was spinning so fiercely she started to faint. Emily put a cool hand on her neck and encouraged her to bend her head low. She heard yelling, but she couldn't track any specific words. A low voice spoke next to her. Lisbeth took a deep breath; her head still bent downward, she opened her eyes and looked to the side. Out of the corner of her eye, she saw William kneeling next to Emily, Willie hugging him from behind.

Slowly Lisbeth raised her head, testing her ability to stay upright. Her equilibrium was returning. She blinked her eyes to clear them. Jack was on the ground, the rope wrapped around his body and a gag covering his mouth. Samuel and Emmanuel stood over him, Samuel looking like he was getting ready to shoot Jack.

Mattie walked up to her son and placed a calming hand on his arm. "God don' like ugly, even when it deserved. God love mercy."

Samuel glared at his mother. She stared right back.

Mattie said, "You gonna feel better for one moment if'n you hurts him right now. But you gonna sleep better next year, and all the years to come, if'n you jus' walk away."

Samuel looked at his mother, then back at Jack. Indecision wrestled on his face.

"For Lisbeth," Mattie said calmly. "How she gonna go on knowin' you kill her brother? Little Sadie? Sammy? You really gonna kill they uncle?"

Samuel looked at Lisbeth, anger burning in his eyes. She took in a shaky breath and exhaled hard. Then she shrugged. She had no right to tell him what to do, but Mattie was right. It would be hard to live with Jack's death if it came from her choices.

Samuel leaned over and whispered something only Jack could hear. Her brother yelled—unintelligible words garbled through the gag. Then Samuel walked away, leaving the rope on the ground. Lisbeth let out the breath she hadn't realized she'd been holding.

William told Emmanuel, "We can bring him farther into the trees. If we tie him up good he won't get free until we are in Washington."

"The laudanum!" Emily declared.

All eyes turned to her.

"If he's found out here, there will be a pursuit," Emily explained. "But if we give him laudanum, we can return him to his study. We will be in Washington before he wakes."

"Laudanum?" Emmanuel asked. "Where you suppose we gonna get that?"

"My father's bedside," Lisbeth stated with a nod.

Mattie clicked her tongue against the roof of her mouth and shook her head. "That sound risky."

Without thought Lisbeth said, "I am expected to be there. I will go back and return with the laudanum. Then Emily and I can bring Jack home after we have given him a nice, strong dose."

Jack yelled through the gag, startling Lisbeth and causing adrenaline to pour into her. She looked at him and quickly turned away. She wasn't going to think about him. Emmanuel tugged on the rope. Jack continued protesting, but it wasn't going to do him any good. Lisbeth set off in a fast walk without waiting for permission or for her own fear to stop her.

Lisbeth's heart pounded with every step. She counted as she walked the two blocks to her parents' home—returning to *one* each time she got somewhere in the twenties. She pushed aside any fearful thoughts and did her best to simply breathe as she walked, but it was difficult to force air into her tight lungs.

The kitchen was just as she had left it, dark and empty. Mother still slept in the parlor. Lisbeth carefully tiptoed up the stairs, rehearsing an excuse should her mother find her.

Father looked smaller and more drawn. His loud intermittent breaths still filled the room. Lisbeth crossed to the bedside, picked up the laudanum, and started to leave; then her soul tugged her back. She placed her hand on her father's chest to send him a silent blessing and perhaps a final farewell.

While she was standing over the dying man, the door opened, making her jump. She composed her face to cover her deceit and looked over to find Julianne framed by the doorway.

"Jack is not here?" the young woman asked, looking around the room, pain and confusion in her voice.

Lisbeth shook her head and lied, "I have not seen him tonight."

Julianne studied the figure in the bed. Staring at her sister-in-law, Lisbeth worked to hide her nerves. Every part of her wanted to rush back to the public square park to get this evening behind her.

Slowly turning her attention away from Father and toward Lisbeth, Julianne stared at her, a vacant look in her eyes. Lisbeth's body thrummed with impatience and anxiety.

"Jack tells me you've convinced your mother to abandon us to live with you," Julianne said, her voice flat.

Lisbeth bit her lip and nodded slightly.

Julianne's eyes filled with tears. "She has been so cruel to me that I should celebrate her departure, but . . ."

Lisbeth waited, not without sympathy.

". . . I do not relish living alone with your brother."

Julianne blinked slowly, sighed, and turned around. She left, the door closing with a click behind her. Lisbeth put her hand on her chest and took steadying breaths. She had no great fondness for her sister-in-law, but Lisbeth felt compassion for the woman. Julianne's life would continue to be marked by sorrow and disorder.

Lisbeth waited for as long as she could bear it, wanting to be confident that Julianne was gone. She felt for the laudanum in her pocket, touched her father's arm goodbye, and walked away from this home for the second time in one night, knowing that it still wouldn't be the last.

She rushed through the dark night to the spot where she had left the others. A rush of love swept over her when she saw that Matthew and Sammy stood with the group of people towering over Jack. Matthew looked greatly relieved when he saw her. He shook his head and walked over to her. He and Sammy wrapped her in an enormous hug.

"Sadie?" Lisbeth asked, worried.

"She's safe. Jordan and Mattie are caring for her," Matthew reassured her. He went on, doubt in his voice. "Emmanuel says you plan to return to the house? With Jack?"

Lisbeth gave a single nod and held up the laudanum.

"Well done." Emmanuel smiled at her.

Lisbeth uncorked the dropper and finally let herself look at Jack. He glared at her with a mixture of fear and rage.

"I'm sorry it had to come to this, Brother. I wish you had not come after me. We won't hurt you, and truly, I hope for the best for you, and Julianne, and Johnny." Her voice cracked. "And Mother. I will pray for all of you. Every day."

Lisbeth filled the dropper all the way to the top and started to lean over. Jack yelled and kicked at her, so she retreated. Matthew knelt down to hold Jack's legs. Emmanuel grabbed Jack from behind, locking his arms and head in place. He nodded at Lisbeth.

She leaned over and grabbed her brother's jaw with her left hand. His mouth was shut tight, but she shoved the dropper between his cheek and gums. When he realized what she'd done, her brother tried to spit, but she held his mouth closed. She squeezed the dropper hard and fast, over and over, emptying it as best as she could. Not moving, she waited until she felt his body slacken a bit.

Then she filled up the dropper and gave him the same dose as her mother. Within moments he was slack. His eyes closed, his breathing slowed, and his muscles relaxed. Matthew and Emmanuel loosened their grips. When Jack didn't lash out, Matthew stood up.

Lisbeth put the dropper back in the bottle and put the elixir into her pocket. She wanted to get Jack back to the house so they could get out of this place as soon as possible.

She looked at Emily, indicating with her eyes that the other woman should move to Jack's right side.

"Jack, we're taking you home," Lisbeth said gently, as if she were talking to a child. "You need to walk, but we will help you." Emmanuel and Matthew got her brother to his feet. He was impaired, but able to walk with support and follow directions.

"We can walk him to the door," Matthew said, looking at Emmanuel for confirmation. Emmanuel nodded.

"No!" Lisbeth was adamant. "We are not risking detection now. No one will be alarmed if they see me and Emily."

Lisbeth slid between her husband and her brother on Jack's left. Emily did the same on his right. He leaned on them, but they managed his weight.

Without speaking, the two women set off for the Wainwright home, Jack stumbling along between them. Lisbeth felt Matthew's worry as they walked away, but she didn't look back; she just kept on moving forward.

Lisbeth readied herself for a fight with Jack, but he was cooperative. The laudanum was serving its purpose. The three of them moved as one, an odd three-headed figure in the dark.

"Do you know she is our sister?" Jack slurred the question, breaking the silence of the night. He swung his head around and stared at Lisbeth, his legs continuing to flop toward the house. Lisbeth looked at Jack, then at Emily over his shoulder.

"Well?" Jack challenged, a little more energy in his voice. "Do you?"

"Yes, Jack," Lisbeth whispered, uncomfortable to be speaking of this directly. She gazed at Emily to see her reaction, but only saw her profile. She was watching where they were going.

"She looks like you," Jack proclaimed. "Every time I see her she reminds me of your betrayal. And now it is complete. I told Mother it was unwise to invite you here."

He looked like he was trying to work up some outraged resistance, but then gave up. His head flopped forward, and he closed his eyes. Silence filled the air again.

Lisbeth breathed deeply to steady her nerves. They crossed Henry Street, and Lisbeth scanned for strangers, but the street was quiet. Once again, they made it to the house without seeing another person.

Emily and Lisbeth brought Jack to his study. Working as one they wordlessly laid him down on the couch, but he popped back up again.

"Sir, it's time to sleep," Emily soothed him.

Jack looked at her with a question in his eyes. "Emily?"

"Yes, sir. You been out drinking again, sir. You jus' sleep it off down here. I make sure Miss Julianne don' learn about it."

Jack looked back and forth at Emily and Lisbeth, confusion in his eyes.

"Your sister here to help you too, sir," Emily said. "Would you like one more?"

She signaled to Lisbeth with her eyes. Lisbeth understood the unspoken direction and searched through Jack's desk until she found a bottle of whiskey and a glass in the bottom drawer. She poured a large portion into the clear cup, her hand shaking so much that liquid spilled over the side, splashing the fragrant amber liquid onto the desktop. Her first instinct was to be more careful, but then she realized she didn't need to be. Emily patted her pocket before Lisbeth handed the glass to Jack. More laudanum? Lisbeth felt alarmed. Would that be too much? Emily nodded emphatically. Lisbeth trusted her judgment and squirted another dropper of liquid into the glass, then handed it to Emily.

Sitting up against the couch, Jack dozed with his eyes closed. Emily held the drink to his lips without saying a word. Slowly she tipped the liquid into his mouth until he'd swallowed half of it; then she turned the glass so quickly that the rest of the whiskey spilled down his chin and ran over his shirt. He opened his eyes and looked at his chest, confused.

"Oh, sir, you spilled a little. No worries," Emily soothed. "You jus' get comfortable right here."

She took his shoulders firmly between her hands and tugged him sideways until he was lying down. He grumbled and muttered, looking around, confusion in his eyes.

"Emily?"

"You jus' go right to sleep, sir." Emily put on a thick accent. "I gonna take care of everythin' for you."

Jack blinked his lids, nestled into the couch, and closed his eyes. The two women stood by silently. Soon the soft sounds of snoring came from his form. Lisbeth felt the tension drain from her body.

"You were very good at that," Lisbeth said, impressed.

"I've had a lot of practice," Emily replied with a wry smile.

Pulling out the bottle of laudanum, Lisbeth said, "Let's return this to Father's bedside."

Lisbeth wanted to rush upstairs, but she forced herself to go slowly. Julianne or Mother might be nearby, and she did not want to alert them that anything was amiss.

Lisbeth paused at the door, uncertain about what she would find on the other side. She turned the knob, Emily close behind. The room was dark, and the air smelled foul. The loud rattle of dying breaths filled the room. Father was still alive. Lisbeth let out a sigh. She didn't relish once again leaving him to face his death alone. She looked at Emily. They crossed to each side of his bed and looked down at the man who had fathered them both. Lisbeth let that understanding sink in a bit further. Emily was her sister. She still didn't know what that meant, but she was glad to have the truth of it.

Lisbeth startled at the sound of fumbling at the doorknob. The two women looked over in unison. Lisbeth expected to see Julianne, but she was surprised to see Mother, disheveled and bleary-eyed. She stared at the two women, looking back and forth between them for too long, hostility and pain in her eyes.

Along with fear and disappointment, a new emotion rose in Lisbeth—sympathy. This woman, her mother, had been forced to live with Emily for decades. How soon after her wedding did the nineteen-year-old bride learn that the beautiful, light-skinned girl was her husband's daughter? Lisbeth could barely imagine the confusion and betrayal she must have felt at the time, and perhaps every day since.

Finally Mother stopped glaring at the two young women and looked at her husband in the bed. She asked, "Is he gone?"

The sounds of his breathing were so loud that the answer was obvious. The question was strange, but Lisbeth answered, not unkindly, "No."

Mother walked to the end of the bed and stared at Father's face. "This is taking forever," she declared. "It is making me ill."

"We can get you to bed, ma'am," Emily said, and took Mother's arm.

"Don't touch me!" Mother jerked her arm away and scolded Emily. "*My* daughter is here, now. *She* will help me."

Lisbeth raised an eyebrow at Emily and signaled with a hand for her to stay there. Lisbeth took the soon-to-be widow's hand and led her out of the room, taking the laudanum with her.

"I have your medicine, Mother." Lisbeth adopted Emily's soothing voice. "We'll get you tucked in, and you won't have to think about any of this."

Despite her newfound sympathy, Lisbeth was still going to abandon this woman. In the morning, her mother's life as she knew it would be over. She'd have to move, dependent on the mercy of her bitter drunkard son. Lisbeth felt sick at her own capacity for deception, to uphold appearances, but from the moment of her birth, her mother had taught her well.

Once again, Lisbeth wished only to escape from this life.

After leaving the house for the third time that night, Lisbeth and Emily made it to the stand of trees and found their people. Matthew and Sammy rushed to her as she walked up and welcomed her back in an extended embrace.

"Momma, Willie says you rescued him!" Sammy beamed at his mother.

"I suppose I did." She smiled back at him. She was no Harriet Tubman, but today she'd done what had to be done, at least for a few people.

"I hope you won't make a habit of it," Matthew said. "My heart can't take the stress!"

"I promise I have no intention of repeating the experiences of this night, ever again," Lisbeth reassured him.

Sammy pointed. "Can I ride in the wagon with Willie?"

She looked at Matthew. He nodded, and she replied, "I don't see why not."

"Thanks," Sammy yelled as he ran off to join his friend.

"Where is Sadie?" Lisbeth asked Matthew.

He pointed to one of the wagons. Her daughter was asleep, curled up with her head resting on Jordan's lap. Lisbeth joined them in the wagon bed.

"Thank you for giving her comfort," Lisbeth said, patting her daughter's back. Oh, to be so innocent.

Jordan smiled and nodded. Most of the time Lisbeth didn't think of this Jordan as the same precious baby she'd loved so many years ago, but in this moment, time folded and she fully felt that the lovely young woman in front of her was the same person as the infant she had carried in her arms.

Lisbeth's heart welled up. "You were the first baby I ever loved, Jordan."

Jordan gave a small laugh. "My mama tells me that. I know you made my blanket, which I still have, but I don't remember." She shrugged.

"Of course you don't," Lisbeth said. "You were so young, hardly more than a year when you left."

The two women sat in silence in the dark, with Sadie sleeping between them. Lisbeth watched the others getting ready to go to Washington. She had more to say, but felt vulnerable.

Eventually she screwed up her courage. "Thanks for sharing your mama with me. I'm not one of her real children. But she's the best mother I had."

"I'm not so sure about that," Jordan replied.

Lisbeth looked at Jordan, her eyebrows furrowed in a question.

"I'm not so sure that you aren't one of her 'real' children," Jordan clarified. "In our own peculiar way, we're a family of sorts."

A sweet warmth passed through Lisbeth. She certainly felt more of a kinship with Mattie, Samuel, and Jordan than she did with her mother, father, and brother. It was sweet to know Jordan might feel something similar toward her.

Sadie stretched her head up and looked around. "Momma! You're back. Did you get Willie?"

Lisbeth nodded at her daughter. Whatever was left of the conversation with Jordan would go unsaid.

"Then we get to go home!" Sadie declared. "Right, Miss Jordan?"

"Sadie," Jordan said gently, her voice full of emotion. "I'm not going back to Ohio."

Sadie's face fell. "You aren't?!"

Lisbeth's heart hurt for her daughter.

Jordan shook her head and replied, "I'm going to be a teacher in Richmond, with the freed little children. And some not-so-little ones."

Lisbeth said to Jordan, "Your mother will miss you."

Jordan nodded.

Sadie looked at Lisbeth, her chin quivering. "Is it bad that I'm sad?"

Lisbeth pulled Sadie onto her lap for a cuddle. "It's never a sin to love."

"I will come for visits," Jordan reassured Sadie. "When I do, will you come to dinner?"

"Can I, Momma?" Sadie asked, looking at Lisbeth with such hope in her eyes.

Lisbeth nodded. "That would be real nice." She smiled at Jordan. "For all of us."

———— ❧ ————

Sadie cuddled up against Lisbeth in the back of the wagon. They were stopped in front of Miss Grace's home, dropping Jordan off. After they said their farewells they were going to drive through the night, heading north into Washington, DC, and through Pennsylvania to Ohio. They were confident they would be safe once they crossed out of Virginia. In the unlikely event that Jack followed them, they would be hours ahead of him. Lisbeth sincerely believed he would be too overwhelmed with Father's death, and his own humiliation, to seek them out so far from home, especially in the heart of the federal government.

Lisbeth watched Jordan saying goodbye to her family. She saw Mattie reach into her bodice and pull out her shell necklace. She slipped it over her own head and placed it over Jordan's. The younger woman started to protest. Lisbeth couldn't hear what Mattie said, but she saw them hug.

Sadie said, "Her necklace is just like yours!"

Lisbeth replied, "It sure is." Lisbeth pulled it out and fingered the shell. "Mattie gave this to me to remind me that her love would always be with me."

"When I grow up will you pass yours to me?" Sadie asked.

Lisbeth looked at Sadie and thought about all that she had already passed on to her; then she nodded, and said, "I sure will."

"Momma," Sadie said, sounding very serious.

"Sadie," Lisbeth replied, matching her daughter's tone.

"Sammy says he's gonna introduce Willie as his friend at school. And he says I get to introduce Ella as my friend, but I don't think that's quite right."

Lisbeth asked, "Why not?"

"I don't know." Sadie shrugged. "They just seem like they are something different than friends."

Lisbeth understood what her daughter was struggling with. What were these people to them? Lisbeth looked around at the faces of the group who would be making the journey back home with them: Samuel, Emmanuel, Mattie, Sarah, Ella, Emily, William, and Willie.

"You can tell everyone they're your kith, Sadie."

"My what?"

"These folks are our kith, the people we are connected to because of our choices. Somewhere between friends and family."

Sadie looked satisfied with that answer. She gave a decisive nod, then lay down by Lisbeth, ready to sleep for the night. Mattie climbed into the wagon on Lisbeth's other side.

Matthew and Emmanuel were in the front, ready to guide the horses out of town. Lisbeth and Mattie would take shifts later in the night, but for now they would get a chance to sleep.

Lisbeth held Mattie's hand as they drove away. Jordan waved, her arm held up high. Miss Grace stood at her side. Lisbeth watched the young woman get smaller and smaller until she disappeared from sight.

"Jordan is going to be all right, Mattie," Lisbeth said. "You raised a strong, and kind, woman. You can be proud."

A sweet smile on her face, Mattie gazed at Lisbeth, like she was looking right into her soul, and said, "I did. And I am."

EPILOGUE

JORDAN

Richmond, Virginia

Teachers aren't supposed to have favorites, but I do. Tessie captured a special place in my heart the first time she boldly declared, "Show me!"

My affection grows each time she takes my hand as we travel the four blocks from our home to school. She chats as we walk, speculating about the morning ahead of us and reminding me of the chores we left unfinished yesterday.

It wasn't hard for me to convince Miss Grace that this precocious girl would be a wonderful addition to her life. She only met Tessie once before agreeing to take her in. They fill a longing in each other's lives, and I'm greatly relieved that Tessie and Miss Grace will take care of one another after I've finished my time here. I wish I could say that I have found permanent homes for all of the children in my school, but saying something is true doesn't make it so.

Eager to please, Tessie helps me get this one-room school ready for the other students. We straighten the desks, tidy the books, and wash the slates clean. When everything is set, she looks at me and waits for my nod. When I give it, she swings open the door with a flourish, stretching her arms wide in a grand gesture of greeting.

I stand in the threshold to welcome each student individually. At the beginning of the term I learned what each prefers, a hug or a handshake, and I respect their boundaries, though I get a special joy when a child comes to trust me enough to seek out an embrace. These children do not have enough affection in their lives.

Most of these children are like Sophia, my little cousin who isn't so young anymore, alone in the world without a loved one to provide daily care for them. Only a few have found a permanent refuge. Their mothers, fathers, sisters, and brothers are lost. And to their families, they are missing children. I imagine some of their names are being called out in churches on Sunday mornings while congregants listen intently, desperate to hear a familiar name.

When my students are seated, I cross to the front of the class and gaze out at all their hopeful faces. Children of all ages and capacities stare back at me. They range in color from nearly white to the darkest of dark. Some are quick and confident, others deliberate and cautious. All of us are former slaves, though they have memories of that experience that I do not. These precious children know the suffering of backbreaking work, forced separations, and grisly warfare.

I have the privilege of opening up the world of education to them, though too often I'm entirely inadequate to the task. I pray that, if only from my example, they will imagine so much more for their futures than they lived with in their pasts.

I'm emboldened by the realization that many, many classrooms just like this one are giving newly freed people tools to succeed in the postslavery world. I am only one of scores of teachers who are educating for the betterment of the Negro race.

Too often this work is overwhelming and seemingly insufficient in the face of so much pain and need. The children casually compare stories of whippings, and killings, and near starvation. They display their physical and spiritual scars as if they are natural and commonplace. And for them they are. I want to shield them from worldly realities that are too distressing for children to learn about, but it is too late. These stories are simply a reflection of the lives they have already lived.

Some of them are so withdrawn I doubt they will be capable of caring for themselves when the time comes. Others are so prone to anger, for understandable reasons, that I fear for their futures. But whenever doubts overwhelm me, I call Sophia to my mind.

I like to imagine that she is in a classroom, similar to this one, being taught with respect and kindness. I remind myself that I alone cannot ensure a good life for these children, but I am one person planting seeds that may encourage them to take steps in the right direction. As Mama says, I will not know which seeds will take root and flourish, but the sowing itself is an act of faith. In the midst of so much ongoing ugliness, these are the faces of hope.

As I do each day, I slip my hand into my pocket and feel the mustard seeds Mama left with me. I say a silent prayer for our lost soul: *God, please watch over Sophia. Keep her safe, and help her to come home to Cousin Sarah.*

And then I recite my prayer for the children that are right here in front of me: *God, help me to be a worthy guide for these hearts, souls, and minds. Amen.*

And then I get to work.

ACKNOWLEDGMENTS

I'm grateful for these resources:

- Louisa Hoffman, Archival Assistant at Oberlin College
- Roslyn at the Library of Congress
- *Help Me to Find My People: The African American Search for Family Lost in Slavery* by Heather Andrea Williams
- "Life in Virginia by a Yankee Teacher" by Margaret Newbold Thorpe
- *Negroes and Their Treatment in Virginia from 1865 to 1867* by John Preston McConnell
- *Plain Counsels for Freedmen* by Clinton B. Fisk, assistant commissioner in the Freedmen's Bureau
- "Richmond Slave Trail," http://www.rvariverfront.com/monuments/slavetrail.html

- *Slavery by Another Name: The Re-Enslavement of Black Americans from the Civil War to World War II* by Douglas A. Blackmon
- *Slavery by Another Name* documentary, http://www.pbs.org/tpt/slavery-by-another-name/home/
- *Worse than Slavery: Parchman Farm and the Ordeal of Jim Crow Justice* by David M. Oshinsky
- *Republicans and Reconstruction in Virginia, 1856–70* by Richard G. Lowe

Thank you to these individuals and groups:

- The people who read drafts, including Heather MacLeod, Jodi Warshaw, Gogi Hodder, Darlanne Hoctor, Amanda Smith, Sheri Prud'homme, Rinda Bartley, Roz Amaro, Aria Killebrew-Bruehl, Jill Miller, Dan Goss, Margie Biblin, Kathy Post, Carmen Tomaš, Sarah Prud'homme
- Terry Goodman for finding my needle in the self-publishing haystack
- The Lake Union and Amazon Publishing teams, including Jodi Warshaw, Tiffany Yates Martin, Gabriella Dumpit, Irene Billings, and the rest of you whose names I don't know
- My Woolsey family for hope, support, and connection in these painful times; I love you all
- The Tijuana Gals for laughter, tears, honest conversation—and names for characters
- The First Unitarian Church of Oakland for challenging me to grow in faith and kindness for more than thirty years

BOOK CLUB QUESTIONS

1. At the start of *Mustard Seed*, Mattie and Lisbeth have a deep love for one another, though they have not been close in many years—even in a community like Oberlin. Why do you believe there was a distance between them? Talk about any people in your life who were like family to you and then you grew apart from.

2. Early in the novel, both Lisbeth and Jordan proclaim that slavery has been abolished and it is time to move forward as a nation. As the story progresses we learn that the owning class is using alternative ways to get reduced-price labor. What are some examples? How did these methods surprise you, if any did?

3. What character did you relate to? Like? Dislike?

4. Faith played a large role in *Mustard Seed*. Talk about any ways you identify with the faith of one of the characters in the book. How did any of the characters make you think about faith in a new or different way, if at all?

5. Lisbeth returned to Virginia to care for her dying father. Mattie returned to Virginia to encourage her niece, Sarah, to move to Ohio. How compelling was each reason to you?

6. Oftentimes it is difficult for a younger generation to really understand their parents' life experiences, as well as the other way around. Discuss a time in your life when this was true, and if you were able to bridge the gap, how that came about.

7. The ongoing, often hidden, effect of war is a subtheme in *Mustard Seed*. How does that resonate in your life? In our nation?

8. Family is a theme in this novel. What are some examples of the various ways people become family to one another in *Mustard Seed*? How does chosen versus inherited (blood, marriage, adoption) family function in your life?

9. How do the life experiences you read about in *Mustard Seed* impact how you understand race relations in the United States today?

ABOUT THE AUTHOR

Laila Ibrahim spent much of her career as a preschool director, a birth doula, and a religious educator. That work, coupled with her education in developmental psychology and attachment theory, provided ample fodder for the stories in *Mustard Seed* and *Yellow Crocus*.

She's a devout Unitarian Universalist, determined to do her part to add a little more love and justice to our beautiful and painful world. She lives with her wonderful wife, Rinda, in a small cohousing community in Berkeley, California, with two other families. Her amazing young adult children, Kalin and Maya, are kind enough to text, FaceTime, and call her on a regular basis.

Laila is blessed to be working full-time as a novelist. When she isn't writing, she likes to walk with friends, do jigsaw puzzles, play games, work in the garden, travel, cook, and eat all kinds of delicious food.